A Piggly Wiggly Wedding

A PIGGLY WIGGLY

Wedding

ROBERT DALBY

G. P. PUTNAM'S SONS

New York

G. P. PUTNAM'S SONS
Publishers Since 1838
Published by the Penguin Group
Penguin Group (USA) Inc., 375 Hudson Street, New York, New York 10014, USA •
Penguin Group (Canada), 90 Eglinton Avenue East, Suite 700, Toronto, Ontario M4P 2Y3,
Canada (a division of Pearson Canada Inc.) • Penguin Books Ltd, 80 Strand,
London WC2R 0RL, England • Penguin Ireland, 25 St Stephen's Green, Dublin 2,
Ireland (a division of Penguin Books Ltd) • Penguin Group (Australia),
250 Camberwell Road, Camberwell, Victoria 3124, Australia (a division of
Pearson Australia Group Pty Ltd) • Penguin Books India Pvt Ltd, 11 Community Centre,
Panchsheel Park, New Delhi–110 017, India • Penguin Group (NZ), 67 Apollo Drive,
Rosedale, North Shore 0632, New Zealand (a division of Pearson New Zealand Ltd) •
Penguin Books (South Africa) (Pty) Ltd, 24 Sturdee Avenue, Rosebank,
Johannesburg 2196, South Africa

Penguin Books Ltd, Registered Offices: 80 Strand, London WC2R 0RL, England

Library of Congress Cataloging-in-Publication Data

Dalby, Robert.
A Piggly Wiggly wedding / Robert Dalby.
        p.   cm.
ISBN 978-0-399-15557-4
1. Weddings—Fiction.   2. City and town life—Mississippi—Fiction.
3. Mississippi—Social life and customs—Fiction.   4. Domestic fiction.
I. Title.
PS3554.A4148P54   2009   2008054627
              813'.54—dc22

Printed in the United States of America
1   3   5   7   9   10   8   6   4   2

Book design by Amanda Dewey

This is a work of fiction. Names, characters, places, and incidents either are the product
of the author's imagination or are used fictitiously, and any resemblance to actual per-
sons, living or dead, businesses, companies, events, or locales is entirely coincidental.

While the author has made every effort to provide accurate telephone numbers and
Internet addresses at the time of publication, neither the publisher nor the author as-
sumes any responsibility for errors, or for changes that occur after publication. Further,
the publisher does not have any control over and does not assume any responsibility for
author or third-party websites or their content.

To Byrnes,
the best brother in the world
and a true champ

A PIGGLY WIGGLY WEDDING

1.

WITHOUT FIREFLIES

*I*n all his seventy-one years living in Second Creek, Mississippi, Mr. Choppy could never recall a summer like this one. Of course, it was hot, humid, dry, and dusty—the requisite four ingredients of every Mississippi Delta summer. But this one had an extra intensity to it. Shortly after his mayoral inauguration the first week in May, the rains had seemingly disappeared for good, as if siphoned up a straw by some retired and thirsty Olympian god frowning down from his perch in the clouds.

No, this summer of 2002 had gotten the attention of every Second Creeker beyond the toddler stage, and it was producing some remarkable fallout. Mr. Choppy's secretary, an appealing young woman with a heart-shaped face and the unlikely name of Cherish Hempstead, was the first to cite the results of the unusually brutal weather.

"You know, Mr. Dunbar," she had begun one afternoon in his office, "I was talking to my husband, Henry, last night, and he agreed with me that we haven't spotted a single firefly this summer. Not a one. It's so sad not to see them winkin' at our bedroom window. I always thought they were sayin' good night to us."

Mr. Choppy had cocked his head and squinted, trying to sort through his own half-formed impressions of the summer so far. "Now that you mention it, Cherish, I don't believe I've noticed one, either."

"Do you think it's because of this awful heat? Maybe those little lemon-lime batteries of theirs have all dried up," she had replied in that innocent, girlish manner of hers.

After that, Mr. Choppy had kept an eye out for the delicate and fanciful creatures of twilight and beyond. They had been an integral part of his childhood, imparting an ephemeral sense of magic to his everyday life. His mother, Gladys, had eagerly pointed them out to him not long after he had begun to master the watershed tasks of walking and talking. "They're flyin' jewels!" she had explained to her wide-eyed little boy. "And if you try hard enough, you can collect enough of 'em to make you a little bracelet. And if you make that bracelet just right, you might even learn how to fly."

So far this particular summer, Mr. Choppy was discovering that what Cherish had passed along anecdotally was turning out to be true. It appeared that Second Creek was indeed without fireflies—perhaps for the first time ever—and that did not bode well. For all Second Creekers it was an axiom: any unusual weather pattern heralded trouble ahead or perhaps the arrival of a stranger who would have a decided impact on their community. And now that he was the mayor of Second Creek, Mr. Choppy would have to preside over whatever loomed ahead, with equal parts good humor and judgment.

The Fourth of July had come and gone with all its fireworks bursting into gaudy parasols of color and raining down to the oohs and ahhs of the citizenry below, but Second Creek was still without fireflies dotting the night. Mid-July was feeling much more like the dog days of mid-August with its triple-digit temperatures and still no drop of rain to cool things down. In the midst of such oppression, Mayor Hale Dunbar Junior, aka Mr. Choppy, had been doggedly balancing his personal life with his new municipal duties. He and his fiancée, Gaylie Girl Lyons of Lake Forest, Illinois, had agreed to get married way back in February on the eve of his photo-finish victory over the now-departed-for-Vegas Mr. Floyce Hammontree. But they couldn't seem to buckle down and set a date, despite their best intentions.

For their part, the Nitwitts were as antsy as beauty pageant contestants waiting onstage with frozen smiles for the emcee to call their names as finalists. Laurie Lepanto Hampton had even paid a visit to his courthouse office one morning to inquire politely, offering the services of each of the club's members in making the event truly unforgettable.

"We've all just been hanging by a thread waiting for your announcement," she had begun. "I've been on long-distance with Gaylie Girl dozens of times just trying to pin her down. And mum's the word when we've been with her on her weekend visits every now and then. What gives? You haven't gotten cold feet, have you? Powell and all the girls would just be crushed if either one of you backed out of this. You two getting together after fifty-something years is the romance of the century, hands down."

He had assured her that their wedding was still on, no need to worry, she and the rest of the Nitwitts would be the first to know when they finally decided to tie the knot. What he hadn't told her was that the disapproval of Gaylie Girl's children, Petey Lyons and Amanda Lyons Sykes, had been throwing cold water on the impending union for several months running. They were utterly horrified at the prospect of their wealthy, sophisticated mother hooking up with someone they regarded as an opportunistic hayseed and were doing everything possible to head her off at the altar.

Meanwhile, Mr. Choppy's mayoral duties had not allowed him much breathing room. He was firmly embedded in the municipal learning curve, getting to know the various department heads and city councilmen, who were used to Mr. Floyce's ways, and discovering by trial and error which ones he could depend upon. No one was out to get him or anything like that, and Mr. Floyce had been more than cooperative during the transition period. But it was a truism that old habits and loyalties die hard, and more than anything else, Mr. Choppy was finding out that he was just going to have to prove himself to the holdovers from the previous administration, one by one. It wasn't exactly trial by fire, but there were a few sparks every now and then.

One sultry, mid-July Friday afternoon, in fact, Mr. Choppy was looking forward to his time off after another week of learning local politics when Cherish buzzed him from the outer office.

"Miz Lyons is on long distance for you. Line two."

Nothing lifted his spirits these days like the sound of his beloved's voice, especially since he had been hoping on a day-to-day basis for a breakthrough in their standoff with Gaylie Girl's children. As a result he always took her calls with his brows arched expectantly and a hopeful grin lifting the corners of his mouth.

"Hello, sweetheart! What's the latest from Lake Forest?" he said, the affection he felt for her generously flowing into the receiver.

"Well, I won't keep you in suspense, Hale. After much clever maneuvering on my part, I've got them off dead-center at last. Both Petey and Amanda have finally agreed to come down to visit Second Creek and meet you." She paused to sigh, and he could easily picture the weight of the world rising like morning mist from her delicate and glamorous shoulders. "I never thought we'd see the day, but it's dawning for us at last."

"Hallelujah and amen! Now, what's our next step, and when are they comin' down?"

"First, I want you to glance at your schedule and tell me what the weekend after next looks like for you."

Mr. Choppy quickly rifled through his appointment calendar and nodded approvingly. "Everything looks clear at the end of the month. It's agreed, then. Two weeks from now?"

"Agreed. As for the next step, I thought I'd ask the Nitwitts to roll out the red carpet. The way I see it, Petey and Amanda will have no choice other than to be swept off their feet when the girls work their magic. Nobody does Southern hospitality better. I know they've made me feel at home on my many trips down."

"Good move. Laurie Hampton has been after me for weeks to spill the beans on our wedding details for her Nitwitts. I was even thinkin' . . ." He broke off, shifting his eyes from side to side as he played with various dates in his head. "Whaddaya say we set the date around Labor Day? That'd give us a good six weeks to plan everything. I don't know much about weddings, of course, but that seems like long enough to me."

"Oh, that will absolutely work, Hale," Gaylie Girl replied. "We certainly don't have to go overboard at our age." She took a deep breath. "And I have more good news for you. I found Harriet Mills, my secretary, a new position with my friend Linda Markham, and I've made another important executive decision. Are you ready?"

He sat up a bit straighter in his chair, reacting to her playful tone. "I'm always ready for good news from my sweetheart."

"I've decided to come down and move in with you permanently next weekend. These trips back and forth are wearing me out, and I see no reason to keep it up. Second Creek is going to be my new home, and I'm going to be its First Lady, so it's time I got my bearings for good. No more stolen weekends here and there. What do you think?"

Mr. Choppy did a quick mental survey of his cramped and dowdy bungalow at 34 Pond Street and grimaced. The fact that it had lacked a woman's touch since his mother's death decades before was the least of it. Gaylie Girl's stylish presence on her visits had only emphasized its inadequacy, and it had caused him to take action, planning a wonderful surprise for her. But now that she had forced the issue a bit with her announcement of an early move-in, he wondered if he should let her in on it or just wait until she arrived to spring the news.

"I think it's a great idea," Mr. Choppy finally said, deciding to withhold further information about the important decision he had made at his end. At any rate, it was going to be his wedding present to his Gaylie Girl, and he was certain that she would like it, given the life to which she had grown accustomed all these years. "Although I don't think you need to bring everything down at once," he added, trying not to give anything away with his inflection.

"Oh, I wasn't planning to. I'll probably end up selling the house when all is said and done. It's one of the many issues I'll need to address with Petey and Amanda. But first let's soften them up a bit down there in Second Creek and see what happens."

When Mr. Choppy hung up after a final exchange of further logistics and intimate pleasantries, he felt like he had just successfully fashioned that firefly bracelet his mother had conjured up for him more than six decades ago. Those little winged darlings might be missing from the summer nightscape, but there were plenty of them blinking inside his head, enhancing the sense of wonder he was feeling at the moment.

Rising from his chair with boundless energy, he summoned Cherish, and she appeared immediately in the doorway—a sunny, yellow vision from blond hairdo to sunflower-print dress to maize-colored pumps, ready to do his bidding cheerfully.

"Good news from Miz Lyons?" she offered, taking a seat. She was, of course, well aware of the nature of their ongoing communication over the past few months.

He quickly brought her up to speed and asked her to enter all the new dates in her calendar as well. After they had double-checked everything in an enviable display of municipal efficiency, Mr. Choppy was surprised to find himself witnessing the sudden evaporation of Cherish Hempstead's dazzling smile. It was her defining trait, something she simply was never without, and he drew back slightly.

"Is somethin' the matter, Cherish?"

"Oh," she began, clearly sounding a note of disappointment. "I didn't know it showed. I was just wondering . . . if I could run something past you, Mr. Dunbar."

Mr. Choppy did not have to think for a second about how to proceed with this delightful young woman who had blown him away during her job interview just before he'd taken office. She'd had the inside track anyway due to a recommendation from none other than Laurie Hampton, whose younger daughter, Hannah, had gone to high school with fellow cheerleader Cherish Elise Holloway, as she had appeared in their senior yearbook. Laurie had promised him then that Cherish would be a "ray of sunshine" and exactly what he needed to weather the many storms of Second Creek, in whatever form, and she had not exaggerated one whit.

"You know you can always come to me with anything you have on your mind," he told her, offering up his warmest smile.

"I appreciate that, Mr. Dunbar." She momentarily averted her eyes, looking down at her small, perfectly manicured hands before resuming. "It's about my husband, Henry, and his job out at Pond-Raised Catfish. He's heard rumors that the plant is having some financial problems, and they might have to lay off some people. Maybe Henry'd be one of 'em. If that happens, it'd be a big blow to us, Mr. Dunbar. He really likes his job as shift manager, of course, but that's not the half of it. You see . . . I've just found out that I'm pregnant. Henry doesn't know it yet, but I'm plannin' on tellin' him tonight. Naturally, I'd want us to be on solid financial ground when the baby comes. We're both of us responsible people when it comes to what's in the bank. So this really makes the situation at the catfish plant kinda critical. Plus . . . I'm a tad bit ashamed to tell you that . . . well, this pregnancy was unplanned. I hope Henry doesn't get too upset."

"He loves you, Cherish," Mr. Choppy said, giving her a playful wink. "When I met him a few months back, it was written all over his face. I know he'll understand and be excited when everything settles down."

There was no change in Cherish's glum demeanor. "But there's somethin' else you don't know, Mr. Dunbar. The first couple of years Henry and I were married, I had two miscarriages. I've always been worried about how it would affect me when I got pregnant again, and I have to tell you that I don't feel confident about this."

Mr. Choppy raised his right eyebrow ever so slightly. "I assume you plan to keep the baby, though."

"Oh, heavens, yes! The alternative never occurred to me, if that's what you were gettin' at. I want to have children—lots of 'em. I know Henry does, too. It's just that between the possible job layoff and my pregnancy history, I'm a big bundle of nerves right now."

Mr. Choppy leaned in and adopted his usual fatherly demeanor. "How's this, then? I'll see if I can rustle up a meetin' with Curtis Ray Keyes out at Pond-Raised real soon. Maybe I can at least help resolve that for you."

"Oh, my Henry swears by him, Mr. Dunbar. Says he's the fairest manager he's ever worked for."

"I've always heard good things about him," Mr. Choppy said. Then he quickly reviewed the history of Pond-Raised Catfish in his head. After the tourist dollar provided by The Square and its myriad attractions such as the Miss Delta Floozie Contest every June, the sprawling catfish plant was the most vital part of Second Creek's economy, and it had been up and running for nearly fifty years. If there was anything at all to these rumors Cherish had revealed to him, he must do everything he could in his official capacity as mayor to see that Second Creek's largest employer continued to prosper.

"Why don't you call out there first thing Monday morning?" Mr. Choppy continued. "See if you can arrange for me and Curtis Ray to get together in the next week or two, and I'll try to find out what's what."

"Oh, that would be wonderful, Mr. Dunbar," Cherish returned, rising from her chair. "I'll get on it next week."

"As for your blessed event, it's just that. Blessed. Think of it that way, Cherish. Don't even consider anything goin' wrong. I'm sure you'll have Henry's support—and mine, too, of course."

Cherish flashed her sunniest smile and exhaled dramatically. "You know, Miz Laurie Hampton told me how much

I was gonna enjoy workin' with you. She didn't exaggerate one little bit, either."

After Cherish had fairly floated out of the office, Mr. Choppy leaned back in his chair and frowned. Things looked like they might have finally broken his way with the wedding plans and Gaylie Girl's children. But the Pond-Raised Catfish issue was a brand-new worry on the horizon. He shrugged and managed his trademark smile anyway. It was all part of his stewardship of Second Creek, a job he had aggressively sought and won against heavy odds.

A COUPLE OF HOURS LATER—just twenty minutes before closing time, in fact—Mr. Choppy was shutting the books on what had turned out to be a mostly satisfactory week for him. The highlights had included meeting with longtime Streets and Sanitation supervisor Lance Walkley about the rising cost of asphalt and therefore increasing the budget for repairing the many potholes around town; going to lunch at the Victorian Tea Room with Morgan Player, the most high-maintenance of the city councilmen, and soothing his ruffled feathers about the current lack of funding for a soccer field on the west side of town; returning a plethora of phone calls as usual; dictating countless letters for Cherish to send out; and still finding time during his few idle moments to daydream about his Gaylie Girl and their impending wedding.

His municipal reverie was interrupted there at the end when Cherish buzzed him, saying that a Mrs. Something-or-Other Simon was on long-distance and wished to speak with him about an urgent matter.

Mr. Choppy chuckled at his secretary's choice of words. "Miz Somethin'-or-Other?"

"I'm sorry about that, Mr. Dunbar. Her first name was a little weird. I couldn't quite catch it." Cherish paused in professional secretarial fashion. "Are you still in or have you officially left for the day?"

"I'll take the call," he replied, while working up a smile in his voice. His father, Hale Senior, had trained him well in that regard. "People can always tell whether or not you're smilin' over the phone," he had told his son from the get-go when the boy had started helping out at the Piggly Wiggly. "So never speak to a customer with a frown on your face or in your head. They'll know it at the other end for damned sure. Trust me on this one."

Mr. Choppy took a deep breath and offered his customary pleasant greeting. "This is Mayor Hale Dunbar. How can I help you?"

An almost musical voice replied quickly—a smile clearly embedded within it. "Yes, Mayor Dunbar, this is Mrs. Euterpe Simon. I have it on some authority that you are looking to lease your campaign headquarters building. Wasn't it the former Piggly Wiggly that your family owned for many decades?"

He assumed a more alert posture, both impressed and surprised by the well-prepared stranger on the other end. He also wondered what "authority" had leaked the information to her, since he had previously spoken only to Laurie and Powell Hampton about the matter behind the scenes. They were considering the possibility of leasing the building and reincarnating Powell's former dance studio, but nothing definite had been decided, and no contract had been signed yet.

"Yes," Mr. Choppy said, trying not to sound perplexed. "I shut down my Piggly Wiggly late last summer and put it to good use during my election campaign, but I'm not quite sure what to do with it now. Are you interested in leasin' the building . . . Miz Simon, was it?"

"Please. Call me Euterpe," she insisted, sounding as if they were just old friends who hadn't talked for a while. "That's E-U-T-E-R-P-E. I know my name is not business as usual, but my mother decided to name me after one of the Muses, and I've been living up to that ever since." She laughed in such a carefree manner that Mr. Choppy couldn't help but find her attractive and compelling, sight unseen. He found himself wanting to hear more from her, unable to resist the warmth of her voice.

"I'm afraid I don't know much about the Muses. But please, Euterpe. Go on. You have my undivided attention, I assure you."

"Well, I'm seriously considering moving to Second Creek and opening a music school," she began. "I teach piano and fancy myself the Mistress of the Scales, if you will. In fact, that would be what I inscribe on my little shingle—Euterpe Simon, Mistress of the Scales. If I'm not mistaken, there is currently no one offering piano lessons in your wonderful little town, and I would like to fill the void."

Mr. Choppy knew that there was indeed no one fitting that description, nor to his knowledge had there ever been throughout Second Creek's storied past. "You just might have some potential pupils here, Miz Simon—uh, I mean, Euterpe. You seem to have done your homework pretty well."

Euterpe offered up her musical laugh once again. "Oh, I never do things halfway, you'll discover." Then she paused momentarily, daintily clearing her throat. "I plan to be in Second Creek week after next. Would it be possible to meet with you and discuss the possibility of leasing your building?"

Mr. Choppy thought it over quickly. He could certainly touch base as a courtesy to Laurie and Powell about their on-again, off-again interest and keep himself out of trouble. "I don't see why not. What about Monday week? Anytime after ten o'clock would suit my schedule."

"Monday week it is. I'll be there promptly at ten," Euterpe replied without hesitation, sounding supremely confident. "I believe you'll like the business arrangement I'll propose."

After the call ended, Mr. Choppy informed Cherish of the new appointment and then settled back in his chair to review what had just happened. He was overcome by the strangest feeling. He had found himself somehow mesmerized by the sound of Euterpe's voice, agreeing with her on every point she had raised and every suggestion she had made. Then he looked down at the green blotter on his desk, amazed to discover that he had been doodling musical notes on his message pad in the midst of his conversation with her. He had never been one to do things like that—he hadn't even doodled in grade school, where it was practically a requirement of childhood. But he nonetheless found himself smiling at what he had done, and he kept right on smiling all the way home to his modest little bungalow.

Later that evening just around dusk, he walked out into his backyard as usual. He stood out in the dripping heat with the sweat beading up on his forehead, just waiting and looking in vain. Still no fireflies to be seen anywhere. Not a one.

He shook his head, clearly disturbed by the phenomenon, but perhaps the long drought and nearly two months of sizzling temperatures were indeed responsible, as Cherish had suggested. He looked down at his grass and winced. Every blade of his Saint Augustine was brown and parched, and no amount of watering with the hose seemed to be helping. There was also a dusty film overlaying all the leaves on his towering pecan trees. He couldn't remember the last time it had rained. Then, perspiring profusely, he went back into his air-conditioning and sat down at his kitchen table, still mulling it all over.

Finally, he rose from the table and headed to the refrigerator to pull out some leftover ham and potato salad for supper, humming a little tune as he made himself a plate. They were a succession of random notes straight out of the blue. He found himself shrugging as he took his first bite of potato salad. He had never been a hummer of tunes, seeing as how he was tone-deaf. This had been judiciously called to his attention by the choirmaster of First Presbyterian when he was but a boy. Nonetheless, he kept right on humming, gathering a growing sense of confidence from the exercise.

2.

THE VIEW FROM
LAKE FOREST

*P*erfectly coiffed and smartly attired, Gaylie Girl sat in the front seat of Mr. Choppy's huffing and puffing Dodge, her expression at once quizzical and amused. She still hadn't really settled in from the move down to 34 Pond Street the day before and would rather have tackled more of the unpacking of the odds and ends she had brought with her in the first of many waves to come, but her husband-to-be had insisted that he had a big surprise in store for her and that it was way past time to unveil it. So they had piled into his car and for the last ten minutes or so had been turning right at this Second Creek street corner, then left at that one on the way to some unknown destination.

"I feel like I'm in a movie script, and you've been driving

Miss Gaylie all over creation," she observed at one point with a certain friskiness in her voice. "Only I'm not in the backseat barking orders at the nape of your neck. I assume this surprise of yours will be worth all the twists and turns we've been taking. Are we almost there?"

Mr. Choppy laughed brightly and managed a quick wink in her direction. "Just one more block. This neighborhood, by the way, is the historic east side of town, which many of our well-to-do Second Creekers call home, including at least one of the Nitwitts, I believe."

Gaylie Girl perked up, noting the gracious parade of wide, white-columned porches, manicured lawns, and gardens passing by. "Our illustrious current president, Renza Belford, right?"

"Right," he replied just as they pulled up in front of a two-story, late-Victorian gingerbread house on North Bayou Avenue that had seen better days. For starters it needed new shutters, a new roof, and a good coat of paint, and the front yard was weed-infested, featuring a muscular wisteria vine wrapped around a dilapidated trellis like some sort of strange, terrestrial octopus. But the house clearly had good bones, as they were fond of saying in the real estate game, being the sort of structure that they "just didn't build like that anymore."

"Well, here's my surprise. Hope you like it," he added, shutting off the engine. "I'd like to buy it for us as a fixer-upper. Consider it my wedding present to you."

Whatever Gaylie Girl had expected his surprise to be, it

was not something as monumental as this. She found herself at a complete loss of words, and too much silence passed.

"Gaylie Girl? Say something."

Finally, she roused herself and said the first thing that came into her head. "It needs a lot of work, doesn't it?"

"So you don't like it?"

Gaylie Girl shook her head emphatically and extended a reassuring hand. "No, no, no. Of course I like it. I can see that it has great potential. It just needs some tender loving care. I'm just wondering what made you think we had to move—and so soon."

"Come on, sweetheart. My little bachelor pad is already strainin' at the seams," he replied, mincing no words. "Besides, I want my First Lady to live in the style to which she's accustomed. You've told me how much you like decoratin' and all that stuff. I thought you'd get a kick outta makin' this place shine and sparkle for us."

An easy smile broke across Gaylie Girl's face, and she gave his hand a solid squeeze for good measure. "That's true enough. If I hadn't wanted to take on a challenge, I would never have said yes to your proposal and moved down South. I'd like you to understand, however, that I don't expect to live in an approximation of my Tudor mansion in Lake Forest. I've been around enough pretension up there to last me a lifetime."

He was staring straight ahead, focusing on the small starburst of a crack in the corner of his windshield that was beginning to send out exploratory tentacles. "I understand,

and I haven't put a down payment on it yet. I told Paul Belford I'd have to get your approval first. But I have the key right here in my pocket. We can do a walk-through, if you'd like."

She released his hand and smiled. "Let's get to it, then. This will be the first of many adventures I'll have down here, I'm sure."

So they trudged through the premises gingerly, wincing a bit at all the faded wallpaper and sagging window treatments. But there was no question the house had a pedigree, what with its high ceilings and elaborate friezes and cornices. Most of all, it had space and plenty of it—for entertaining, for moving about, for living the good life.

"We open a few windows, dust it down, and voilà! No more echoes of the Addams Family," Gaylie Girl observed as they stood together looking down the long central corridor below the elaborate winding staircase. "I only have one condition for taking this on, Hale."

"And what's that?"

"Let's make this a joint wedding present. Let's go in on the down payment together, okay? After all, we're a team, aren't we—Mayor and First Lady, I mean?"

FIFTEEN MINUTES LATER they had driven back to Mr. Choppy's bungalow and were seated across from each other, sipping coffee at his modest kitchen table with the red-and-white-checkered tablecloth, and Gaylie Girl was rambling on effusively about their new fixer-upper.

"Of course, I'll want to take my time renovating it. I'm spectacular at these things, I assure you. Single-handedly, I decorated a summer house Peter and I kept out in Santa Fe, and I know a trick or two about stretching budgets. But I don't mean that in a chintzy way, at least not regarding myself. I do have a few friends in Chicago, though, who go around acting like they don't have a red cent to their names, when the truth is, they're way beyond set for life. They just seem to want to nickel-and-dime everyone to death."

Mr. Choppy managed a cautious smile. "Must be nice to have that luxury. Of course, I grew up workin' at the Piggly Wiggly knowin' the full value of a dollar, so I guess I could never be that casual about money. I've never been real big on creature comforts as a result. Can't even seem to get rid of that rattletrap of a car parked outside. But I do appreciate what a generous person you are. Hell, you gave me the seed money to finance my campaign, even if you didn't know at the time that I was gonna use it that way. I guess I just gotta get used to bein' around someone who has your kinda wealth and not try to read between the lines too much."

"Fair enough, Hale," she replied, heaving a sigh of relief afterward. "Never forget that one of the reasons I'm marrying you is because you are a very direct and straightforward man. I'm more than ready for someone like you at this time in my life."

"It's true. I've never put on airs, but I've learned to dress the part of mayor of Second Creek. You know—tradin' butcher's aprons for three-piece suits. I feel a little too stitched and hemmed in at times, but I've gotten used to it." Then he freshened each of their coffee cups and changed the subject. "Now, tell me more about how you finally convinced your children to come down here and give us a look-see."

Gaylie Girl briefly inhaled the fresh coffee aroma and that seemed to invigorate her further. "Well, Amanda has always been the bigger problem. She's developed a somewhat aloof personality lately. Some might even call it snobbish. I'm afraid she's just never given the South a second thought, except to turn up her nose at some of the more sensational civil rights headlines over the years. The truth is, she's bought into all the Southern stereotypes—particularly about Mississippi."

"I'll admit we don't get the best press in the world. All it takes is for one crazy redneck to show his spots, and the media's on it like white on rice," Mr. Choppy replied, shaking his head in reluctant agreement. Then he caught her gaze intently, removing the frown from his face. "But things have changed for the better, for the most part. People work really hard at gettin' along with each other down here—particularly in a town like Second Creek. There's a real sense of community."

Mr. Choppy was momentarily distracted as he ran a ticker tape in his head concerning the past eventful year. Sometimes he still found it hard to believe that the summer before, he had been managing his family grocery store, never dreaming that he would become a politician. "So Amanda was harder to convince, huh?" he finally remarked, resuming his train of thought.

"I had to be more creative with her, that's for sure. With Petey, I just kept mentioning that the real estate opportunities in Second Creek looked promising to me," she continued. "Petey's always had his father's eye for investment and making a buck. So I proposed that he consider making a trip down to see for himself. As for Amanda, I kept tempting her with descriptions of all the specimens of Greek Revival and Victorian architecture. Oh, and all those wonderful brick and lacework balconies on The Square, of course. She does like traveling around and viewing historic districts and buildings—although she favors Europe in that regard. She's become quite addicted since her father left her all that money. I've told her to think of visiting Second Creek as another one of her little junkets, and she finally bought into it."

Mr. Choppy nodded thoughtfully. "That's light-years away from the hysteria you described when you first told 'em about my existence a few months back."

Gaylie Girl averted her eyes and shook her head slowly from side to side. "Oh, as I told you, Amanda in particular was inconsolable at first. She went on and on about how I was defiling her father's memory and, oh, how could I have carried on like that with you years ago, and, now, why was I going back for more at my age? I'm afraid my daughter has become quite the diva. She's been known to peer over the servants' shoulders while they polish the silverware for the dinner parties she gives." Gaylie Girl broke off, tossing her head back with a chuckle. "Not that I haven't been guilty of certain excesses myself in my lifetime. Sometimes your genes come back to haunt you in the most unexpected ways."

"Down here in the South, we just cut to the chase and say, 'What goes around, comes around.'"

She gave him her customary sociable smile and added, "You Southerners do have a way of simplifying things—especially you, Hale."

He leaned back in his chair with a look of contentment. That Labor Day wedding couldn't come soon enough for him, and right now he wanted nothing more than to iron out all the pesky details. "Speakin' of simplifyin' things, those six weeks to our wedding will go by pretty fast. Don't you think we need to make a few decisions soon? I know Miz Hampton and the Nitwitts will wanna pitch in and help."

Gaylie Girl offered an introspective grin as she cocked her head. "I remember way back in February when you first popped the question, we were both leaning toward a civil ceremony with no fanfare. But that was before I'd spent more time down here and gotten to know all the girls a little better. I think we'll need to add that unique Second Creek touch."

Mr. Choppy laughed heartily. "You mean like a wedding in a grocery store? We've been there and done that with Laurie and Powell Hampton."

"Rumor has it," Gaylie Girl began with a sly edge to her voice, "that a certain Nitwitt will offer her elegant house and grounds for our ceremony. Need I say more about the considerable maze of details that would involve?"

Mr. Choppy had no trouble reading between the lines, as he always enjoyed hearing the latest from the Nitwitts. "Miz Myrtis Troy and Evening Shadows, I take it? You don't know how happy I am that the ladies took you into the club back in February and that you've been gettin' along so well with every one of 'em on your visits. That's easier said than done, believe me, but I told Miz Hampton way back then how important it was to me that you felt a part of Second Creek as soon as possible."

"Oh, indeed I do," she replied, her face lighting up and a hint of mischief in her eyes. "The girls have taken me into their bosom, or rather, bosoms, I should say. There are lots and lots of bosoms present whenever we get together, you know. So, yes, I'll meet with the girls real soon and see who wants to do what for us. Of course, I'm sure you realize we're going to have more suggestions than we'll know what to do with. But I'm equally sure we'll be up to the challenge and negotiate things without hurting anyone's feelings."

The mention of negotiations jogged Mr. Choppy's memory

of the arresting phone call he had received the previous week from Euterpe Simon, and he quickly rattled off the gist of their conversation. "I'm glad you're here with me now. I've gotta pay a visit to Laurie and Powell Hampton about their interest in leasin' my buildin', too, and I believe it'll help to have you tag along with me. That'll keep you in the loop."

"Of course. I'd be delighted. All part of our teamwork."

Mr. Choppy liked hearing those words. It brought the reality of their impending union closer to the surface. All they had to do was finesse Gaylie Girl's difficult children and get some sort of peremptory blessing from them, mostly for her sake. After that, he felt sure everything would be a piece of wedding cake, and he knew the Nitwitts would be their ace in the hole in that regard.

"Onward and upward, then," he answered, his tone at once playful and emphatic.

3.

WHITHER THE DANCING PIG?

*T*he firefly-less weather continued to bear down upon Second Creek with a vengeance, causing all its citizens to drag their heels trying to cope with it. Nonetheless, Laurie and Powell summoned the energy to go all out for their meeting with Mr. Choppy and Gaylie Girl about leasing his building. They had both been surprised to hear from him over the phone that the former Piggly Wiggly and Hale Dunbar Junior Campaign Headquarters suddenly had another prospective tenant.

"I'm lettin' y'all know about this right now as a courtesy," Mr. Choppy had explained. "The last time we talked, Miz Hampton, I believe you said that you both weren't really sure you wanted to lease my buildin'. You said you were just thinkin' about openin' that new dance studio a' yours. Now, what was that name you said you were gonna call it?"

"The Dancing Pig," Laurie had replied. "In honor of its illustrious grocery store past, as I'm sure you can appreciate. Of course, Powell's original studio in Memphis was called Studio Hampton, but we decided against bringing that name out of mothballs. We'd like to make a fresh start. That is, if we go through with this."

"That's right cute, Miz Hampton," Mr. Choppy had added after a brief chuckle. "The Dancing Pig. I like the sound of that. But I guess I'm at a juncture here where I need to know if The Dancing Pig is gonna get to hoofin' or not anytime soon."

And so Laurie and Powell had decided to invite Mr. Choppy and his fiancée over for Saturday dinner and a more in-depth discussion of the leasing issue. Laurie had planned an elaborate gourmet feast—cheese-and-bacon mini-quiches as appetizers, followed by salmon steaks grilled on cedar planks, spinach soufflé, confetti rice, and key lime pie for dessert. No matter what the outcome of their negotiations, she figured, everyone would go away pleasantly sated.

"I just adore this cottage of yours, Laurie," Gaylie Girl was saying, once they had all settled in around the parlor, sipping cocktails. "What style is this? I know I've never run across this kind of architecture on the shores of Lake Michigan."

Laurie put down her glass of muscadine wine and made

a dismissive gesture. "Oh, it's just a simple raised cottage circa the 1870s, I'm told. We haven't actually ever gone down to the courthouse and researched the deed, but this is pretty much typical of that mid- to late-Victorian period here in the South. White clapboard, green shutters, lots of gingerbread filigree, and a dormer window or two for that dollhouse touch."

"We've hosted many a cozy little party since I moved in," Powell added, winking. "There are all kinds of nooks and crannies where people can pair off and get to know each other better. And it seems Laurie is always having the Nit-witts over for some kind of powwow with the usual Bloody Marys and lots of nibbles."

Gaylie Girl wagged her impeccably sculpted brows. "Sounds like my kind of fun."

Mr. Choppy put down his Maker's Mark on the rocks on a nearby coaster and said, "Speakin' of fun, folks, have y'all come to a decision about teachin' Second Creekers how to trip the light fantastic once again?"

It was Powell who initially tackled the question with another mischievous wink. "Yes and no. We're pretty certain we want to start up the old studio again, but we were thinking around the first of the year and not right away. There are a couple of trips we want to take first before we settle back into a teaching routine. Once you open for business, you're pretty much locked in. But I've been dying to show Paris to Laurie. I have so many fond memories of ballroom dance competitions over there, and I have the opportunity to catch up with a few people I've heard from just recently."

Laurie was oozing with excitement as she elaborated further. "Powell knows such interesting people in the ballroom dance trade. He's told me several times about this larger-than-life personality he met over in Europe who bills himself as the Great Buddha Magruder. Powell's always described him as an Orson Welles type—only much lighter on his feet, as you might expect. Don't you just love that name? And believe it or not, Powell got a letter from him a few weeks ago, inviting him to an insider's view of Paris. We'd really like to take him up on that, so we were wondering if we could delay leasing the old Piggly Wiggly just a little bit longer."

Mr. Choppy nodded sympathetically, looking amused. "I can sure appreciate your wantin' to travel like that and all. Only I feel I should bring you up to speed on this Miz Euterpe Simon that's interested in leasin' the buildin', too. Before she called me this past week, you folks were the only game in town."

"Euterpe?" Laurie said, tilting her head with a curious smile. "What an unusual name!"

"Well, it's a blast from the past for me!" Gaylie Girl replied, cutting in with some authority. "I was a huge Greek mythology buff in high school, and if I remember correctly, Euterpe was the Muse of Music. There was a picture of her in our textbooks, holding a flute and looking quite otherworldly wearing something that looked like it was made of tissue paper or maybe even spun sugar. I was quite taken with that fanciful image for a while and thought I just might take up the flute or maybe even the piano and join a symphony orchestra for some sort of artistic career. Instead, I settled for hawking Tommy Dorsey records and Frank Sinatra sheet music at Evanston Popular Tunes, and that was the end of that."

"Well, I don't know squat about mythology," Mr. Choppy added. "But this Miz Simon did tell me over the phone that her mother named her after one of the Muses, and it seems she wants to open a piano school in my buildin'. Says she wants to advertise as the Mistress of the Scales. She's comin' to Second Creek soon to discuss it all, and I just wanted to be sure how you two stood on the issue."

Laurie looked momentarily puzzled, but then a particularly humorous image seemed to flash into her head. "I wonder if she'd be willing to share the building with us at some point. Maybe play the piano while we teach people dance steps."

"Don't know about that," Mr. Choppy replied, sounding somewhat amused, himself. "But my first obligation is to you good folks. I owe you so much. If you don't lease it from me, is it gonna upset you if I lease it to her?"

Laurie and Powell quickly exchanged glances, and he spoke up first. "I have to confess that I truly don't know yet if I want to return to the 'feets do your thing' business. I'm not sure my bunions have recovered from all that waltzing at the Piggly Wiggly. Maybe we just ought to defer right now.

There are other buildings in town we could use if we decide to start up The Dancing Pig later on after we get the travel bug out of our systems."

"I really am looking forward to Europe," Laurie added with girlish excitement. "I think that's where my heart is for the time being. I agree we should take a rain check."

"Then I have your permission to proceed full speed ahead with Miz Simon?"

Powell and Laurie nodded simultaneously. "By all means," he replied. "I'm sure this will all work out the way it's supposed to."

A HALF HOUR LATER, Laurie and Gaylie Girl had retreated to the kitchen, leaving the mayor and his former campaign speech writer to their own devices in the parlor discussing the trials and tribulations of municipal politics.

"It smells perfectly divine in here, Laurie," Gaylie Girl had said after finishing off the gin and tonic she had carried in with her to a roomful of appetizing aromas. "I've always said kitchens can be more comforting than churches. And I simply must get your delicious recipes. Perhaps I can impress my Yankee daughter with some of your unique Southern dishes. She's convinced all of you eat nothing but grits and fried chicken down here, not that there would be anything wrong with that. Amanda doesn't know what she's missing."

It was only after Laurie had assigned Gaylie Girl the

task of stirring the rice, however, that the real reason for her voluntary KP duty emerged. "I wanted to catch up on the rest of the girls with you, Laurie. I've just gotten bits and pieces on my weekends down, and I'm not the least bit ashamed to tell you that I need my fix."

Laurie was gingerly peeking into the oven at her soufflé. Seeing that everything was bubbling up nicely, she carefully closed the door, straightened up and chuckled. "I know what you mean. I never really thought of it that way, but you're right—being a Nitwitt can be positively addictive, with or without the gin mill spirits."

"So what's the latest on all my wonderful new friends? First, how is our dear Wittsie doing? She's just the sweetest thing I've ever met, and I keep hoping against hope that something miraculous will happen."

Laurie removed her oven mitts and gestured toward the nearby breakfast nook, where they took their seats. "Oh, big news there. She's having a bit more trouble now. The medication seems to be slowing things down, but it is Alzheimer's, after all, and it isn't going to get better. Her daughter, April Thurman, finally came down and conferred with us. She felt the time had come to take more definitive action, and the gist is that Wittsie's now in an assisted-living, memory-care complex near Greenwood. We all take turns visiting her throughout the week. I go on Mondays, and we have lunch together. Renza goes on Tuesdays, Denver Lee on Wednesdays, Myrtis on Thursdays, and Novie on Fridays. We all show up for a right festive Sunday brunch, but we've got Saturdays open. Would you like to volunteer? I don't think Wittsie's ever had so much attention in her entire life, and I can sense it's helping her deal with this."

"Oh, absolutely. Sign me up," Gaylie Girl said without hesitation.

"You'll love the food, too. It's quite good," Laurie continued. "In fact, I do believe Wittsie's put on a pound or two, which she probably needed to do. She's always been the spindliest among us. Of course, we miss having her in our daily routine, but it really was the best thing for her as her condition worsens."

"It must be a comfort to her to know that she has so many friends who care."

Laurie's sigh was loud and plaintive. "I think we're all bearing up well under the reality of it all. Fortunately, she still knows mostly who we are and is glad to see us when we show up. I guess we'll have to deal with the latter stages of the disease when we get there."

"It's sobering, isn't it?" Gaylie Girl reflected. "Watching someone slowly disappear before your very eyes, I mean."

Laurie rapped her knuckles on the table and said, "I trust this awful thing won't visit any of the rest of us."

"If you have your health, you have it all at our age," Gaylie Girl added. "Gather ye rosebuds, as they say."

"Speaking of flowers," Laurie began, pursing her lips rather coyly, "are you any closer to setting a date for that second-time-around wedding bouquet of yours?"

"Ah! Your timing is perfect!" Gaylie Girl exclaimed. "Tonight's the night I'm breaking the news to everyone. Hale and I have chosen Labor Day weekend for the ceremony, and I'm calling up the rest of the girls when I get home."

Laurie perked up and clasped her hands together dramatically. "That's wonderful news. I thought we'd never pin you two down!"

Gaylie Girl managed a diplomatic smile, but it soon faded. "It took us a little longer than we'd anticipated. I won't mince words. I've been having a little bit of trouble with my children. They don't approve of the marriage. At least not at this juncture. Petey and Amanda keep on telling me that they just don't understand what on earth I'm doing down here. Or why I would want to pick up my life and move it so far away from everything they know. They just think Second Creek, Mississippi, is beyond the pale, and while I don't need their approval, I don't want to cut myself off from my family, either. I'd like to think I'm that strong, but I'm just not."

"I can certainly understand that."

Gaylie Girl resumed with a dramatic intake of breath. "I can't help but think this is karma. I had nearly the same opinion of this town fifty-odd years ago when my cousin Polly and I were trapped here for a couple of days on that infamous War Bonds tour. That's when Hale and I first got involved, of course. I'm afraid my children just haven't been

ROBERT DALBY

able to put themselves in my shoes. Much to my chagrin, they've grown up long on wealth and short on empathy. I know Peter spoiled them, and maybe I did, too."

"Oh, dear," Laurie replied, slowly shaking her head from side to side. "It seems that getting our children to see things through our eyes is one of the greatest challenges of being a parent. You don't want them to finally understand you after you're gone and it's too late to do you any good. I really shouldn't complain, though. Both my Lizzie and Hannah seem to be getting more and more on the same page with me as time goes by, and the older I get, the more I really appreciate that."

Gaylie Girl drew back and gave her an admiring glance tinged with envy. "You must be sure to give me some of your tips to use on Amanda and Petey when they arrive next weekend. I finally got them to agree to come down for a visit, and I'll want you and Powell and the rest of the girls to be a huge part of putting out the welcome mat, of course. We'll all have to get together and formulate a plan soon." Then she quickly switched gears. "Any other Nitwitt news I should know about?"

Laurie thought for a moment before striking a triumphant pose. "Oh, Novie has some wonderful news. Her son, Marc, and his companion, Michael, are about to move from California to Second Creek, and are opening up a plant boutique on The Square. It seems landscape architecture and plant materials are Michael's thing. They say they're going to do their part to restore some of the

38

charm that's been lost because of the Bypass and the Mega-Mart. They've even picked out a right catchy name for their little business—H-O-W-apostrophe-S, then P-L-A-N-T-S-question mark."

Gaylie Girl grinned.

"Yes, well, the main thing is that Novie is just thrilled to pieces that she has Marc back in her life after what was a very long period of estrangement. It seems she had problems for years with the gay angle, but she's put all that behind her now and can't wait to do everything possible to help the two of them make a go of it. I assured her that all of us Nitwitts would be lining up at their door for all our houseplant needs."

Then Gaylie Girl ran on excitedly about the fixer-upper on North Bayou Avenue that she and Mr. Choppy had agreed to buy. "I'm sure I'll need more than a few indoor green friends to water and talk to once we finish with the major renovations. I've always had an ongoing relationship with my houseplants," she concluded with a pleasant smile. "And how nice for Novie to have her son finally settled in life like that. I wish I could say the same for my Petey." She paused briefly for an exasperated sigh. "Forty has come and gone for him. He's been married and divorced twice, and personally I thought his two wives were just gems as daughters-in-law. I got along just fine with both of them. But he didn't, as it turned out. As I've told Hale, I just don't think he knows what he wants out of life, and his father leaving him some money of his own has made things worse,

I'm afraid. It's enabled him to indefinitely postpone buckling down to make something work. He needs a project in the worst way."

Laurie was nodding sympathetically. Both her daughters had taken their time tracking down spouses, and she had wisely resisted the generational impulse to pressure them, refusing to resurrect that time-honored "girls should be married by a certain age" rule of thumb that her own mother had imposed upon her from the moment she graduated from high school. "Just give him more time," Laurie finally replied. "I predict he'll find his niche sooner or later."

"I hope so. Of course, his sister, Amanda, is a little too settled, I think," Gaylie Girl added, continuing to surprise Laurie with the unsolicited review of her children. "Oh, she's quite happily married to Richard Sykes, and she's given me three lovely grandchildren, but she's not cutting me much slack about my friendship with Hale."

Laurie leaned in on her elbows with a confidential air. "Well, I trust we can turn that around for you. We Nitwitts are especially good at scheming, you know."

"I'm counting on that. Now, was there any other significant news I've missed?"

Laurie quickly scanned the lineup of Nitwitts in her head and said, "It's pretty much status quo for Renza and Denver Lee. Renza's enjoying her reign as Nitwitt president—she's a natural at lording it over everyone, you know. Denver Lee is trying her dead-level best to lose more weight and keep that diabetes diagnosis at bay. Nothing new there. But Myrtis has added a new wrinkle. She's turned Evening Shadows into a luxury bed-and-breakfast, and I have to say I think it's a marvelous idea. The woman does know how to entertain, and the food she serves is scrumptious. But that house is way too big for Myrtis to be rambling around in all by her lonesome listening to her husband's old Frankie Valli records. She needs the company."

"Evening Shadows was my first real taste of Second Creek hospitality the day after Hale's election, so naturally I'm thrilled Myrtis has already offered such a gracious setting for our wedding. She called me long-distance some time ago and wouldn't take no for an answer," Gaylie Girl said, pausing to sniff the air curiously. "Is everything still okay in the oven?"

"Oops!" Laurie exclaimed, shooting up out of her chair and heading over to the stove and its warm, concentrated aromas. "I run my mouth and do this all the time!"

THE DINNER CONVERSATION among the two couples was predictably lively, punctuated here and there by anecdotes from Mr. Choppy about the perils of municipal politics. "Councilman Player, for instance, is just obsessed with the soccer mom thing," he was explaining to the others between bites of his savory salmon. "He keeps insistin' that he would never have gotten elected without all those busy women in their station wagons. They gotta have their own soccer field for their children on his side of town. We just can't swing it in the budget right now, of course, but the other day over lunch, I just about sprayed my sweet tea all over him when he says to me, 'It's just unfair that the kids in my ward have to go across town to kick their balls.'"

The table erupted with laughter, and then Powell spoke up emphatically. "If that's the worst you have to deal with, you're one lucky mayor."

Mr. Choppy put down his fork and frowned. "Well, I am a bit concerned about some recent Pond-Raised Catfish lay-off rumors. I've got a get-together with Curtis Ray Keyes down the line to find out what's goin' on out there. My secretary is pretty worried these days about her husband's job, and he's one of their best shift managers. I have to say, I'm puzzled as I can be. Pond-Raised never had any problems before that I heard of. But I intend to get to the bottom of it real soon."

"I'm sure you will," Laurie offered. "And I know we'll all help you win your children over, Gaylie Girl. So let's toast to a whole handful of Second Creek solutions—the best problem-solving there is."

Filled to the brim with Laurie's delicious food, they all quickly smiled and raised their glasses to the successful resolutions they felt certain were on the way.

4.

THE MISTRESS OF THE SCALES

Euterpe Simon stood in the doorway of Mr. Choppy's office, striking a pose that was at once unconventional and riveting. She was stroking a spotlessly manicured toy poodle, which was draped over her shoulder like a sleeping baby. The effect of her aquamarine ensemble was both ethereal and soothing, matching her easy smile and arresting blue eyes; and though it was clear that she was a mature woman, it was virtually impossible to tell just how old she actually might be. Some indefinable quality about her somehow suggested that the passing years were of little consequence to her.

After introducing herself to Mr. Choppy and Gaylie Girl, Euterpe glided across the room to the visitor's leather armchair. "And this is my Pan," she added, continuing her gentle stroking. "I'm sure he's dreaming his little doggie dreams right now."

"He certainly is well behaved. Not a peep since you arrived. Did you have a pleasant journey to Second Creek?" Gaylie Girl said, striving for small talk from her nearby chair.

"Oh, I never mind travel," Euterpe replied, leaning back against the supple leather and then sighing contentedly. "All life is travel, you know."

Mr. Choppy settled in behind his desk comfortably. "Somebody wiser than me once said that it's all about the journey."

"Indeed it is. And now my journey has brought me to your wonderful little town. I would very much like to make my mark here with music. The harmony of the scales, if you will. I want to sound just the right note for the people of Second Creek, and I'm very much interested in using your building for that purpose, Mayor Dunbar. I think a quick, modest renovation will do the trick—a coat of paint here, a few potted plants for good measure. Then I'll move in my practice spinet and my grand piano for recitals and put out my shingle. 'Euterpe Simon, Mistress of the Scales.' That's how I've occupied much of my time since my husband, David, died."

She paused briefly to allow Mr. Choppy and Gaylie Girl to digest what she'd proposed and then resumed. "You know, I don't think there's anything in the world quite so easy on the eyes as a grand piano, nor quite so satisfying to master. It lifts people to new heights, I always say. It's part of why I want to teach and illuminate."

Energized by Euterpe's vision, Gaylie Girl spoke up quickly. "You make me want to take lessons right this instant, Mrs. Simon."

"Please. You must call me Euterpe."

"Euterpe it is, then. And you must call me Gaylie Girl. But the fact is I've always wanted to learn to play the piano. I've even had one all these years in my house up in Lake Forest, but it's just been standing there, soaking up the furniture polish. Perhaps I should consider becoming your first pupil."

"I don't see why not," Euterpe replied. "And I imagine your recommendation will go far in Second Creek."

Gaylie Girl gently wagged a finger and smartly arched her brows. "The truth is, I'm a relative newcomer to Second Creek, myself. But when I believe in something, I'm capable of a mean testimonial."

"Then, shall we get down to the leasin' figures and arrangements?" Mr. Choppy cut in, rustling papers on his desk. "I had a certain price range in mind to open things up." He paused to proffer a sheet of paper, which Euterpe accepted with her free hand.

Within fifteen minutes or so, a leasing arrangement agreeable to both parties had been worked out, and Mr. Choppy's Piggly Wiggly had been put to yet another adaptive use, ensuring that it would continue as a focal point of

Second Creek activities for many years to come. For her part, Euterpe would begin advertising in *The Citizen* to solicit pupils right away for an early August opening.

"You haven't mentioned where you'll be living," Gaylie Girl said to Euterpe after the various papers had been signed. The two of them had just headed out the door while Mr. Choppy stayed behind huddling with Cherish. "If you need help finding something suitable, one of my friends has a brother-in-law in the real estate business. I can guarantee you that Paul Belford won't let you down. He recently did a bang-up job for me and Hale on a fixer-upper we've just closed on."

Euterpe gave her a gracious smile as they walked down the hallway. "Oh, thank you so much for your concern, but I'm where I need to be for a while. I'm staying at a gorgeous bed-and-breakfast called Evening Shadows. I've booked it for at least two months, until I get the lay of the land a bit better."

"What a small world!" Gaylie Girl exclaimed, clearly delighted by the revelation. "Your hostess, Myrtis Troy, is another of my new Nitwitt friends, and I just know you're going to love her. Hale and I have had the pleasure of spending the night out there ourselves. It's decorated to the rafters, and the food is to die for."

"Oh, I wholeheartedly agree," Euterpe added. "I arrived day before yesterday and have gotten to sample some of the goodies for myself. The way your friend has it set up, you can pay a little extra and sit down to a multi-course dinner as well. Last night, I had this shrimp and grits dish that may have been the best thing I ever put in my mouth. Your friend Myrtis said, 'It's a little something I invented a few years back when I couldn't think of what on earth to do with some shrimp left over from one of my parties.' At any rate, the way you Southerners mix unusual ingredients together boggles the mind. But I like that. I've always been a believer in yin and yang and that sort of thing."

"Well, I can't claim to be a bona fide Southerner yet, but I fully appreciate every one of those juxtapositions you just ran by me." Then Gaylie Girl stopped in her tracks as they neared the courthouse entrance and gave a sudden gasp. "I have the most fabulous idea, Euterpe. You simply must meet the rest of the Nitwitts. We're all getting together day after tomorrow so the girls can divvy up duties for my approaching wedding and entertaining my visiting children soon. It would be the perfect way to spread the word about your new studio as well."

"How very gracious of you," Euterpe replied. "I believe I'll have to take you up on that."

Gaylie Girl was chuckling to herself as they walked down the courthouse steps into the pedestrian traffic milling about The Square. "Maybe the rest of the girls could end up taking lessons from you, too. Maybe they'd make so much progress they could even take turns playing the standards I grew up with at my wedding. Sounds corny, I know, but it should fill the bill. When I'm wrapped up in my favorite music, I always feel like nothing bad could ever happen to me. At any rate, my wedding is going to be staged out at Evening Shadows, where you're staying, you know. I'm really beginning to like the symmetry of all this."

"Oh, I'm quite the fan of symmetry, you'll discover," Euterpe explained. "I couldn't be otherwise, teaching the scales as I do and billing myself as their mistress. Each note is its own perfect interval and self-contained universe, as well as proof that there is a grand design out there for all of us to experience and enjoy. I do not settle for merely teaching piano. I consider that I also teach patience, rhythm, and balance—everything that's necessary to lead a happy life."

"Well, there's no way I can turn you down now. You're more convincing than one of those late-night motivational infomercials and far more intellectual to boot!" Gaylie Girl exclaimed. "When can I sign on the dotted line, so to speak?"

Euterpe chuckled richly. "Why not at your upcoming club meeting? We could accomplish quite a number of things all at once."

"Then it's settled. Day after tomorrow. Noon at Renza Belford's house on North Bayou Avenue. You and Myrtis can ride in together, I'm sure. It's just down the street from the fixer-upper that Hale and I bought."

"I've always felt moving into a new house is such an exciting time. I think I enjoy beginnings much more than conclusions. So many possibilities ahead and no way of knowing how they're going to turn out, even though I always err on the positive side." Euterpe paused and pointed to a narrow side street. "My car is parked down there. So if you'll excuse me, I'll just be moseying on off to Evening Shadows to get Pan and myself a bit more settled. Do you need a ride?"

"Oh, no. I've got my own car one block over."

And with that the new friends said their good-byes and went their separate ways.

THAT EVENING, Mr. Choppy and Gaylie Girl were snuggling on one of his well-worn sofas surrounded by several of her still unpacked boxes. They were also in the midst of sipping cocktails and discussing Euterpe and her perfectly balanced poodle. "It's the oddest thing, Hale," Gaylie Girl was saying. "I don't think I've ever been around someone as compelling as Euterpe."

He sat up a bit, stretched his legs, and blinked. "What do you mean?"

"Oh, I know it sounds like nonsense, but there's just something about her that I can't put my finger on. I think I had the sense that there was no way I was going to be able to resist her. She's awfully good at speechifying, if there is such a word. Suddenly, I found myself committed to piano lessons—not that I didn't want to do it, of course."

Mr. Choppy frowned, considering very carefully before he answered. "Yeah, I think I know what you're gettin' at. She had the same effect on me first time I talked to her over the phone. It was kinda hypnotic."

Gaylie Girl had a distant, dreamy look on her face as she

spoke. "I just adored her clothes. I must remember to ask her where she got that marvelous aquamarine creation. I thought it made her look like some sort of classical painting come to life. She's obviously a very cultured woman. Second Creek will be lucky to have her."

"So you're serious about takin' up the piano?"

"Absolutely. Way back in the day, Peter and I used to watch Liberace and all his candelabras on television, and I remember thinking how marvelous it would be to master such an impressive instrument. Then Peter bought a grand piano for our Lake Forest house on an impulse, even though neither of us could play. Such a waste, I always thought. But now I've reached the stage of my life when I'm supposed to do the things I've always wanted to do. I've raised my family, and now it's time for me—with maybe a metronome thrown in for good measure."

"A metronome?"

"That's standard equipment for piano teachers, I believe."

Mr. Choppy gave her a philosophical shrug of his shoulders. "I'll betcha anything the rest of the Nitwitts'll be interested in lessons. I know you're new to the group, but I can assure you that what one of 'em does, all the others want to do eventually—and with a vengeance. They're all polite and genteel on the surface, but they're also competitive as hell underneath."

"So I've noticed," Gaylie Girl replied, pleasantly amused.

"They always talk like they're at a tea party, but there's a lot of tension just below the surface."

Then Mr. Choppy embarked upon an impromptu but humorous review. "I know all those wonderful ladies pretty well by now. First, I can just picture Miz Denver Lee McQueen poundin' away at the ivories to beat the band, sendin' everybody runnin' for their earplugs. She's always been pretty determined about everything she does."

Gaylie Girl enjoyed a good laugh. "And how do you see the rest of them?"

"I'm picturin' Miz Renza Belford now. She'd make a huge fuss about the keys bein' too dusty for polite company and insist on havin' everything sprayed with Lemon Pledge. Then she'd play with latex gloves."

"And shout, 'Horse apples!' every time she made a mistake!" Gaylie Girl interjected with a giggle.

Mr. Choppy continued through his laughter. "You got her nailed there. Now, Miz Myrtis Troy would call up half the town and throw a party every time she sat down to a tune. I think Miz Novie Mims might find a way to trot out slides of various antique pianos she's come across in her extensive travels. Miz Laurie Hampton, well, I think she'd figure it all out quicker than any of 'em without any fanfare. I'd figure her for a star pupil, along with you, of course. As for Miz Wittsie, well, bein' out at the home and all now, I don't think piano lessons are somethin' she could manage too well, bless her heart."

"Oh, I meant to tell you!" Gaylie Girl added with an apologetic edge to her voice. "I've agreed to go over to Greenwood every Saturday and look in on Wittsie. All the other girls have their own days of the week for a little visit and lunch. Naturally, I want to do my part. You're welcome to come with me. It just breaks my heart, of course."

Just then a sudden clap of thunder startled them both, magnifying the distress they were both feeling over the mention of their ailing friend.

"Is that what I think it was?" Mr. Choppy exclaimed, rising from the sofa with a sense of urgency. More rumbling followed, and soon the two of them were standing out on the front steps of his bungalow, gazing up incredulously at a bank of angry, fast-moving clouds.

"I can't believe it. It's rain on the way. Blessed, honest-to-goodness rain!" Gaylie Girl exclaimed. "You've been keeping me posted on all the heat and the drought you've been having, and I must admit your summer weather is quite a change from what we usually get off Lake Michigan. But I could swear there was nothing in the forecast about precipitation in either the paper or on television today."

Mr. Choppy concurred. "No two ways about it, though. We're about to be deluged right now."

As if on cue, the wind picked up dramatically, whipping hundreds of tree branches into fits of swaying choreography that kept flashing the underside of their leaves. Soon enough, the first big drops began to splatter along the sidewalk and out on the street, with little wisps of steam rising and the pungent smell of nitrogen assaulting nostrils every-where. Five minutes later, every square inch of the heavens had opened up, and the parched and thirsty Second Creek landscape below soaked it all up like a sponge.

Nestled safely inside on their sofa once again, Mr. Choppy and Gaylie Girl were content to listen to the bar-rage on the roof and at the windows. "We seem to go from one extreme to another," he observed as the rhythm of the rain continued to lull them into complacency.

Gaylie Girl managed to rouse herself, shaking her head slowly. "I've been told people like to make their grand en-trances here in Second Creek. I believe it was Laurie who gave me a complete rundown once. Mr. Floyce, Lady Roth, maybe even myself—we all made a lot of noise coming to town, she told me."

"Are you sayin' this rainstorm is Euterpe's grand en-trance?"

Gaylie Girl patted his hand and managed an endearing little smirk. "Indulge me, Hale. She floats in on air, dressed as blue-green as the ocean, sweet-talks everybody to get her way, and the next thing we know, the wand is waved and the drought is over."

"A wand, huh? Nah. It's just a coincidence, most likely. The rain couldn't stay away forever," he added with a wink. "But I am still on the lookout for fireflies."

5

ONCE MORE,
THE NITWITTS

*R*enza Belford's elegant home was on North Bayou Avenue. Decades earlier, Renza and her late husband, Lewis, had sunk a large portion of their personal worth into saving this late-Victorian gem from being condemned. Now, with its fanciful turrets and inviting veranda, it was one of the showplaces of Second Creek. Impeccably furnished with period antiques, paintings, and Aubusson and Savonnerie area rugs over polished hardwood floors from top to bottom, it had become one of the favorites of the "fixed-income-little-ole-lady" bus tours that chose Second Creek as their destination every spring and fall.

At the moment, Belford Place, as Lewis and Renza had christened it shortly after its spectacular rebirth, had been buffed to within an inch of its life by a promising new housekeeper whom Novie had recommended, and the current meeting of the Nitwitts had come to order with a confident President Renza presiding.

"Ladies," Renza was saying, standing in the middle of her spacious downstairs parlor addressing the group seated around her. "We have a full and most interesting agenda today, so let's get started, shall we? First, I'd like Myrtis to step up and formally introduce our guest, Mrs. Euterpe Simon, even though I'm sure each of you has had a chance to chat with her briefly over cocktails before I called the meeting to order."

Dutifully, Myrtis abandoned her Bloody Mary and rose from her spot on one of Renza's cozy Belter love seats, motioning Euterpe to accompany her to the middle of the room. "Ladies," Myrtis began, nearly mesmerized by Euterpe's shimmering, peacock blue ensemble, "all of you know by now that Euterpe is stayin' with me out at Evening Shadows. She's come to town to teach all willin' spirits how to play the piano and has leased Mr. Choppy's Piggly Wiggly building for that purpose. It'll soon be open for lessons—all scrubbed and shiny, I'm told—and Gaylie Girl has already informed me that she will be Euterpe's first pupil. And I'm makin' it known right here and now that I'm signing up, too."

Euterpe flashed a smile as she gave Myrtis a gracious nod. "What a wonderful gesture, dear. The more, the merrier, I'm sure." Then she took the floor from Myrtis and formally worked her way through her Mistress of the Scales spiel. "Look upon it as an adventure, ladies," she concluded. "You should never stop learning and striving as the years roll by."

There was a visible stirring and buzzing among the group, and Denver Lee responded first. "Oh, I've always wanted to take piano lessons, but I just never got around to it somehow. Although I did take voice lessons my freshman year at Ole Miss. My teacher said I had real potential."

"Now, that I would love to have seen. And heard," Renza said. "You tryin' to sing, I mean. I'm gettin' a very Wagnerian vision right now—Viking helmet, horns and all."

Denver Lee bristled, heaving her bosom in nearly operatic fashion. "Scoff if you must, but I was told I could be a coloratura if I pursued it seriously."

"I suppose I could picture you loudly stompin' around a stage without too much trouble," Renza added.

As usual, Laurie stepped in to restore a semblance of order. "Ladies, I believe Euterpe still has the floor."

Renza looked properly contrite and cleared her throat. "Oh, yes, do continue, Euterpe."

"No, I was substantially finished with my pitch to you ladies. I'm now in the midst of sprucing up the building a bit. It did look slightly worn from its Piggly Wiggly and campaigning days, but I'm painting the walls a bright gold and taking up the linoleum and replacing it with hardwood flooring. It's not going to take long. Meanwhile, I'd like to invite each of you to drop by anytime during the renovation.

Perhaps some of you will even have some decorating suggestions."

Novie's hand shot up immediately. "I don't know if this qualifies as decorating, but I do have a suggestion for houseplants, if you wanted to go that way. A few green things might make interesting accents, and my son, Marc, and his friend Michael Peeler just moved to town and opened up their new plant boutique, How's Plants?, on The Square last week. I know they'd love to show you what they have in stock."

Euterpe silently continued to stroke her poodle for a while. "I would very much like to see what they have to offer."

"Well, gettin' back to the piano lessons issue," Renza put in, "I think I'd be interested in considering it, too. Maybe all of us could take lessons, as you suggest, Euterpe. Not together, of course."

"Of course not together. It isn't a cooking class, Renza," Myrtis said, giving her a disdainful glance. "It's not a stick of butter here and a pinch of salt there with a group looking on in cutesy aprons with their mouths watering. It's one-on-one, just teacher and pupil, along with black and white keys and sharps and flats."

"Nor is it to be considered a competition," Euterpe added, quickly picking up on the rivalry between the two most recent Nitwitt presidents. "Each pupil progresses at her own pace."

Laurie spoke up next. "Oh, Euterpe, I definitely want to

take lessons from you, too. But Powell and I are trotting off to Europe soon, so I'm wondering if I should start right away or postpone things."

"You can start and then resume later. Won't hurt a thing."

"In that case, I'll start up with the rest of them."

Novie was the last to volunteer. "Of course, I'll want to start lessons the same time as the others. So it looks like you'll have all of us Nitwitts eventually, except for Wittsie. But I have an idea there, too. On my last visit to the home, I noticed they have a grand piano in the library just off the lobby. Perhaps we could show Wittsie what we've learned every now and then when we go over for lunch. I think it would certainly add a more personal touch to our visits. That, and keeping her posted on all of Gaylie Girl's wedding hoopla."

"I think that's a charming and generous idea," Euterpe said, "and I think it will also serve as a motivational tool for each one of you. Imagine your sense of accomplishment when you've actually mastered a little tune to play for Wittsie's entertainment. You'll lift her spirits as well as your own."

"No singing and stomping about, though, Denver Lee," Renza quipped, offering up a naughty wink. "You'll wake everybody up."

"You're incorrigible," Denver Lee said, cracking a smile in spite of herself.

Euterpe intervened quickly. "Ladies, I do feel I must bring up a practical consideration to all of you. There's the matter of being able to practice what I'm teaching you. How many of you have access to a piano at home in between lessons?"

An impromptu survey was quickly taken, and it turned out that Renza, Denver Lee, and Myrtis had pianos in their homes, while Novie, Laurie, and Gaylie Girl did not.

"I did leave one behind up in Lake Forest, though. It was mostly for show," Gaylie Girl explained. "It's in storage right now. Perhaps I can arrange to have it shipped down here. That would give us one more to play with, even though it'll be a tight squeeze fitting it into Hale's living room. Still, we'll manage somehow."

"Excellent," said Euterpe. "Meanwhile, perhaps you ladies can work out schedules among yourselves for practice. It will be essential once we get started."

"Of course. We could just think of it as another one of our club projects," Renza offered. "And may we all produce a pleasing din for Second Creek."

"I accept the challenge, ladies," Euterpe replied, executing a curious little bow before them. "But cacophony is not in my vocabulary. Let the lessons begin."

AFTER A CHATTY BREAK in which finger sandwiches, rémoulade deviled eggs, and more Bloody Marys were passed around, Renza corralled the group's attention and again took up the day's agenda. "It seems Gaylie Girl's two children will be visiting Second Creek for the first time next weekend," she continued. "And she has asked for our help in welcoming them in the very best traditions of Southern hospitality." Renza then nodded in Gaylie Girl's direction, giving her the floor.

"Don't misunderstand, ladies," Gaylie Girl began, surveying the room with a pleasant smile. "I do love my children. But my Petey and Amanda are handfuls. They have their doubts about the choice I've made so late in life, and neither of them has any experience at all with the Deep South. That's where I need the Nitwitt expertise in wowing them for the weekend. After that, I think we can go all out to plan my wedding, which I know you've all been just dying to do. So, any suggestions?"

Gaylie Girl should have known better, even though she was still relatively new to the group. Asking the Nitwitts en masse for suggestions on any given issue was akin to blowing up the dam that held in the reservoir, and she was soon inundated with input.

Myrtis was up first, immediately calling everyone's attention to the fact that she had already agreed to host the wedding and reception out at Evening Shadows. "I was thinkin' we might also want to use my house as the starting point to welcome your children, Gaylie Girl. I have several luxurious guest rooms to offer, and Sarah and I can put together everything from simple brunches to seven-course extravaganzas. If it's pampering they're lookin' for, they'll get it with me."

"I can certainly vouch for that," Euterpe added. "I've

enjoyed accommodations all over the world, from cottages in Wales to palaces in India, and Evening Shadows compares favorably with the best I've sampled, from cuisine to ambience."

Myrtis looked supremely pleased. "Thank you for the testimonial, dear. So what do you say, Gaylie Girl? Shall we put them up at my place?"

"If you have the room, I don't see why not. I know Amanda will appreciate all the lovely pieces you and Raymond collected over the years. Hale and I absolutely loved the four-poster we slept in just after he won the election. There's something very luxurious about sleeping in a bed surrounded by posts. Makes me feel like royalty."

"Well, I insist on doing something, too," Renza interjected. "After all, I am the president of the Nitwitts, and as such I feel it is my responsibility to lead the way. Let's have a little dinner party for them here at Belford Place one night."

The challenge was on, and Myrtis quickly fell to. "Now, Renza, if Sarah and I go to all the trouble to plan meals for them out at Evening Shadows, there's no reason to cart them off elsewhere for dining purposes."

"And . . . why . . . not?" Renza asked evenly, injecting every ounce of presidential authority into her tone. "Second Creek has other options besides your B-and-B menu, Myrtis. There's the Victorian Tea Room, for instance. Vester Morrow and Mal Davis could stage quite a feast for them there. I'm sure they'd be happy to reserve the whole restaurant for us on a moment's notice. And what about Laurie? I think we all know she's the champion gourmet cook among us. It would be a shame not to let her contribute."

Having been drawn into the fray somewhat against her will, Laurie lost little time in trotting out her trademark diplomacy. "Well, how about this? Why don't we stage a progressive dinner one night? That way we can include several venues in one evening."

"Progressive?" Renza replied. "I don't think we should bring politics into this. It gives people indigestion at mealtime."

Laurie's expression teetered between surprise and bewilderment. "Renza, I can't believe you've never heard of the concept. It has nothing to do with politics. It's sort of a movable-feast arrangement. You have cocktails and hors d'oeuvres to open the evening at one establishment, then you move on to another house or restaurant for the entrée, and finally you end up at a third venue for dessert and coffee. You spread the dining experience around, in other words."

Renza lowered her haughty profile somewhat and tried for nonchalance. "Oh, of course I've heard of that before. We just called it something else years ago, as I recall."

"May I offer a suggestion?" Euterpe said. "Myrtis, you have that lovely Steinway out at Evening Shadows in the drawing room underneath the chandelier. Perhaps I could give a little recital before or after dinner one evening.

Something classical on their first evening here? It will make a memorable impression, I assure you."

Gaylie Girl clasped her hands together excitedly. "Perfect. Petey's largely indifferent to music of most any kind, but I'm afraid Amanda thinks the South consists of one big, smoke-filled honky-tonk. I'm sure a classical piece would open her eyes just a bit."

Laurie tactfully intervened, sensing that Euterpe's suggestion had lightened the mood while standing down the combatants. "Why don't we leave it at this, then? Myrtis, you and Sarah will plan most of the meals for them, just as you do for your other guests. Then let's pick a night—Saturday, for instance—for the progressive dinner. We could all have cocktails at the Victorian Tea Room with Vester and Mal, then come to my house for the main course, and finally we'll have our dessert and coffee at Belford Place."

Renza toyed with her ever-present fox fur, looking slightly uncomfortable. "Belford Place would be anticlimactic under those arrangements, wouldn't it? I know people who don't even eat dessert."

But as usual Laurie had the perfect rejoinder on the tip of her tongue. "That depends on what you mean by dessert. You could serve whatever sweets you wanted, of course. Perhaps petits fours or marzipan or even something as elaborate as tiramisu. But you and I both know that everyone in this crowd loves their after-dinner drinks. You could have scads of other cordials, dessert wines, and several different kinds of coffee drinks besides. To my way of thinking, that would put the exclamation point on the entire evening!"

"Well, when you put it that way," Renza replied, her tone sufficiently softened, "it does sound more appealing. I'm onboard, then."

Laurie surveyed the room expectantly, locking eyes with Gaylie Girl first. "So is the Saturday progressive dinner approach to your liking?"

"Absolutely. And Euterpe's Friday recital, too!"

Renza asked for a verbal show of support from the other Nitwitts and received it, while Novie, who had taken over as club secretary from the institutionalized Wittsie, duly noted the proceedings amid the careless banter that ensued.

"I had something else I wanted to mention," Gaylie Girl resumed when things had quieted down somewhat. "Amanda just adores traipsing through historic homes, and I was wondering if we might be able to arrange an impromptu tour for her. Maybe two or three houses that would give her a sampling of the various types of architecture here in Second Creek."

Novie put down her pen, puffed herself up, and abandoned her notes with what could only be described as a smug demeanor. "As it happens, I'm chairing the Springtime in Second Creek Historic Homes and Cottages Tours this year, so I believe I can convince a couple of the homeowners to accommodate us here in the off-season."

"And don't forget about my Belford Place," Renza was quick to point out. "My house is one of the favorites on the tour every season."

"Of course," Gaylie Girl replied, careful to keep a smile on her face and in her voice. "I meant in addition to Belford Place when I brought up the matter. Novie, why don't you try to line up some houses late Saturday morning into early afternoon? With all that touring, I'm sure Petey and Amanda will work up quite an appetite for the progressive dinner later on."

"Then it looks like we have Friday and Saturday pretty much planned out for you," Laurie added. "Anyone have any thoughts about Sunday? Gaylie Girl, would your children perhaps enjoy going to church?"

Gaylie Girl closed her eyes with a sigh of resignation and the suggestion of a shudder. "Oh, Amanda likes to gawk at cathedrals in foreign countries, but that's the extent of her interest in salvation, so to speak. I don't think Petey's darkened an altar since he was dismissed as an acolyte for guzzling too much communion wine behind the rector's back. That was the last straw after he had previously smuggled unleavened wafers into show-and-tell at school. He's always had a sneaky rebellious streak."

Then Laurie snapped her fingers and smiled. "One of my schemes just came upon me, ladies. Perhaps it would be a nice, homey touch for all of us to go out and have Sunday brunch over in Greenwood with Wittsie. It might be reassuring to your children to see that you're already part of a

very special group of friends who look after each other—
and you, of course. It might help bring the Nitwitts to life
for them a bit more, and I think that's the goal here, isn't it?"

"Yes, and I'm also hoping to make them understand why
I've chosen to live out the rest of my life here in Second
Creek with Hale," Gaylie Girl added. "Maybe I'll never be
able to get through to them on that particular issue, but I'm
bound and determined to try my best to keep the family
peace. So for the record, I like the idea of visiting our sweet
Wittsie for all the reasons you mentioned."

Renza quickly surveyed the group, and Novie added
Sunday brunch to the upcoming weekend agenda. "Do we
need to plan anything else?" Renza continued. "Or should
we leave your children a little free time, Gaylie Girl?"

"Let's leave some room for spontaneity. We don't need
every second accounted for. After all, this is Second Creek.
You never know what will happen."

ANOTHER HALF HOUR PASSED, during which Novie
and Denver Lee had to make their manners for a pressing
beauty parlor appointment and another diabetes prevention
checkup, respectively. The remaining Nitwitts, plus Euterpe, were now in the midst of officially discussing the actual wedding and reception details, and Myrtis was holding
forth with aplomb. Every other sentence, it seemed, found
her gesticulating wildly and gushing about the arrangements
she had made so far.

"A little birdie in the public relations office at the Peabody Hotel told me how to get in touch with Larry Lorrison and His Big Bad Swing Band," she was explaining to the group still gathered around the parlor, focusing particularly on Gaylie Girl. "That's our era, of course, and I also happen to know that you and Mr. Choppy enjoyed dancin' to his music up there last year. Well, to make a long story short, I've taken the liberty of engaging the band for the reception, Gaylie Girl. I was sure you wouldn't mind."

Gaylie Girl put down the Bloody Mary she had been nursing and applauded softly. "Mind? I'm delighted, and I'm certain Hale will be, too. That little outing up in Memphis last Christmas was the centerpiece of our courtship. The truth is, nothing can beat a musical memory, particularly if something absolutely wonderful happens to you while you're listening. Or dancing. It all gets delightfully hardwired into your brain."

"I couldn't agree more," Euterpe added. "Music overlays and infuses our lives constantly, and I'm in the business of seeing that that shall ever be the case."

Never one to be out of any given exchange for long, Renza offered up her usual edgy insight. "My God, but you're well spoken, Euterpe. I feel like I'm listening to dialogue from an old Katharine Hepburn movie whenever you open your mouth."

"I'll take that as a compliment," Euterpe replied, not missing a beat with the impromptu impression that followed. "I've always adored Katharine Hepburn. Really I have.

Among all the actresses of Hollywood's golden era, she always made the most indelible impression on me with those cheekbones and that accent. Really she did."

Gaylie Girl was giggling like a schoolgirl. "Katharine Hepburn. Larry Lorrison. They're both oldies but goodies in my book. Myrtis, what else have you come up with?"

Taking her cue, Myrtis rattled off her plans for the buffet table on the glassed-in back porch. "Basically, Sarah and I intend to offer bits and pieces of our entire B-and-B menu with a few special surprises thrown in. I've been dying to try out this new, hot curried chicken recipe and also a crème de menthe black bottom pie instead of a traditional wedding cake."

"Oh, Myrtis, that sounds divine!" Gaylie Girl exclaimed. "You'll have us all waddling away from Evening Shadows!"

"And there's more," Myrtis continued, clearly feeling her oats. "I've decided to put up a big air-conditioned tent around the boxwood maze outside and decorate it with gardenias and other fresh flowers. That way, everyone will have a place to take a little walk and get away from the throng. I often use the maze to work out my tensions."

"Well, I'm certainly impressed," Gaylie Girl said. "But are you sure you want to go to that much trouble?"

Myrtis leaned forward with a no-nonsense expression on her face. "Now, you just listen to me. How often do women our age get to walk down the aisle again? Why, I read these depressing clinical articles all the time in those women's magazines that claim our chances of gettin' remarried are more remote than gettin' struck by lightning under the apple tree. Don't spoil my fun here. Just let me spoil you and Mr. Choppy. You both deserve it, and so do we. You'll see. It'll be one helluva wedding."

"Sold. Down to the last detail," Gaylie Girl said, playfully pointing her finger at Myrtis like an auctioneer.

"Do you intend to let any of the rest of us get in on this?" Renza inquired.

Myrtis wasn't about to let Renza get under her skin. "Of course. Whatever you'd like to contribute. It will take all of us pullin' together to make this work. Which reminds me, I must tell Novie that I want to give her son's new plant boutique all my wedding flower business."

Finally, the busy agenda of the Nitwitts came to an end, with Renza declaring the entire session to be a smashing success. "Let's all keep in touch on everything as the big wedding weekend nears. And don't you worry about a thing, Gaylie Girl. We're going to make your children feel like they grew up here."

SOMEWHERE ALONG THE WAY during her pampered existence over the past half-century, Gaylie Girl had learned how to cook. Although she and Peter had employed famed Chicago chef Myron DeMille, formerly of the Palmer House, to plan and prepare all the meals they took in their

Tudor mansion, that had not prevented Gaylie Girl from sneaking into the kitchen now and then to observe him at work. She had always asked Myron's permission, and he had always granted it cheerfully. She never did anything more than make mental notes, but she had always been an observant person with a photographic memory, and it had served her well. When the mood struck her, she could turn out a steak au poivre or trout amandine with the best of them, although she knew from last year's Christmas tryst at the Peabody Hotel in Memphis that her accustomed cuisine was a bit on the rich side for Mr. Choppy's small-town tastes.

"Teach me to cook something Southern tonight," she told Mr. Choppy shortly after he'd walked through the door after work and she'd given him a peck on the cheek. "The girls were just so wonderful to me at our Nitwitt meeting today, I just feel I should do everything I possibly can to fit in. Our wedding out at Evening Shadows is going to be spectacular, and everyone is pitching in to roll out the red carpet for Petey and Amanda as well. I just know we're going to win them over."

They strolled into the kitchen together, dodging more of her newly arrived boxes along the way, and he pulled out a beer from the refrigerator, taking a hearty swallow straight out of the bottle. "Ahh, yes, that hits the spot!" He waited for the beer to settle before sitting down and continuing. "Well, I had a productive day, too. I finally got to meet with

Curtis Ray Keyes out at Pond-Raised, and I got the low-down on what's going on there."

"Is it bad news? Is it fixable?" Gaylie Girl said, taking a seat across from him at the kitchen table.

"Not sure yet," he replied in between sips of his beer. "But at least now I know that the layoff rumors I've been hearin' about have some basis in fact. Curtis Ray says that their womanizing owner, Elston Graves, has just plain lost interest in runnin' the plant. His lack of attention to detail has resulted in losin' a lucrative contract to supply catfish fillets to one of the big restaurant chains."

Gaylie Girl sat back in her seat, frowning. "So there will be layoffs, then?"

Mr. Choppy looked suddenly uncomfortable, fidgeting in his chair. "Maybe. Maybe not. Curtis Ray did suggest that Elston might be interested in sellin' Pond-Raised, if the price is right. With new blood and new money out there, maybe the layoffs could be avoided. I thought maybe I could put out some feelers—" He stopped abruptly, finished off his beer, and then looked directly into her eyes. "I wanted to run somethin' past you, too. What would you think about my mentionin' Pond-Raised to your Petey as an investment? You've been sayin' for months now that you think what he really needs is some sorta project to settle him down in life."

"I have said that, yes. And I do think that's what he needs to perhaps put an end to his restless behavior."

"So I thought maybe I could bring it up on his visit

down here, maybe take him out there, get Curtis Ray to rustle up some figures and convince him that Southern fried catfish is the best thing since corn bread. Do you think I might be on to somethin'?"

Gaylie Girl leaned in on her elbows, matching the intensity of his gaze. "You know, I think you just might be. It couldn't possibly hurt to light up those dollar signs in Petey's eyes. I say go for it, Hale. While we have Amanda touring the homes with her digital camera, you can have Petey touring the catfish production line."

Mr. Choppy settled back, enjoying the pleasant buzz from his beer. "Great. Now I feel like I'm doin' my part to help you and the Nitwitt ladies pull all this off."

"Back to my original question, however," Gaylie Girl said, elaborately gesturing toward the stove in television-spokesmodel fashion. "What are you going to teach me to cook tonight? It has to be something quintessentially Southern, you understand."

"Funny you should ask," he replied, rising from his chair and heading over to the pantry. "I had a pretty big lunch with Curtis Ray today out at Pond-Raised—some pork tenderloin and a baked potato and some green beans with some bread pudding for dessert. So I was thinkin' somethin' on the lighter side for supper. How about cheese grits and omelets, and I'll show ya how to whip up the cheese grits?"

Gaylie Girl laughed brightly and joined him just as he retrieved a box of instant grits from the shelves. "Grits and fried chicken! That's all Amanda thinks we eat down South, and here I am proving her half-right. Okay, I'm ready, willing, and able. What do I do first?"

Mr. Choppy retrieved a measuring cup from one of the cabinets and handed it over to her. "Here. Pour out one cup. That'll be more than enough for us."

Gaylie Girl carefully followed his instructions, holding the cup of grits in front of her face and then squinting as she held it up to the light. "This doesn't look like nearly enough for even one person, much less two."

"A beginner's misconception," he explained, adding a playful smile and a wink for emphasis. "Grits expand like you wouldn't believe. Sometimes I think Hollywood is missin' a bet not makin' a horror movie about some dumb bachelor who pours a whole box of grits into a pot, and it bubbles up and conquers the world."

They both enjoyed a good laugh, and Gaylie Girl's cooking lesson proceeded smoothly after that. Soon, she had a small pot of water boiling, and they both watched as the dry, innocent grits descended to the depths of the salted maelstrom.

"Just keep on stirrin'," Mr. Choppy advised. "They'll eventually thicken up, and that's when we'll take 'em off the stove and add the cheese and butter and garlic salt."

"Garlic salt? Oh, well, as long as we're both going to be eating it."

While meticulously tending the grits, Gaylie Girl continued to trot out more details of the Nitwitt meeting, and

Mr. Choppy busied himself cracking eggs into a bowl. "Sometimes I wonder if I should be going to all this trouble to win the children over," she concluded. "But then, I've learned the hard way about tying up loose ends, haven't I? Haven't *we*, I should say?"

He looked up from beating the eggs with a fork and smiled. "You said a mouthful. My life has turned around one hundred and eighty degrees. Hey, if we can get back together after fifty-odd years, the rest'll be a piece a' cake. As in wedding, I mean."

"Oh, I meant to tell you," Gaylie Girl added. "Myrtis is going to make us a crème de menthe black bottom pie for our wedding reception, instead of the traditional almond-flavored Kilimanjaro with icing. I think I'd marry you just to get a little taste of that."

"Sounds like a memory in the makin' to me." He sidled up to her to inspect the progress of the grits, nodding approvingly. "See how thick they've become with a little lazy bubblin' up here and there? They've always reminded me of a junior-high science project at this point." Then he gave her a mischievous wink. "Good ole Southern comfort food. There's nothin' like it."

6

THE OFFSPRING MATTRESS

*T*he long-awaited visitors from Lake Forest had arrived at last for their big weekend, but it had been an awkward ride down from the Memphis Airport, from Mr. Choppy's point of view. Though Gaylie Girl had tried to act as a tactful buffer between her children and her fiancé, the tension filled his Dodge like the secondhand smoke in some political back room. Totally overdressed for the occasion in female CEO fashion, Amanda had set the tone with her first comment as Mr. Choppy kept the engine running curbside at the airport while helping Petey load their luggage.

"Is this one of those wrecked rentals?" she had said quite audibly to her mother, who was sitting on the front passenger side and trying her best to smile. In his business suit Petey looked equally skeptical as he and Amanda subsequently piled into the backseat.

"No, it's Hale's car. He keeps it around for sentimental reasons," Gaylie Girl had answered, the irritation creeping into her voice. "We were going to come up in my car, but it's in the shop."

From that point forward, the conversation was very strained and clipped. Mr. Choppy made a game effort to rescue it, trotting out one of his best stories once they were out of Memphis and heading down Highway 61 South. It was the tale of Grace Fong, who had moved to Second Creek with her family during the Eisenhower years.

"There'd been quite a few Chinese families in Second Creek around the turn of the century, but they all seemed to have moved away for one reason or another. Miz Fong was a single mother with three children, and my own mother, Gladys, quickly befriended her. She even threw a little neighborhood shebang for her to make her feel at home. Miz Fong sent along a little thank-you note in the best English she could muster, but it didn't end there, no sir. Mama called her up to tell her how charmin' her thank-you note was, and the Ping-Pong match was on. Miz Fong sent her another thank-you note, thankin' her for the phone call about the first note. It prob'ly shoulda ended there, but Mama called her again and told her no note was necessary for the phone call. So then—you guessed it—Miz Fong sent a third note thankin' Mama for lettin' her know what the correct thing to do was. I'm sure it was all due to Miz Fong's polite upbringin'. She was a very sweet woman."

Gaylie Girl interrupted the story with her typical sparkling laugh, perhaps a bit too obviously, but Mr. Choppy could see in the rearview mirror that neither Amanda nor Petey seemed particularly engaged. Nonetheless, he forged ahead.

"At that point I believe Mama attempted to end the exchange, but not before Miz Fong had called her up to find out if anything was wrong, since she hadn't heard from her lately. I think it woulda gone on forever if Mama hadn't finally reassured her that they could put the whole thing to bed and resume their routine lives as housewives—on a thankless basis."

"Thankless. Yes, that is clever," Amanda had managed. But her tone was reminiscent of a crumb she was throwing out because it was expected of her. There was the barest hint of animation in her face, and Petey's smile seemed restrained as well.

But once Amanda and Petey had walked into the living room of the cluttered little bungalow at 34 Pond Street, Mr. Choppy could sense that they were working hard to bite their tongues. It was all there in their surprised expressions and eyes searching for a place to focus and land.

"So this is the family home," Amanda stated evenly, giving Gaylie Girl a surreptitious glance.

"With all these boxes everywhere, I can't tell whether you're packing or unpacking, Mother," Petey added.

Gaylie Girl was quick to counter. "A little of both, I guess. But Hale and I will soon be up to our eyeballs in renovations with the new fixer-upper we've bought. I'll let you get a glimpse of it before you leave."

After freshening up from the drive down, they all finally settled in around the living room, where Mr. Choppy was fidgeting on the sofa beside Gaylie Girl, closely observing Amanda and Petey seated across from him. Neither of them resembled their mother very much. He'd come to the obvious conclusion that they must have favored their late father, Peter Lyons. Both were dark-haired and olive-skinned with a facile yet intense demeanor that made them look like they might be angry about something. Still, they were definitely attractive—especially Petey, who was tall and lanky with the crisp style of a business executive.

Gaylie Girl had just resumed her seat after serving them all glasses of muscadine wine with a cheese and fruit plate for good measure, but the conversation remained stilted. "We grow the grapes for this little wine right here in the Delta," Mr. Choppy was explaining, after taking a healthy sip. "We hope you'll like it."

Petey lifted his glass perfunctorily and sampled it. "Yes. It is a bit different. On the sweet side, I'd say. I like my wine a little drier."

Amanda nodded and agreed, then politely mentioned her husband, Richard Sykes, and three children, whom she'd left behind in Chicago. "And there was a cool feeling in the air when we left, but I can hardly catch my breath, it's so hot down here," she continued, sticking with the small talk while making a histrionic fanning gesture.

"It was a lot worse earlier in the summer," Mr. Choppy added quickly. "Record heat and no fireflies."

Both Amanda and Petey looked puzzled, and he said: "Fireflies? Uh, I don't get it."

"When I was growin' up, we used to call 'em lightnin' bugs," Mr. Choppy explained. "Anyway, they seemed to have mostly disappeared this summer, and we think it may be due to the extreme heat. We have had some rain lately, and I've spotted maybe one or two around since, but they're still not out in full force like they usually are."

"Fascinating," Petey said. But then there was nothing further from either him or his sister. The tension that had filled the Dodge had now followed them into the house.

Mr. Choppy decided that the moment had arrived to switch gears and proceed with the agenda that he and Gaylie Girl had concocted. "Well, whether our muscadine wine's too dry or too sweet for your taste, it's not the only thing we're famous for. Second Creek is the land of soybeans and catfish, too."

Amanda made a face. "Ewww. Catfish. I think I remember reading in the newspapers somewhere that they're nasty, bottom-feeding trash fish."

Petey quickly chimed in. "And I read a magazine article once that said everything from license plates to Nikes to mallard ducks have turned up in the slit-open bellies of some of those whopper Mississippi River catfish. The big ones are practically like sharks. They'll eat anything."

"Well, you're both mostly right about all that," Mr. Choppy said. "The river cats are certainly different from the pond-raised, though. Much more aggressive. But they're all really delicious, I can assure you."

"Oh, they're beyond tasty," Gaylie Girl explained. "Especially the way they're prepared down here. My good friend Laurie Hampton, whom you'll soon meet, is going to contribute her wonderful lemon-pepper catfish to our progressive dinner tomorrow. I'm quite sure you're going to fall in love with it just like I did. Why, I hear you raving all the time about these fabulous dishes you've discovered in your frequent travels, Amanda."

But Amanda was having none of it, lifting her profile dramatically. "In Tuscany and Alsace-Lorraine and places like that, yes. I really can't see putting catfish in the same category. Or in my mouth."

Mr. Choppy saw where the conversation was headed and wisely short-circuited any defensiveness on his part with an easy smile and a change of emphasis. "They're a pretty down-home staple here in the Delta, no two ways about it. Maybe our most dependable comfort food. Easier goin' down than fried chicken." He deliberately caught Petey's gaze. "Did you know we have over a hundred and fifty-five thousand acres of catfish ponds in this part of Mississippi?"

"Had no idea," Petey answered in a rather emotionless tone. "So it's a big business?"

"Lotsa money in it. Over five hundred million pounds of the tasty critters comin' outta the Delta every year."

Mr. Choppy shot Gaylie Girl a conspiratorial glance, and she joined in on cue. "I think the entire country has discovered the benefits of aquaculture, as they're calling it these days. It's a real investment opportunity."

There was a slight uptick in Petey's vocal inflection as he put down his wineglass and turned toward his mother. "Really?"

"Why, just the other day, Hale was telling me something about the local processing plant, weren't you, dear?"

"Yes. That would be Pond-Raised Catfish. They've always been a vital cog in the local economy, and they ship those catfish fillets and nuggets to restaurants and supermarkets all over the country. But they could probably use some managerial help these days to get to the top of their game. Maybe tomorrow I could drive you out to see a few things for yourself, Petey—just the two of us."

Amanda remained clearly above the fray, her eyes roaming around the room in a detached manner, but Petey continued to perk up. "Maybe so. Of course, I've never even tasted catfish before, but you've got me curious about it now. I'm game."

"And if you really like it," Amanda said, "I'm sure you can have most of my helping when the time comes."

Gaylie Girl delicately rolled a grape between her thumb

and index finger and gave her daughter a disapproving glance. "That's not very adventurous of you, Amanda. Where's my experienced traveler?"

Fortunately, Amanda chose not to argue the point further and moved on. "I'm much more interested in this tour of the antebellum homes you've promised me, Mother. You said that happens tomorrow?"

"Right after breakfast. My friend Renza Belford will be showing you her Belford Place, and I've gotten special permission to visit our Lady Roth's house, Cypress Knees. Now, that will be quite an experience in itself—Lady Roth as our historical hostess."

For the first time all afternoon, Amanda's face and tone of voice became truly animated. "Lady Roth? You mean you have royalty here in Second Creek? You know, I've actually met royalty on my many trips to Europe. Countess Mady Gertrude Gutenberg in Heidelberg, for instance. She took Richard and myself to the Mannheim Opera to see *Tales of Hoffman* in German. We sat in her box seats next to Dianne Carlton-Rhys Diefenbach—she goes by DeeDee, you know—and her cousin Hans Klaus Victor von Zimmers. Everyone calls him Zimmy. Then we drove to Alsace-Lorraine for lunch the next day. At least the chauffeur did. He went over a hundred and twenty miles per hour. I thought surely we would get a ticket, but the Europeans don't care about such traffic nitpicking the way we Americans do. All in all, it was just a fabulous outing."

It was Mr. Choppy who continued the narrative on Lady

Roth. "I'm afraid Lady Roth's title is all in her turban-wrapped head, Miz Amanda. But she's a fascinatin' person. Very theatrical in everything she does, and your mother says her house is filled to the rafters with all kinda treasures from the Vanderlith and Roth families. It'll probably be the highlight of your schedule tomorrow."

"Speaking of schedules," Gaylie Girl added, "I see by my watch that it's almost time for us to get you both out to Evening Shadows and checked into your rooms. My friend Myrtis Troy will have the red carpet rolled out for you. Her place is absolutely the most luxurious bed-and-breakfast in Second Creek."

"Another of your Nitwitts, right?" Amanda said, quickly rising to her feet. "I'm still not sure why you want to call yourselves something like that, Mother. It sounds positively addled."

Gaylie Girl managed a diplomatic smile. "You'll understand better when you've met all the girls a bit later today. I'm fortunate to have made such wonderful friends so quickly. They've all really made it possible for me to embrace Second Creek the way I have."

Amanda shrugged, clearly indicating with her body language that she could not wait to escape from the drab clutter of 34 Pond Street to something much more upscale.

"YOU WERE QUITE LITERAL about the welcome mat, weren't you, Mother?" Amanda was saying as Sarah also ushered her brother, Mr. Choppy, and Gaylie Girl into the enormous foyer of Evening Shadows some twenty minutes later. Myrtis had, in fact, purchased a red carpet and rolled it out Academy Awards–style down the hallway in honor of the occasion. "But I could have sworn we were doing Deep South this weekend, not Hollywood."

Gaylie Girl fought through a wave of irritation at her daughter's flippant remark. "I think it's a very thoughtful touch. Myrtis has done such an elegant job of decorating this house. There are striking pieces in every room. Hale and I found it very comfortable and relaxing when we stayed here the night of his mayoral victory."

Fortunately, Amanda herself managed to rescue the situation. "Oh, I was just kidding, Mother. I'm sure it's all going to be very lovely."

Wrapped in an alluring gold sari, Myrtis suddenly appeared in the jasmine-scented hallway, and a flurry of gushing introductions ensued all around. "We have a delightful evening planned for you," Myrtis continued. "First, cocktails. Then a piano recital by our Mistress of the Scales, Euterpe Simon, who's upstairs gettin' her beauty rest for the occasion. We Nitwitts have actually started our piano lessons with her down at the old Piggly Wiggly building, and some of us already know our scales. Not that it sounds very melodious, but we all take it one note at a time."

"Yes, Mother's been telling me about what she's learned so far," Amanda remarked. "The scales, sharps, flats, middle C—that sort of thing."

"Oh, it's gone beyond that, hasn't it, Myrtis?" Gaylie Girl said. "Some of us have twisted Euterpe's arm to teach us a couple of simple ditties which will come in handy when we visit our dear Wittsie Chadwick over in Greenwood for Sunday brunch. I can't wait to see her reaction."

Myrtis tilted her head smartly to one side and grinned. "We hope we can pull it all off, of course. Anyway, to get back to our evening, we have a delicious dinner party as the finale with the menu prepared by Sarah and myself. She and I both decided that we'd go ahead and try this hot curried chicken and saffron rice recipe we've wanted to serve for just ages. If it goes over, we'll have it at your wedding, Gaylie Girl. Of course, I'm wearin' this sari in honor of the occasion. Meanwhile, just think of yourselves as my gourmet guinea pigs."

"At least she's not serving catfish," Amanda whispered out of the side of her mouth to her brother as Sarah led the way to their upstairs rooms.

"Come on, Sis," Petey countered under his breath. "At least give these people a chance. They seem to be going all out for us."

Gaylie Girl and Mr. Choppy remained behind, retreating to the drawing room, where Sarah offered them wine on a small silver platter before departing for the kitchen.

"Well, how do you think it's going so far?" Gaylie Girl said, making herself comfortable on a corner love seat that Mr. Choppy had already claimed for himself.

"Sweetheart, you didn't lie. Your kiddies are a tough act,

but I do sense we're softenin' them up a bit. I mean, I've got Petey agreein' to go with me out to Pond-Raised to meet with Curtis Ray Keyes tomorrow. That's a great start."

Gaylie Girl nodded while sipping her wine thoughtfully. "Amanda's harder to handle, though. I think what I'm going to do is introduce her to Euterpe before the recital and let them get to know each other. I think a large dose of Euterpe will put my name-dropping daughter in the right frame of mind for all the festivities this weekend."

"I wasn't gonna bring that up," Mr. Choppy said somewhat tentatively. "But I did kinda get a kick outta all those royal nicknames Amanda threw around. Hey, I didn't know those people from Adam and Eve, but she made it sound like a lotta fun, zippin' around Europe in fast cars like that."

"Amanda likes everyone to know she lives in the fast lane. I wish she were more down-to-earth, and I'm hoping this weekend will make her see that you can have just as good a time in Second Creek, Mississippi, as you can in the capitals of Europe. Right now I'm afraid she thinks I'll be exiling myself to one long ride on the turnip truck down here." Gaylie Girl took another sip of her wine and then laughed gently. "But I think Laurie and Powell Hampton will be just the right tonic for that European connection Amanda covets so. They'll both be telling her tonight all about their upcoming trip to Paris to party and dance with the Great Buddha Magruder."

"And I have a surprise maneuver I haven't mentioned to you," Mr. Choppy added, looking quite smug.

Gaylie Girl stirred in her seat, clearly intrigued. "I didn't think we were keeping secrets from each other anymore."

"Trust me. If what I have in mind works, we're home free."

AN HOUR LATER, Gaylie Girl sat at Myrtis's Steinway, running quickly through her scales while Amanda and Euterpe stood on either side of the piano bench, giving her their undivided attention. Mr. Choppy had returned to his office for a brief wrap-up of the week with Cherish; Petey was still upstairs napping; and Myrtis was tending to a few last-minute odds and ends before the cocktail hour and the rest of the guests arrived.

"You have great dexterity, Gaylie Girl," Euterpe was saying, her own fingers gently stroking the recumbent Pan's fur as usual. "You're a fast learner—in fact, the fastest of the Nitwitt group and all my other pupils combined. I have a dozen at this early stage."

"Well, at least you're finally putting that piano that Dad bought to good use," Amanda said, sounding slightly reproachful. "It just took up space all these many years."

Gaylie Girl gave her daughter a knowing glance and sighed. "I've put it in our fixer-upper on North Bayou Avenue, since it wouldn't fit in Hale's place. I go over every day to practice, and between my banging away and the workmen banging away, we produce quite a racket. I think I may have already learned the 'Anvil Chorus.' It does make me wonder if I'll ever really sound like I know what I'm doing."

"All beginners feel that way," Euterpe explained. "At first, piano lessons do seem like a lot of tedious banging, almost like the noises a piano tuner makes. Just note after note and not terribly pleasing to the ear. But one day, after much practice, it all clicks in, and suddenly you're playing recognizable songs. It all flows through your fingers into the keyboard, and you feel such a sense of accomplishment."

Gaylie Girl rose from the bench with a smile. "I can't wait for that day to arrive, I assure you. But now, why don't we all take a break and have a nice little chat?" The three of them took their seats around the room, and Gaylie Girl continued her social orchestration. "Amanda, you might like to know that Euterpe is quite the world traveler, just as you are."

Amanda sat up a bit straighter in her armchair. "Where all have you been?"

"Where haven't I been is more like it," Euterpe said, throwing her head back and laughing with gusto. "Almost all of Europe, Japan, Singapore, South America, Australia—really, just about anywhere you care to name. Bright lights, big cities—that's my mantra."

Amanda produced a skeptical frown in knee-jerk fashion. "If that's the case, then why are you here in Second Creek? Isn't this a bit off the beaten path?" She gave her mother a piercing glance for emphasis.

Euterpe looked particularly pensive for a while and then said: "Let's just say that Second Creek is my kind of town. It presents challenges that I eagerly accept. And, of course, rewards that I definitely anticipate."

Amanda nodded, but the look on her face indicated she had no idea what Euterpe was talking about, and she switched subjects. "May I ask you about your little dog there? He's so still lying on your shoulder like that. When you first swept down the stairs a few minutes ago in that dazzling blue gown, I thought he might be a prop—like a stuffed animal."

"Yes, I have had people tell me that from time to time," Euterpe replied with a note of amusement in her voice. "Pan just likes being next to his mommy."

Gaylie Girl kept the conversation going when it lagged, which was quite often, mostly due to Amanda's indifference, but eventually both Amanda and Euterpe were exchanging pleasantries about their families.

"I never had any children," Euterpe was explaining. "David and I tried many times, but I guess it just wasn't meant to be. I concentrated on my teaching, and then, after David died, my travels. I was determined to get out of the house and out of the darkness that enveloped me."

"My goodness! That's quite a dramatic way of putting it," Gaylie Girl said, looking as puzzled as her daughter this time. "Almost gothic, I think."

"Oh, no, I meant the comment about the darkness literally. David had his inexplicable quirks, and one of them was his obsession with the light bill. He was a real penny-pincher, even though we were never hurting for money. Often, after dinner, we'd sit in the living room talking to each other across the darkness, since he didn't like to turn on the lights. It's amazing how you can misinterpret things when you can't see the face of the person who's talking to you, no matter how well you think you know them. It's also a wonder I didn't stumble and break a hip or something. I became very adept at lighting candles, though. It more or less became my theme."

Gaylie Girl arched her brows momentarily, leaned back in her armchair, and said: "And you had Pan on your shoulder besides."

"No, I didn't have Pan back then while David was alive. My dear little doggie came later. But early on, he developed this habit of crawling right up onto my shoulder and lying there perfectly still. He's done that ever since—without prodding. I eventually got to the point where I considered Pan one of my accessories that I would never dream of being without—like my best gold earrings, my most bewitching perfume, and my aquamarine nail polish."

"Aha!" Gaylie Girl exclaimed. "Another explanation of someone's delightful quirk. It seems Second Creek truly does attract people who swear by them. If we're lucky, we may get another revelation out of Lady Roth tomorrow on our tour."

"I'm definitely looking forward to that," Amanda said with a bit more warmth in her voice. "I really haven't seen many examples of provincial architecture, but I've been told they're worth a look or two."

"Lady Roth's Cypress Knees is no Palace of Versailles, of course," Gaylie Girl added. "But even if it were, I have the feeling she'd be what we were looking at in all those mirrors."

MYRTIS HAD FINALLY GOTTEN everyone's attention amid their cocktail sipping, hors d'oeuvre nibbling, and sociable small talk from one end of her drawing room to the other. The time had come, she announced, for Euterpe to entertain them all spectacularly with a few classical selections, at which point the accomplished teacher approached the piano to the polite applause of the gathering of Nitwitts, Amanda, Petey, Powell Hampton, and Mr. Choppy. Carefully lowering Pan to the rug, where he quietly curled up into a furry white ball, Euterpe then bowed politely and took her seat. Moments later, she turned around and addressed her audience.

"I know that classical selections were just announced, and I do hope I'm not disappointing anyone, but I've taken the liberty of changing the program to something a bit more Broadway-ish. I have no idea what came over me. Perhaps the Muse of the Great White Way decided to channel herself. In any case, I will begin with Cole Porter's 'I Concentrate on You' from *Broadway Melody of 1940*. It's always been one of my favorites."

Euterpe's first selection was played with a flourish and enthusiastically received, and then she started in on "You'd Be So Nice to Come Home To." This was followed by an energetic rendition of "From This Moment On," and an equally spirited finale of "I Love Paris" from *Can-Can*.

After the appreciative applause had ended, Euterpe retrieved her Pan and said, "For those of you who may have been keeping track—yes, that was an all–Cole Porter medley. He was my absolute favorite modern composer—gifted but wounded. I think that's what made his music so universal in its appeal. It had that touch of heart as well as heartbroken. I seem to have homed in on that quality throughout my life."

Euterpe was handed a fresh Manhattan by Myrtis, took a healthy sip, and then stepped forward to mingle. The first little knot she encountered consisted of Amanda alongside Powell and Laurie Hampton, and she entered the conversation on a deferential note.

"I hope you didn't mind my getting so carried away with show tunes."

"Not at all," Laurie said. "It was just lovely, and I can't believe you played 'I Love Paris.' So incredibly timely. As Myrtis may have told you, Powell and I are off to the City of Lights next week for a wonderful visit with that Continental ballroom dancing wizard, the Great Buddha Magruder."

Amanda's head jerked sharply to the right where Laurie stood nursing her glass of wine. "Oh, do you actually know him? I went to Cannes last year with a friend of mine who happens to be an independent film director, and I saw this amazing short subject on ballroom dancing. It featured the Great Buddha Magruder, and he really was quite frisky for such a large man, I thought. And such a deep voice!"

Powell stepped up and offered more details. "Actually, Buddha is an old friend of mine. He and I once played the infamous Folies Brassiere together when my first wife, Ann, was still alive. That show was a parody of ballroom dancing, cabarets, nightclubs, and such, and we had great fun doing it together. I remember Buddha getting himself up as a rather hefty version of Josephine Baker in one segment, though drag was definitely not the usual thing with him. Anyway, though a little time has passed, he's invited Laurie and myself to join him for a week or so to see Paris from his point of view. We both expect to be swept off our feet, so to speak, but we also firmly expect to be back in time for Mr. Choppy's and Gaylie Girl's wedding. We wouldn't be forgiven for missing it, you know."

"Indeed, you wouldn't!" Denver Lee exclaimed, bursting bosom-first upon the scene with a small plate of half-eaten hors d'oeuvres in one hand and a glass of wine in the other. "You absolutely cannot miss the conclusion of the past century's most romantic interlude resumed."

Amanda maintained a suggestion of a frown as she pointed to Gaylie Girl and Mr. Choppy across the room, feeding each other party nibbles. "They certainly can't keep their hands off each other, can they?"

Ever-diplomatic Laurie stepped in immediately. "Powell and I can testify to what a wonderful experience it is to get that second chance at love." Then she quickly changed the subject. "I'm very impressed that you know all about the Great Buddha Magruder, Amanda. Your mother was certainly right when she told us how well traveled you are."

"I try," Amanda said, the frown completely disappearing from her face. "I do have a thing for old houses and architecture, and I've already seen some interesting examples as we've driven around town."

Renza and Novie sidled up to the group, and Novie quickly ran through the tour schedule. "I couldn't help overhearing, Amanda, but everything is ready for you tomorrow. First, we'll see Morningside, which is currently unoccupied but has become Second Creek's museum of sorts. Then we'll visit Lady Roth out at Cypress Knees, and finally—"

"You'll end up at my house—Belford Place," Renza interrupted. "Saving the best for last, of course. And then you'll be returning that evening for coffee and dessert."

Seeming to soften her attitude by the minute, Amanda said, "I'm very big on a full day of activities when I'm out and about. Mother told me what good friends she's made down here, and I'm beginning to see why."

"Your mother is a charming and sophisticated addition to Second Creek," Novie added. "We jumped at the chance to invite her to become a Nitwitt."

Just then, Gaylie Girl managed to pull herself away

from Mr. Choppy and approach the group, catching the tail
end of Novie's praise with a satisfied smile on her face. "Did
I hear my name being taken in vain?"

Renza adopted a playful tone, hardly her usual behavior.
"We've been saying absolutely scandalous things about you.
Now flit on over to Mr. Choppy so we can continue our
wicked ways."

Gaylie Girl and the others responded with a polite sprin-
kling of laughter, at which point Sarah appeared in the
doorway and announced that dinner was served in the dining room across the hall.

GAYLIE GIRL AND MYRTIS had spent the better part
of an hour the afternoon before working out the place set-
tings for Friday's dinner at Evening Shadows. They had
concluded that it would be most advantageous to their "win
over the children" campaign to put Amanda between Laurie and Powell, while Petey would dine between Mr. Choppy
and Euterpe. So far—as Gaylie Girl was observing between
bites of her marinated asparagus salad—things were humming along beautifully beneath the Waterford crystal chandelier, which accented Myrtis's commanding dining table;
and Laurie was just beginning an anecdote about her
now-departed, octogenarian cousin, Miss Kittykate.

"I would have preferred to call her Kitty all those years,"
Laurie was explaining for the benefit of Amanda and Petey.
"But she wouldn't hear of it. She took Kittykate to her

grave." Laurie paused for a sip of water, and the gleam in her eye promised a payoff for yet another memorable Second Creek story. "Which is my seamless segue into the details of her funeral."

Laurie gave Amanda and then Petey another quick glance for good measure. "Most everyone in Second Creek knows that Kittykate expired after staying up all night drinking sherry and rolling the lawns of her neighbors. She had just become the first woman in her eighties to win the Miss Delta Floozie Contest in The Square, and I suppose she wanted to celebrate in her own inimitable style—which she most definitely did."

Both Petey and Amanda looked expectantly amused as Laurie allowed a riff of giggles to run its course around the table. "As out of left field as that was," Laurie resumed, "it paled in comparison to what happened at her funeral. According to the terms of her will, her ashes were to be scattered somewhere along the banks of the Mississippi River—although no specific location was named. So, an intrepid little band of her family and friends, including yours truly, trudged all the way over to Greenville one miserable afternoon in our raincoats for the ceremony."

"Didn't you end up at Lake Ferguson rather than the Mississippi River, though?" Powell interjected.

"Yes, we did. But Lake Ferguson is an oxbow lake, which means it used to be the channel of the Mississippi, so everyone figured that would satisfy the letter of her last will and testament and prevent her from returning to haunt us.

Believe me, if you knew her, you definitely considered that a possibility. To put it bluntly, she was a scary, intimidating woman, and I can say that about her because she was my cousin.

"Anyway, there we all stood, some in tears, some smiling as they remembered all of Kittykate's antics over the years. The Reverend Zane Somerby of St. Luke's Episcopal Church said his prepared words and then proceeded to scatter the ashes along the bank. Just then, the *Delta Queen* appeared on the horizon in the midst of one of its many voyages with its calliope going full-bore and by chance playing 'Toot Toot Tootsie, Goodbye.' Everyone started roaring with laughter, and I could just picture Kittykate orchestrating the entire scenario from her heavenly post above. It was exactly the way she would have wanted to be remembered. All in all, it turned out to be the quintessential Second Creek farewell that no one will ever forget."

The unexpected punch line cemented the camaraderie that had slowly been building throughout the evening, which proceeded seamlessly. Here and there amid the incessant chatter and clanking of silverware as people finished off their salads, peals of laughter rang out. Then Sarah brought out the hot curried chicken dish she and Myrtis had toiled over so lovingly all afternoon long, and the guests lost no time in eagerly sampling the menu.

"You don't think it's too spicy, do you?" Myrtis asked, scanning her long table solicitously.

It was an opening Renza couldn't resist. "Oh, you know

it's perfectly delicious, Myrtis. You were just fishing as usual."

"I've always liked Indian food," Petey chimed in, dropping a dollop of chutney onto his chicken and rice. "Mother exposed us to just about everything growing up, didn't you?"

Gaylie Girl beamed, seizing the opportunity. "I certainly tried. Whatever comes along in life, I've always stressed the value of being broad-minded." She was uncertain whether her children truly got the gist of her comment, but at least they still had smiles on their faces, which was a favorable sign.

Whatever the case, it was another of Laurie's anecdotes about Miss Kittykate that put an exclamation point on this evening of calculated offspring schmoozing. Coffee and crème brûlée had just been passed around when Gaylie Girl signaled to Laurie with a subtle wink. Time to serve the pièce de résistance.

"I think the funniest, most unbelievable thing Kittykate ever did—which is saying something, by the way—was the time she couldn't get her old Hudson in gear after getting slightly tipsy at a dinner party much like this one," Laurie began, vigorously stirring a spoonful of sugar into her coffee. "Of course, she had no business driving at all in that condition, but back then in the thirties, there was no campaign to chastise people about such things. Besides, everyone else was just as tipsy off the local muscadine wine or even something stronger. At any rate, attempts to wrest the keys from her were unsuccessful, and she stubbornly backed out of the driveway onto the street. Only at that point, she couldn't get the car out of reverse no matter how hard she ground and stripped those gears."

People around the table who were familiar with the tale had already started to nod their heads conspiratorially and chuckle, while Amanda and Petey appeared to be trans- fixed like little children at a library story hour.

"To put this in further perspective," Laurie continued, not about to forget her objective, "there exists in our strange Second Creek universe something called the Second Creek solution. It's just the way we solve things around here, and I'd venture to say that people in other towns, states, and, yes, even countries would never operate like this. Anyway, since no one could get the car out of reverse, it was decided by everyone on hand that Kittykate should just go ahead and back on home. Which, by the way, was a distance of several miles involving several different streets. Don't ask me why someone didn't just offer to drive her home in their car and park her problem overnight. That would have been the safe, logical thing to do. But, you see, that wouldn't have been a genuine Second Creek solution."

"So she actually drove all the way home in reverse?" Petey said, completely hooked at that point and putting down his fork in amazement. "Safely?"

"Not a scratch on her. A brigade of friends whose houses were along the route ran the gauntlet with her, in a manner of speaking. Oh, they made an absolute production out of it!

They were informed of Kittykate's dilemma and told to hoist a drink or two in her honor, then go turn on the front porch lights and sit out there sipping and watching for her arrival. Once she had passed by safely, they were to phone in and confirm that she was still alive and steering backward. The story spread quickly, as it is apt to do in Second Creek, and for the next hour or so, people were calling each other up all over town with progress reports. 'Kittykate just went by,' was the phrase of the evening."

By now the entire table was belly-laughing, and this time it was Amanda who pursued things. "And she didn't even get a traffic ticket?"

"Oh, in a town as unique as Second Creek, the police would have shrugged it off, had they witnessed any of it—which they didn't as far as I know. Kittykate had a great deal of money, not to mention social position, and the rule of thumb was that you simply didn't mess with her about anything. At any rate, she made it all the way home safely, but I'm told she did develop a terrible crick in her neck that lingered for days from looking over her shoulder all that distance."

"I have to admit, you do things very differently down here," Petey said, his face sporting a ruddy glow from all the laughter. "That's pretty funny stuff!"

"Every now and then, we go for the dull and straightforward, though," Mr. Choppy added, patting Petey's shoulder. "Our visit to Pond-Raised Catfish tomorrow, for instance. That'll just be the plain vanilla business side of Second Creek."

Myrtis waved him off. "Now, don't you two go discussing business right now. That's not good for the digestion. But I do have a splendid suggestion. Perhaps Euterpe will be kind enough to treat us to an after-dinner selection at the piano."

Euterpe graciously agreed and roused Pan, who had been sleeping at her feet throughout the meal. She then proceeded to deliver a stirring rendition of "Sunset" from "Grand Canyon Suite" by Ferde Grofé for the evening's entertainment finale. The only off-key note was provided by an overly sated Denver Lee, who seemed to have dozed off in her armchair at one point, adding percussive snoring to the composition. But a gentle elbowing by a nearby Novie put an end to the unwanted accompaniment as the rest of the snickering Nitwitts watched without comment.

"I THINK YOU'RE MAKIN'" way too much of this," Mr. Choppy was saying emphatically to Gaylie Girl as the two of them walked through the front door of his bungalow on Pond Street around ten-thirty that evening.

But his Gaylie Girl was not in the mood to be consoled. On the way home from Evening Shadows, she had agreed that their determined cast of characters had put on a terrific dog and pony show for her children, but she was still very annoyed with some of Amanda's smart-aleck remarks scattered throughout the evening. "I just thought I had brought her up better than to be rude and condescending under any circumstances." They both headed into the kitchen, where Gaylie Girl laid her stylish beaded clutch bag on the counter and folded her arms in a huff.

"I was payin' close attention," Mr. Choppy continued, pouring himself a glass of water at the sink. "And Amanda definitely got more with the program as the evenin' wore on. Plus, Petey seemed to be havin' a good time all along. He's a cool customer. Sweetheart, the overall result was what we'd hoped for, so why are you still so upset?"

Gaylie Girl said nothing at first, then expelled her frustration with a burst of air. "I know my daughter too well, Hale. When she didn't think I was looking, I caught her lowering her guard. I saw it clearly in the way she dropped her face. She was still tolerating the evening for the most part."

"You're not sayin' you could read her mind, are you?"

This time, Gaylie Girl produced an ironic little chuckle and drew herself up as if she were about to make an important announcement. "No, but please follow me closely on this. I was thinking just now about something my friend Linda Markham up in Lake Forest once mentioned to me when we were discussing our various family problems. She has an unusual way of breaking things down that I admire quite a bit.

"First, she said, you trot out your innerspring mattress

with all the passion you can muster. And voilà! There come your children. Then, by the time they're all grown up, you find out what you've actually produced, and what they're all about. Linda christened that the offspring mattress. As in—you made your bed, and now you have to lie in it. And sometimes you like the results, and sometimes you don't. I was reminded of just how savvy and appropriate all of that is when I observed Amanda's roller-coaster behavior tonight."

Mr. Choppy was scratching the crown of his head, allowing himself the mere suggestion of a smile. "You don't figure you're overthinkin' this a bit?"

"Maybe I am. But is it so wrong to want my children to understand me at this pivotal point in my life? I don't want my choices here in Second Creek to be merely tolerated by them. After making so many surface decisions throughout my life of leisure, I truly want them to see what a commitment I've made to you and to this wacky little town you rule. I mean, where else can people get away with driving backward tipsy for blocks and blocks with no harm done?"

Mr. Choppy couldn't help laughing and moved to her to put his arm around her waist. "I fully appreciate what you're sayin'. But it's also very possible that tolerance is all they'll be capable of, at least for a little while." He gave her an energetic peck on the cheek. "I think time'll be on your side, though. Our side, I should say, since I'm in this, too."

Just before dropping off to sleep that night in bed,

however, Mr. Choppy reviewed once again his surprise ma-neuver, his ace in the hole. Of course, he had no intention of revealing it to his Gaylie Girl until the results with that off-spring mattress of hers had been duly registered at the end of the weekend. Naturally, he hoped the results would be successful. And maybe Gaylie Girl wouldn't approve of his little ploy when he finally told her about it. But he had made up his mind, and that was the way things were going to play out.

7

CATFISH HEADS AND CYPRESS KNEES

Mr. Choppy and Petey Lyons were chugging along Lower Winchester Road on the way to their Saturday meeting with Curtis Ray Keyes, the longtime plant manager of Pond-Raised Catfish, Inc. "It wasn't so long ago that this part of the road was full of right dangerous potholes," Mr. Choppy was explaining to his attentive passenger. "But my predecessor in the mayoral office, Mr. Floyce Hammontree, was nothin' if not a born asphalt paver, and so we got us a smooth ride all the way out to the plant as his legacy."

Petey cracked an unassuming smile and continued looking out at the unfamiliar scenery passing by. The occasional tintype tract house had given way to row upon row of some sort of dust-covered crop. "Is that cotton out there?" he said, turning back to Mr. Choppy. "Doesn't quite look like it."

"Nope. That's soybeans. They're right up there with catfish as Second Creek's biggest export."

"So I'm really going to get the skinny on the catfish business today?" Petey continued, managing to sound both amused and skeptical at the same time.

Mr. Choppy had his response at the ready, stopping just short of sounding a bit rehearsed. "We're all at your disposal."

"Yes, and I hope you don't mind my saying that everything so far has been quite enjoyable, if lacking a bit in spontaneity. My sister and I compared notes last night before we went to bed, and I, for one, certainly appreciate the hospitality."

Mr. Choppy had no trouble picking up on the way Petey had carefully phrased his response and decided to press further. "And how does your sister feel, if you don't mind my askin'?"

"I don't mind at all. I guess it's old news to you that Amanda marches to a very elitist drummer. I'd have to say that she's still working things out in her head. And her heart, I would hope."

Mr. Choppy didn't answer right away, sensing that he was being tested. "Your mother thought the tour of homes might just be the ticket for her." He glanced down quickly at his watch. "They ought to be well under way by now back in town."

Petey seemed to be mumbling something and chuckling under his breath at the same time. "Was that grizzled troubadour part of the plan?" he finally said.

Mr. Choppy was still shaking his head in disbelief about that one. It was odd how Second Creek always seemed to be pitching in with its own mysterious signs and embellishments. Earlier, he and Petey had spent a little time walking around The Square before setting off on their journey, and they had witnessed a curious sight. There, strolling in front of them, was a street musician, strumming his guitar and singing what sounded like a homemade ditty in a very hoarse voice. Mr. Choppy could only remember bits and pieces of the free-flowing lyrics. Something about "havin' the catfish blues and singin' 'em all day long." Folksy music about being tired and sweaty.

To be sure, there had been street musicians patrolling The Square from time to time, spouting that infamous phrase "Got any spare change?" They usually appeared before, during, and after the annual Miss Delta Floozie Contest in June, but Mr. Choppy could never recall having seen that particular lean, scraggly-bearded specimen before.

"Petey, I had absolutely nothin' to do with that man, I assure you," Mr. Choppy answered. "But I can understand why you thought some of us might have put him up to it, since he was makin' a point of singin' about catfish."

"Well, considering all those hilarious anecdotes I heard last night at Evening Shadows explaining Second Creek solutions, I just thought this might turn out to be another one. I mean, for all I know, you might have a booking agency for talented homeless people down here. He certainly looked like the poster boy."

Mr. Choppy sported a wide grin as he gripped the steering wheel with a tad bit more confidence. He definitely liked the way the conversation was going, and he could sense Petey relaxing more and more in his presence by the second. "I appreciate the way you seem to be embracin' certain things about life way down here in Mississippi. Your mother and I have discussed the culture shock issue more than once."

"Culture shock for her or for me and Amanda?"

"Both, I suppose. Believe it or not, I understand your reluctance to accept what your mother is doing. What she and I are doing together, I should say. I've never been married before, and so I have no children. But I grew up as part of a small family that ran the local Piggly Wiggly and got to know lots about all the tight-knit families who came to shop with us through the years. So I know how family members like to look after each other. Maybe I'd be just as protective of my own mama if I was in your shoes."

Petey was flexing his fingers in an odd configuration reminiscent of the old church-and-steeple game. "So . . . you really do love my mother, Hale? That has to be the bottom line for me here. As the man in the family now, I feel it's my duty to ask."

Petey's question coincided with the precise moment Mr. Choppy pulled into the sprawling parking lot of Pond-Raised Catfish. He quickly found a visitor's spot but continued to idle the engine to keep the air-conditioning going. Meanwhile, he gave Petey his undivided attention. "And it's my duty to answer you honestly and directly, as the new man in your mother's life. You see, I've loved your mother for more than fifty-five years now. Even all those decades she was married to your father, and I had no way of knowin' what had happened to her or if she'd dropped off the edge of the earth. She was the first and only love of my life, even though I was basically just your average teenage sap when we first met. Still and all, she never left my heart and my memories and dreams." Mr. Choppy allowed himself to tear up for a brief moment when he came to that particular phrase, but he soon regained his composure and dabbed at his eyes with his fingers.

"Somehow, some way, all kinds of crazy things aligned in the Second Creek universe that I've always called home, and we traced a path to each other's doors again. I know this won't make much sense to you—but it took a bank of dark clouds here, some dancin' in the aisles of my Piggly Wiggly there, maybe a dash of somethin' never meant to be understood. Life just doles it out anyway. I would never have believed it remotely possible had I not just lived through the past year or so, but it's happened. Maybe the Nitwitt ladies are right when they call this the longest interrupted love story of the past century. I certainly hope that answers your question, Petey."

There was only the sound of the engine idling for a while. Then Petey extended his hand, and the two men shook firmly. "It does, Hale. And I think I see why you won that election. You don't mince words. You make a strong case for yourself."

Mr. Choppy enjoyed an introspective laugh. "I had some excellent coachin', though. Mr. Powell Hampton helped me with my grammar and my projection, but the words I spoke to the voters about the things I believe in were the genuine article. My love for your mother is the genuine article, too."

Petey heaved his chest while staring at the processing plant looming in the distance. "That's good enough for me, then. And I guess I'm as ready as I'll ever be for my intro- duction to catfish guts and all these hefty profits you say will fatten my bank account."

"Well, I believe I'd put it in more appetizin' terms, but we'll give you the grand tour inside and out." Mr. Choppy then shut off the engine and pointed to the security guard- house ahead. On the way over he silently reviewed the gist of the conversation with Petey and concluded that perhaps they were well on their way to winning over half of Gaylie Girl's offspring mattress, no matter what happened at Pond-Raised Catfish today.

AMANDA'S VISIT TO the Morningside Museum was proceeding without incident. Her mother and Novie Mims were acting as her guides, but Gaylie Girl was finding it difficult to get a read on her daughter. Amanda's remarks about the *Godey's Lady's Book* display of poetry, costumes, and other antebellum paraphernalia had been polite but reserved; the drawing room filled with enlarged photos and daguerreotypes of Second Creek scenes dating back to the mid-nineteenth century caught her fancy a bit more. But Amanda seemed unusually antsy by the time they wound up at the tacky, touristy gift shop, where a hunched-over, bespectacled woman did her best to interest them in a pack of postcards and a cluster of Wajeelia's Famous Pralines wrapped in wax paper.

"Not today, I don't believe," Gaylie Girl said, trying to maintain control of the situation to keep them on schedule. And then they all headed out to Novie's car and piled in for the next stop on the tour—Lady Roth's home, Cypress Knees.

They were about five minutes away from that eagerly anticipated destination when Gaylie Girl noted a hopeful musing from Amanda, even if it seemed to be something of a non sequitur. "Are Wajeelia's pralines really that famous?"

It was Novie who took on the question excitedly, homing in on Amanda's quizzical face in the rearview mirror. "Oh, we've all grown up on Wajeelia Evans's pralines down here. I probably got my very first sugar high off them when I was a little girl. Wajeelia was a very enterprising black woman who came up with the idea of selling those sinful goodies to the tourists who showed up for the Springtime Tour of Homes and Cottages—which I currently chair, as you know. Anyway, Wajeelia used to peddle the pralines around town in a wooden cart until local health officials made her establish a definite place of business. She's no longer with us, but her daughter LaWeesa carries on the family tradition and does quite well. Needless to say, there've been many imitators over the years, but if you want the real thing, you go with Wajeelia's Famous in waxed paper. Not any of those see-through cellophane varieties."

"Maybe I should treat the children, then," Amanda said with a conflicted edge to her voice. "I could take the pralines back as souvenirs. Only I'm not sure about the 'sugar high' part. Richard complains that the kids are wild enough as it is. They do take after their mother—always on the go."

"One or two in moderation won't hurt," Gaylie Girl added, intent on keeping Amanda on a positive track. "Anyway, they sell the pralines practically all over town. You'll be able to pick up some at the last minute if you want."

"Oh, speaking of sugar highs," Novie said, "I received some bad news from Denver Lee last night. She phoned and said that her doctor has finally had to put her on oral medication for diabetes. Hard as she's been tryin', she just hasn't been able to lose enough weight to fend off the full-blown condition. No more diet-managed now. And if she doesn't behave herself this time, she'll have to put up with those awful injections. Another Southern belle going through the rest of her life sticking herself, bless her."

"By any chance, was she the one snoring after dinner last night during the recital?" Amanda asked, her curiosity getting the better of her.

Novie nodded. "One and the same. She was terribly embarrassed after I nudged her to wake up. I didn't keep tabs, of course, but she probably had way too much food and drink that she wasn't supposed to touch. She's just never been much good at restraint. Denver Lee has that all-or-nothing personality."

Gaylie Girl's sigh was deep and empathetic. "Time marches on, and sometimes cruelly so. Wittsie's Alzheimer's is worse than ever, and now Denver Lee's diabetes has finally arrived full-blown. Perhaps a big dose of Lady Roth will be just the medicine we all need right now."

"You've all been building up this Lady Roth so much since I came down yesterday that I can't help wondering if she's going to be a disappointment."

"Lady Roth a disappointment?" Gaylie Girl replied. "Highly unlikely, Amanda. I've been told that no one in Second Creek has concocted more surprises over the years than she has."

MR. CHOPPY, PETEY, and Curtis Ray Keyes had just wound up their tour of the facilities, exiting the massive production line room at Pond-Raised. It was an unsettling scene for most visitors to the plant. It wasn't at all unusual for many people to insist cavalierly that they wanted to see how the catfish were decapitated and cut up. But those same folks would frequently blanch, avert their eyes, and move along quickly at the sight of the actual bloodletting.

Petey Lyons, however, had not batted an eyelash while watching hundreds of workers in their spattered shower caps and smocks performing the precision surgery in virtual lockstep.

"Not the weak-stomach type, I'm happy to see," Mr. Choppy observed, giving Petey a playful nudge with his elbow.

"Not me. But I am curious as to how they'll taste when we have them for dinner tonight."

"Hey, they don't look too tasty at this stage, but it takes a little over thirty minutes from start to finish for us to make the fillets that everybody craves so much these days," Curtis Ray quipped. They all followed his lead and headed down the metallic green hallway to his office, taking their seats quickly.

"Looks like a pretty efficient operation to me," Petey said in his most businesslike manner. "You breed them and feed them in those farm ponds out there. You process them in here and ship them out all over the country—all the way up to my stomping grounds in Chicago, I'm guessing. So bring on the numbers, and I'll do some serious crunching once I get home and get together with my accountant."

Curtis Ray, who was basically an overfed country boy used to taking orders and not much else, leaned across his desk and handed over a manila folder to Petey. "Mr. Elston Graves hisself has authorized this proposal for your eyes only, Mr. Lyons. It's got everything you'd wanna know about liabilities and assets, our product line, payroll, employment statistics, and such as that. The website address is in there, too. Mr. Graves would be here today to meet with you, but he's off on a trip this weekend. He told me to tell you that he'd be happy to discuss everything further when he got back—that is, if you're still interested."

Petey began slowly thumbing through the papers while Mr. Choppy and Curtis Ray exchanged expectant glances. After a few more minutes of silent study, Petey looked up and said: "I won't be making any decisions right this minute, but I expect Mr. Graves will be hearing from me soon."

Curtis Ray stood up and offered his hand, followed by a spontaneous invitation to lunch in the plant cafeteria. "If you have time, we have right good food, don't we, Mr. Mayor?"

"I can vouch for that," Mr. Choppy answered with a ready smile. "And I hear you can even sample a real tasty catfish dish or two."

AT THE MOMENT, Gaylie Girl, Novie, and Amanda had no clue what Lady Roth was about to unleash upon them. Shortly after their arrival, she had been the picture of decorum, leading them around her exquisitely appointed two-story Cypress Knees. Built during the Federal period, it was filled to overflowing with Adam mantels, secretaries, linen presses, frowning ancestral portraits, and sturdy four-posters. There was even an enormous, dusty harp that took up most of the room in the well-stocked library. Lady Roth was quick to claim that she had once fancied it during her youth while harboring her show business ambitions as that great entertainer for the ages, Vocifera P. Forest.

"I went through this brief, impulsive period when I thought if I practiced hard enough, I could maybe end up being a female Marx Brother," she had confessed to her astounded guests without missing a beat.

Novie recited the lineup and was barely able to keep a straight face. "Groucho, Gummo, Harpo, Chico, Zeppo, and Vocifera. Blends right in."

Brushing the comment aside, Lady Roth further explained that the vast majority of the pieces throughout the house had been part of the inheritance from her late husband's estate, and with a moniker like Heath Vanderlith Roth, there was no shortage of one-of-a-kind treasures. She had been full of details about which artisan had constructed which piece of furniture, what style it was and when it had been made, omitting nothing. All well and good.

But after Lady Roth had served everyone midday nibbles and drinks and settled them around her downstairs parlor, she had them exchanging bewildered glances and rendered them speechless with what followed. She had left the room briefly while they were all enjoying their refreshments; then practically floated back in wearing a sequined flapper costume and proceeded to attach a small cymbal to the side of each of her extremely bony knees.

"I wanted to prove something today to all of you," she

announced after modeling her strange outfit in awkward fashion for a few moments.

Novie was still blinking in disbelief. "I can't imagine what you're going to say or do next."

Lady Roth broadly wagged an index finger as if it were a windshield wiper. "Then let me take this opportunity to clear things up for you." She moved slowly and noisily—cymbals and all—to an old-fashioned turntable in the corner of the room, carefully lifted the needle onto a worn LP, and that old standby Charleston began to play loudly, startling her guests.

"Ever since moving to Second Creek, it's always been about knees for me," she continued, raising her voice slightly to be heard above the din.

"Aha! I get it!" Novie interrupted, matching her decibel level. "You mean the bee's knees!"

"Not exactly. But I do mean Cypress Knees on the one hand, and my own bad knees on the other. Moving here to Second Creek and naming this house was one thing, even though people pointed out there wasn't a cypress tree any-where on my particular acreage to support my choice. But my poor, damaged knees were quite another proposition."

This time, it was Gaylie Girl who gathered her wits and took a stab. "I take it you are going to do the Charleston for us in that getup?"

"I'm waiting for just the right chorus. Then I'm going to pick up where I left off last summer at Mr. Choppy's Piggly Wiggly." True to her word, Lady Roth proceeded with her best effort, crossing her knees several times and clashing the cymbals now and then as an unabashedly amusing accent.

When the show was over, everyone applauded politely, and Lady Roth resumed the explanation of her performance. "I was so embarrassed last summer when I danced in the store with Mr. Powell Hampton as Bonnie, and he was Clyde. Arthritis has dogged me for many years now, and I just know I let all my supporters down when I just couldn't seem to cross my knees properly. It was that group that liked to stand nearby in the next aisle and rate me with those big placards. That one time as Bonnie was the only time I didn't get perfect tens from my audience, but I'm on a new, improved medication now. My range of motion is to beat the band, and I feel like showing off. So indulge me."

Gaylie Girl and Novie were nodding after plastering smiles on their faces that were far too obvious. "Well, that was certainly worth a top score this time," Novie offered as Lady Roth busied herself trying to remove the cymbals. "You've definitely closed the circle as far as I'm concerned."

Only Amanda seemed lost. "I didn't understand what she was talking about the whole time," she whispered to her mother out of the side of her mouth just as Lady Roth was leaving the room. "It was like I had walked in on the middle of a movie or a play."

"Life in Second Creek frequently feels like that, I've discovered. I'll try to explain it all later," Gaylie Girl whispered back. "We'll find a moment between the visit with

Renza at Belford Place up next and cocktails with Vester and Mal at the Victorian Tea Room to begin our progressive dinner."

But Amanda set her jaw firmly and cleared her throat. "Never mind all that. But I do think we should definitely find a moment or two, Mother. There's something very important I've been wanting to discuss with you for quite a while."

A FEW HOURS LATER, Gaylie Girl was perched on the edge of the antique daybed at the foot of Amanda's guest room four-poster at Evening Shadows. She was hoping for a productive discussion with her daughter but sensed that she just might be in for an uncomfortable session instead. Unfortunately, Amanda did not disappoint.

"How to begin. First, I fully appreciate the fact that this is your life, Mother," she was saying, moving about the room in restless fashion almost as if she were a busy executive dictating a letter. "And I can see why you find these people so funny and fascinating. The Europeans I've met have the same kind of quirkiness about them—that unexpected, over-the-top, what's-coming-next quality. I'll give you that in a New York second."

"Not that I need your permission," Gaylie Girl began, fighting off the urge to bristle, "but I do enjoy these Nitwitts of mine—hell, I'm one myself now. I wanted very much to share them with you this weekend. What did you think of Renza's house? It's the same style as my fixer-upper just a few doors down." She knew exactly what she was doing with that last remark—briefly postponing more of the confrontation she would not be able to escape.

Amanda plopped herself down at the other end of the daybed and gave her mother a no-nonsense glance. "Belford Place was charming and impeccably kept. Your friend Renza is very sure of herself and has no shortage of opinions, but I admire that in people. I'm quite aware I'm like that myself. All of these houses you've shown me have been interesting showplaces. I'll be honest enough to admit that Second Creek is nothing like I thought it would be, and I'm quite sure I've taken some wonderful pictures for my travel scrapbook. But I'm still worried about something, and you and I haven't really sat down and discussed it since you shocked me and Petey with all those revelations about yourself and this Mr. Choppy Dunbar."

Gaylie Girl was careful to maintain a firm but light-hearted tone. "I would prefer it if you would start calling him Hale, but let's get everything out in the open right here and now. What's really on your mind? Is there something about all this that you just can't get past? Of course, I still hope this weekend will help you see how important this wedding really is to me. Call me a better-late-than-never romantic—but I imagined that we could all head into this as a real family, all of us on the same page. Corny and clichéd as it may sound, I want your brother to give me away, and I want you to be my matron of honor. It would be just perfect."

Amanda managed a weak smile but took her time to speak, bringing her hands together prayerfully in front of her face. "It's quite obvious how you feel about . . . Hale, Mother. But it's the other half of that equation that bothers me. You're a very wealthy woman and owner of a very successful company that Dad left behind. He worked at it all his life, and I'm sure he would want to see it protected at all costs. The truth is . . . well, I wouldn't like to see Lyons Insole out of the family, especially for the sake of generations to come. Even if Petey never settles down with the right woman—and he's certainly had his chances—you have three beautiful grandchildren to consider right this instant, you know."

An awkward amount of time passed before Gaylie Girl was able to answer. Somewhere in her innermost core, she had always known it would come down to a discussion of money and property—offspring angst over her considerable estate. "So there it is, rearing its ugly head after all. Where there's a will, who's in the way? A very base but predictable sentiment, to say the least."

"Don't you think Petey and I have the right to know? That doesn't seem very unreasonable to me. We're not strangers who just walked in off the street asking for the details of your bank account."

Unexpectedly, something inside Gaylie Girl snapped, and her tone suddenly took on a harsh edge. "Your father left both you and your brother a life-changing amount of money. Neither of you has wanted for anything since then.

Or growing up, for that matter. But you might as well know that I didn't agree with his decision at all. I was quite adamant about it, even though my opinion didn't change his mind in the least. Not even on his deathbed, when he was at his most vulnerable, making all those puns he enjoyed making all the time and still finding the strength to kiss me good-bye."

Amanda ignored the sentimentality and drew back, looking both angry and surprised. "Why were you so adamant about it?"

"For the most part, I'd say the attitude you've been displaying all weekend sums things up quite nicely. I told your father shortly after we knew he was terminal that I didn't think either one of you would be able to handle great wealth so early on in your lives. As it turns out, I was quite prescient, and that makes me very sad."

"There are things you don't understand, Mother. I don't think you'd be saying these things to me if—" She broke off for a moment and then said, "Oh, let's just forget it."

The silence that ensued was stunning, finally shattered by an urgent-sounding knock at the door and Petey peering in without an invitation to enter.

"Are we all decent in here?" he said, obviously full of himself and unable to pick up on the tension yet.

"Let's just say we're civil and leave it at that," Gaylie Girl answered, rising from her seat. "I assume Hale is downstairs waiting for me."

Petey lowered the smugness several notches and moved

to the daybed quickly to intercept his mother. "Yes. He said to tell you he's ready to roll on home. But what's going on? Here I am just bursting with tales about bloody catfish heads, and I can tell there's no one in the mood to listen to me. I've had a very interesting and educational morning, but you two have definitely been fighting about something, haven't you? What—did your camera break, Sis?"

"I'm sure Amanda will fill you in on everything," Gaylie Girl said, this time without a trace of emotion. "As for myself, I'm going to go home for a little nap with Hale before we begin our progressive dinner this evening. I'll see you both then." And with that, she was out the door without looking back—leaving both her daughter and her son confounded.

Petey waited a few more moments to collect himself. "What did I just walk in on here?"

"I decided to bring up the subject of her will, and she more or less flew off the handle."

"I thought we agreed to soft-pedal that while we were down here," Petey answered, looking slightly disgusted by the revelation. "'Let Mother shine' was supposed to be our mantra."

Amanda was distractedly smoothing out a wrinkle in the bedspread, avoiding her brother's gaze. "That was your idea, not mine. I don't know how you can be so blasé about the company. Suppose she does decide to leave everything to Mr. Choppy? I just couldn't accept that. My life is very different from yours."

Petey sat next to his sister and began gently rubbing her arm. At first she recoiled at his touch, but he kept at it. "It's Mother's adventure, and at first I had my doubts, too. But it's touching the way Hale cares for her. I don't think it's an act, and I don't think he has any ulterior motives. He is what he is and maybe not the sort of person we're used to in our lives. But after spending the morning with him, I believe he's genuine and genuinely in love with our mother."

Amanda finally managed to look into his eyes, and some playful sibling connection passed between them, bringing a surprising hint of a smile to her face. "You got all that out of a trip to a catfish plant?"

"There. That's better," he said. "I think Mother probably got so upset with you because you're raining on her parade, Sis. Something tells me that her financial plans—and ours—will work themselves out."

Amanda did a subtle double take. "Wait a minute. Are you actually considering investing in this catfish plant?"

"Haven't decided yet. I'm taking the proposal back to Lake Forest with me, though."

Amanda swallowed wrong and coughed several times, causing Petey to stop massaging her arm. But eventually she recovered and spoke to her brother firmly. "I still want to know where I stand, Petey. Where my children stand. And you should want to know, too. We're not ogres for pursuing this. I don't feel the least bit guilty about asking Mother the practical questions. You were always off on a lark somewhere, and you never would do that after Dad died. I was always the one, and it looks like I still am."

Petey stood up and for some reason actually brushed himself off. To an outside observer, it would have given the impression of brushing off his sister as well. "Let's just try lightening up a bit for the rest of the weekend, okay? You've made it pretty clear how you feel about everything, but I don't mind telling you that I'm having a blast so far. I like these people. I like this place. I think Mother's done well for herself here."

MR. CHOPPY WAS BOUND and determined to get the lowdown on Gaylie Girl's ruffled mood. He had never seen her this disturbed before, and it was hardly becoming. He found himself flashing back to the temper she had displayed over a half-century ago during their brief but torrid affair as teenagers in the Second Creek Hotel. She had sent him packing with a vengeance then, and it was that sort of fury that seemed to be burning in her eyes now that they had returned from Evening Shadows.

"What do you mean you have half a mind not to attend the progressive dinner tonight?" Mr. Choppy asked. "Everybody went to all this trouble, so it'd be kinda counterproductive to abandon our plans now."

Gaylie Girl had just taken off her pumps and stretched out on his bed with her clothes still on. "It's just that here I am, lying on my offspring mattress again, and I'm not comfortable with the lumps I'm feeling."

It took a second or two, but he eventually got the reference while climbing into bed next to her. "Oh . . . that. You mind telling me what's got you so riled up? You hardly said two words in the car. Of course, I didn't, either. I was too afraid you'd snap at me."

"Oh, Hale. I'm sorry about that. I'm certainly not upset with you." Then she propped up her pillow, sighed, and quickly reviewed the morning tour. Predictably, Lady Roth's antics brought some much-needed laughter into the mix.

"What will she think of next?" Mr. Choppy concluded.

Then Gaylie Girl went into great detail about the exchange with Amanda. When she had gotten it all out of her system, Mr. Choppy found it hard to suppress his sense of relief. He wanted so much to tell her she would probably have absolutely nothing to worry about, but he couldn't be premature. He must be patient and wait for the right moment, which would be coming soon.

"Let's forget about all that for a while," he suggested instead. "We have a little time on our hands. Why don't we make the most of it?"

Gaylie Girl could not help but notice the unmistakable twinkle in Mr. Choppy's eye and inched closer. "A nap by any other name, Hale."

And then he gave her the sweetest kiss, feeling the afternoon's tension melting away throughout her body as he took her in his arms.

8.

ALL ON A
SATURDAY NIGHT

*I*t was ten past five at the Victorian Tea Room. Vester
Morrow was in the midst of overseeing the exclusive
cocktail party he and the Nitwitts had planned as the first
step in the evening's progressive dinner for Petey and
Amanda. Only customers held in such inestimable esteem
by the veteran restaurateur could have convinced him to
close down his pride and joy for an hour or so on a Saturday
night—prime time in Second Creek.

The rangy, fastidious Vester was a virtual tuxedoed
blur moving beneath the whirring ceiling fans, orchestrating his spiffy corps of waiters balancing their silver trays
filled with drinks and nibbles. Here and there he would
pause long enough to schmooze with one of the Nitwitts,

Mr. Choppy, Powell Hampton, or even gently pet Euterpe's poodle, dozing on her shoulder as usual. Such effortless socializing was his trademark gift and quite essential to his success, considering that his partner, Mal Davis, stayed behind the scenes crunching numbers all the time with mousy efficiency.

At the moment, Vester's buzzing and flitting around had landed him right beside a quartet comprised of Gaylie Girl, Mr. Choppy, Petey, and Amanda, and he quickly adopted his most solicitous demeanor. "Do you all have everything you need? I do see lots of happy faces, but it's my duty to double-check for forthcoming frowns. I pride myself on avoiding customer snits at all costs."

"Not so much as a hint so far," said Mr. Choppy, who was drinking beer out of a frosted mug. "Everything's as smooth as this brewski here."

"We're just fine, Vester. Everything is delightful," Gaylie Girl added. "This Cosmo I'm sipping is to die for, and I may very well decide to treat myself to another."

Vester seemed to shiver with excitement. "I'll pass all that along to my bartender. Gregg has been with us since we opened, and I always like to say that he knows his mixology so well he practically has call brands coursing through his veins. In fact, the last time they drew his blood for a checkup, he was found to be type B and B."

"I'll remember that next time I need a transfusion!" Petey exclaimed, enjoying a good laugh while hoisting his martini glass. "But I do have a question for you, if you don't mind."

"At your service."

Petey pointed to a corner of the room where a very tall, blond-haired young woman was sipping a drink in front of a stained-glass window flanked by an assortment of ferns. "Do you happen to know who that Amazonian beauty is over there? I just can't seem to take my eyes off her. Mother has no idea who she is, either. I thought maybe you would."

"That's Miz Renza Belford's daughter, Meta," Vester answered after a brief glance. "I was just introduced when they arrived a few minutes ago, but then Miz Belford mentioned something about making a quick visit to powder her nose, and I had some waiters to track down, so we parted company at that point."

Fortuitously, Renza emerged from the ladies' room and was headed in Meta's general direction when Petey, Vester, and Mr. Choppy dramatically motioned her over. Though looking puzzled at first, she stopped in her tracks and then approached the group with her imperious demeanor at full strength. "I had no idea my activities of a more pressing nature were being so closely scrutinized by the opposite sex. If I'd known that, I wouldn't have tugged at my dress so indiscreetly when I walked out of the bathroom. Now, what on earth can I do for all you gentlemen?"

It was Vester who stepped up to explain. "I believe Mr. Lyons here wants to meet your daughter, Miz Belford. He's already noted how well she sets off my ferns."

"She does, indeed," Renza said, glancing back momentarily. "I like to call her my artsy-craftsy girl from Florida, but she marches to different Muses, I can assure you. She just showed up at my doorstep a couple of hours ago, if you can believe it. She does that sort of thing now and then. Not so much as a phone call to her mother for months on end, and then she gets it into her head to pop in on the spur of the moment. Why, I could have gone off to Timbuktu with Novie for all she knew, but that's of no consequence to her! Of course, I had to tell her about the progressive dinner tonight and then run it past Laurie quickly, so we're setting an extra place for her throughout the evening."

"She certainly is tall," Petey observed, his tone brimming with lusty portent as his eyes ran up and down the length of her body.

"Come right along, then," Renza said. "I'll take you all over and introduce you."

The group moved en masse across the room, and a flurry of introductions ensued. It was soon obvious to all concerned that Petey wanted a one-on-one with Meta, so the two of them were left alone to flirt while the others moved on to circulate around the room.

"YOUR MOTHER described you as artsy-craftsy," Petey was saying to Meta after the two of them had taken their drinks to a table and settled in for small talk. "Would you care to elaborate?"

Meta tossed her long blond mane and almost seemed to be laughing off his question. "That's just my mother's way of saying that she thinks I can't settle down with any one thing—or person, for that matter. But actually, I do have a plan for my art degree. I've been dabbling in watercolors and paper sculpture and have even gotten a couple of shows at galleries in Saint Augustine. I go by the name of Meta, Unlimited—which I like to think I am. Of course, like all women of her generation, my mother thinks I'm totally rudderless without a husband. She describes me all the time as 'still playing around in my early-thirties sandbox.'"

Petey nodded and took a measured sip of his martini. "I like the way you cut to the chase, and I won't mince words, either. I'm twice-married and merrily divorced and grazing forty-two, but I'm not ready to be put out to pasture yet. Bet that was more information than you needed to hear."

She caught his gaze and locked in with a deliberate intensity he could not fail to notice. "I'm a 'wipe the slate clean' kind of girl, if you know what I mean."

"Interesting." There was a pregnant pause. "Do you mind my asking just how tall you are? I hope you don't think that's a rude question."

"I don't. People ask me all the time. I'm a whisper over six feet, but the reason I look even taller is because I refuse to hunch over. I refuse to throw away my heels, and I also wear my height like a badge of honor. If a man is threatened by that, then he's obviously not for me." She sat back in her chair and observed him closely for a moment. "And now it's my turn to ask you a personal question."

"Shoot."

"What happened with you and those two not-so-merry wives of yours?"

Petey returned the good-natured laugh she had given him earlier and then answered forthrightly: "Apparently, they were too short."

IN ANOTHER CORNER of the restaurant, Denver Lee was holding forth on the subject of her battles with the sugar bug while Gaylie Girl, Laurie, and Amanda surrounded her, listening attentively. "In case you were wondering," she was saying as she pointed to the clear drink that she'd been nursing, "this is innocent club soda with a twist of lime. My gin-and-tonic days are way past over, I'm afraid. Of course, it's the Bloody Marys and mimosas at our Nitwitt gatherings I'll miss most. Alcohol of any kind just sends my blood sugar right to the top and rings my bell like a muscleman showin' off to his girlfriend at the state fair."

"Good heavens! You must have stayed up all night thinking up that one. But it's effective. I can almost hear that bell clanging right this instant!" Laurie exclaimed, trying her best to duplicate Denver Lee's lighthearted tone.

But Denver Lee soon went all somber on them, gazing down at her drink as if into the bottom of a deep well. "I'm afraid the prize I've won is no fun at all. The fact is, I thought of my diagnosis as a game and really didn't take it as seriously as I should have. I know I didn't usually go off my diet in front of all of you too much, but it's the things you sneak when you get home that do you in. The things you get up in the middle of the night to indulge. Why should I give up all the goodies I've adored all these years? I thought. But all the backslidin' and rationalization have finally caught up with me. I really have to be on my best behavior from now on, or it's here comes the needle, for me."

"I know there are things you can have here tonight, though," Laurie put in. "I've seen scads of crudités circulating around the room on those platters. And I know you can have the grilled catfish I'll be serving at my house later."

Denver Lee's sigh of exasperation signaled the diatribe to come. "I'm sure there'll be no problem with the catfish, Laurie. You've been more than mindful of my special dietary needs. But how many raw veggies can one person crunch in a lifetime? I'm beginning to feel like one big, bosomy rabbit. Is that to become my lot in life? Next thing you know, I'll be restricted to those pellets. I suppose I should be thankful for the little things. I still have all my teeth—every last one of them, fillings and all. But what on earth do people with dentures do when their doctors tell them, 'Oh, you can have all the carrots and celery you want!' All well and good, but you just try and find interesting ways to dress up carrots and cucumbers and such. They're garden-variety dull, duller, and dullest. How I ever thought it would be interesting to paint them, I'll never know!"

At that point, Denver Lee spied one of the waiters carrying a tray of fresh hors d'oeuvres out of the kitchen and visibly perked up. "If you'll excuse me, girls, I think I'll follow that waiter and see if there's something benign on his tray I can spear with a toothpick." And off she went on her tidbit safari.

"She's certainly passionate about food," Amanda said once Denver Lee was clearly out of earshot. "Does she always go on and on like that?"

"She's always been that way about anything she does. For a while there she was engrossed in doing oil paintings of various vegetables," Laurie quickly explained. "The Fates, however, did not smile down upon that fledgling career of hers, even though I actually have one of her most sincere efforts. It was given to me as a wedding present last year. Whatever Denver Lee does, she either goes all out, or she won't play the game at all. For health reasons now, I do hope she'll finally pay attention to doctor's orders. As the years go by, that's something many of us have to learn to do."

Laurie's face dropped further as she paused for a moment. "I was reminded of our Wittsie again and what a devastating thing she's having to endure. On my visit over there last week, one of the nurses told me that she's going downhill rapidly, not that I couldn't see it for myself. It's frightening how fast something like Alzheimer's can progress in the latter stages. We've all been dreading this day."

Gaylie Girl was shaking her head, lost in thought. "The nurses told me the same thing. Maybe our brunch tomorrow and the little entertainment we've planned will brighten things up for her just a bit."

"It's the least we can do as Nitwitts," Laurie added, giving Gaylie Girl a hopeful glance. "By the way, do you think we've practiced enough?"

"Euterpe seems to think we're as ready as we're ever going to be."

PETEY AND META had chosen to pair off to do the remainder of their mingling and mixing, and it was clear to everyone who encountered them that they were fast becoming an item. There was even an amusing presumption of sorts when Euterpe, herself very much the newcomer to the Second Creek milieu, told them what an attractive couple they made.

"You two are glowing like you've just returned from your honeymoon," she continued. "You haven't, by any chance, have you?"

Petey almost seemed to be blushing, but Meta conjured up that infectious laugh of hers and said: "Now, there's a picture that might be fun to paint. But no, we just met tonight, right here on the premises in typical Second Creek fashion, and we've been talking back and forth like we're old friends or leftovers from another lifetime."

Wherever they went throughout the rest of the evening, a sexual undercurrent continued to swirl around them; they began leaning into each other for emphasis as they spoke, even punctuating the end of certain sentences with light, affectionate bumping. Hand-holding soon followed, but they thankfully stopped short of swinging their arms to and fro like schoolchildren with crushes. As the end of the cocktail hour and the time to move on to Laurie and Powell's cottage finally aligned, a few last-minute promises and suggestions were hurriedly bandied about.

Trying to atone for her previous minor gaffe with a more businesslike approach, Euterpe suggested to Meta that she find time to drop by the Mistress of the Scales Studio before leaving Second Creek. "I have a few bare spots on the wall," she added. "Perhaps I could take a look at your portfolio sometime, and you could do a watercolor or paper sculpture that would be the perfect accent. I'd like to use Second Creek talent as much as possible in decorating my business. I've already given all my houseplant orders to Novie's son, Marc, and that wonderful new plant boutique he's just opened on The Square."

A masculine voice rang out from the adjacent throng. "I wondered why my ears were burning!" Marc exclaimed. Then he and Novie, who had accompanied him to the party, broke away and approached Euterpe with gracious smiles on their faces. "I want to thank you again for all that bamboo and bougainvillea you bought for your studio," Marc continued. "Not to mention the potted palms in the copper pots. If Michael were here, he'd thank you, too. You got us off to a great start!"

"Where is your better half tonight, by the way? I've had an eye out for him all evening. I love looking at big, strapping redheaded men."

"So do I," Marc replied with an impish grin and a wag of his eyebrows. "But to make a long story short, Michael's in bed with a heating pad. We had a huge shipment of ficus come in today, and I think he pulled a muscle or two dragging them around the showroom. He has this obsessive thing about symmetry for sales purposes."

"Oh, symmetry can be an absolute bugaboo," Meta chimed in enthusiastically. "I struggle with it all the time in my artwork. You know—whether to bow down to it or let it take a backseat. Mostly, I end up doing things a bit off-center."

At which point Euterpe and Meta definitely agreed to meet at the studio on Monday for "artistic purposes."

No sooner had they done so than Laurie made the final announcement that it was time for everyone to head over to her little cottage for the main course. "Does everyone have rides and know the way? If you don't, Powell and I have room for one more in our car."

There seemed to be no blank faces nor any odd guests out among the group, and after many effusive compliments to Vester, who stood at the door pumping hands and patting shoulders in assembly-line fashion, the intimate and lively cocktail party at the Victorian Tea Room came to a successful end.

LAURIE'S DECISION TO let her guests serve themselves buffet-style from her granite kitchen countertop was working to perfection so far. The plan had been to get people to mingle further, creating a more relaxed atmosphere than a formal, seated dinner would have produced. Of course, neither she nor anyone else had foreseen Petey pairing up with Meta Belford—a development that had everyone buzzing, whispering, and nudging as they sampled the delicious menu of grilled catfish with buttered shelled edamame and sweet potato fries. There were also two big pitchers of chilled sangria and a selection of wines to wash it all down.

"Just sit wherever you like," Laurie kept saying, handing out big bamboo serving trays as each guest reached the end of the line with a heaped plate. "Dining table, parlor sofas, easy chairs in the corner—whatever strikes your fancy and looks most comfortable. And please, don't be shy—go back for seconds or even thirds. We've got plenty, as you can see."

Powell stood beside her, carefully observing the proceedings. When the last plate had been helped, he said: "Now it's finally our turn. I'm starving. Vester's tidbits just teased the hell out of my stomach. I assume you want a little bit of everything?"

She nodded. "I'll go claim a spot for us on the afghan sofa while you take care of that."

As Fate would have it, Laurie and Powell ended up sitting beside Petey and Meta, who were making constant eye contact before, during, and after each bite they took. They even indulged that romantic cliché of taking turns feeding each other with their own forks. Keeping the primary week-end objective in mind, however, Laurie continued to romance her cuisine with her best hostess smile.

"It looks like you're enjoying my catfish recipe, Petey," she began. "Of course, I have so many different ways I like to prepare it. That's the beauty of catfish, though. It's so versatile."

Powell couldn't resist and whispered out of the side of his mouth, "Uh, don't overdo it. You sound like a script from one of those Food Network shows you watch all the time to get recipe ideas."

On the other nearby sofa, Mr. Choppy had already picked up on the gambit and was running with it. "Oh, we had catfish once or twice a week when I was growin' up in our little house on Pond Street. Mama breaded it with corn-meal and swore it had to be God's favorite food. I think most Southern families think of it as a staple just like they do biscuits and gravy or butter and grits."

Petey put down his fork, finally managing to take his eyes off his brand-new love interest. "Speaking of grit, Hale, I got a letter from Mother a week or so ago telling me that you taught her how to cook it."

Everyone following the exchange looked either puzzled or amused, but Mr. Choppy quickly tackled the faux pas. "Cook *them*, Petey. It's grits, not grit. There are thousands, maybe millions, of 'em in one box. They're tasty little flecks of ground-up hominy."

"How many what?" Petey said. At first it was impossible to tell if he was truly joking. But he soon ditched his straight face, and ripples of laughter broke out among the group.

"What's so funny?" Gaylie Girl asked, entering the room with her tray at just that moment. "I have the feeling I'm missing all the fun in here."

"Just discussin' the grammar of grits," Mr. Choppy explained, patting a spot for her on his end of the sofa. "Where's Amanda?"

"Oh, she's at the dining table, but she's not in a very good mood. I'm reluctant to draw her out, though, considering the little tiffs we've been having lately."

"You don't think it's my catfish, do you?" Laurie said. "I believe someone mentioned to me off-the-cuff that she might be a bit squeamish about eating it."

"Maybe I shouldn't have brought it up, but that would have been me," Petey explained. "Sis made a big to-do about it when we first arrived, but I assume she's past that now." He took another bite of his catfish and wagged his brows for effect. "As far as I'm concerned, this stuff is the catfish's meow. I can see why people like it so much and why it's gotten to be such a lucrative business. And I'd also like to compliment you on these lima beans, Laurie. They're the freshest I've ever tasted."

"Thank you for the compliment, Petey. But those aren't lima beans. They're edamame—which is just a fancy way of saying boiled green soybeans."

Petey looked both surprised and impressed. "Wow! I

thought you had to doctor up soybeans to make them work, so to speak. You know, fool around with them to make them taste like something else. You Southerners sure are creative with food."

"Actually, edamame is a Japanese favorite," Laurie explained, pausing briefly for a little giggle. "And all the kudzu you see covering everything from gullies to telephone poles in this part of the South was imported from China. So I guess you could say the Deep South owes quite a bit to the Far East these days."

The conversation continued to flow in an effortless manner, and Laurie was particularly pleased that Petey seemed to be enjoying himself to the hilt. But, as everyone had discussed tirelessly in planning the weekend, he was only half the equation and objective. As the evening progressed, Laurie indulged stolen glances at Gaylie Girl and was reasonably certain that it was Amanda who was causing the distraction reflected in her mother's face from time to time. Perhaps the coffee and dessert course at Renza's would sweeten things up nicely for everyone.

THE INTENSE COFFEE and dark chocolate aromas swirling throughout Belford Place were enough to make a grown man swoon. In fact, Mr. Choppy could not remember when he had been presented with such a dazzling array of choices—a veritable feast for the eyes and sniffer alike. Renza's dessert table was groaning with sinful concoctions that would be nearly impossible for anyone to resist, and Mr. Choppy had already decided that he wasn't even going to try.

There were platters of New York cheesecake miniatures, huge walnut chocolate chip cookies the size of small Frisbees, and white chocolate and marzipan petits fours. As if that were not enough, there was an enormous fondue pot of hot, bubbling chocolate, alongside an assortment of fresh pineapple chunks, maraschino cherries, strawberries, bananas, and dried apricots for skewering and dipping. There were four types of coffee drinks available—a regular and decaffeinated cappuccino and the same varieties of latte. A selection of liqueurs such as Kahlúa, Grand Marnier, Courvoisier, Baileys Irish Cream, and two types of port wine rounded out Renza's sumptuous offerings for the finale of the progressive dinner.

"I don't believe I've ever done fondue," Mr. Choppy was saying to Gaylie Girl as they surveyed the dessert buffet together in the downstairs parlor just off the kitchen. "But I did have a thing for lickin' my sticky fingers when I was a kid. If it's anything like that, I'm in."

"Well, you know me," Gaylie Girl said, giving him a devilish grin and gently pressing up against him. "A splash of Kahlúa in my cappuccino and I'm in after-dinner heaven."

The two of them fussed at the table for a while, eschewing the assistance of Renza's servant-of-the-month—a thin young woman with a timid smile. They finally emerged with their drinks and chocolate-dipped fruit intact and then approached Renza, Petey, and Meta in a cozy corner of the parlor. The trio was standing around holding their after-dinner drinks, and a lively conversation already seemed to be in progress.

"Mind if we join you?" Mr. Choppy said, taking a seat on a sofa near them with Gaylie Girl in tow.

"Please do," Renza responded, swirling her snifter of brandy almost as a reflex action. "I was trying to find a way to ask Petey about his company and his interest in following in his father's footsteps. But no matter how I phrased it in my head, it kept coming out too much like a pun, and I didn't want to be guilty of such corny horse apples."

Gaylie Girl momentarily rested her Kahlúa and coffee in her lap. "Oh, my Peter absolutely adored his puns. He managed to come up with one on his deathbed, and it made me appreciate his odd sense of humor all the more. Deep down where it counted, I think he thought the success of Lyons Insole was the funniest thing in the world."

"That's true, you know," Petey added, chuckling and nodding at the same time. "Dad once told me that he really thought his success had all boiled down to avoiding 'stepping in it' with the company from the get-go. I thought that was pretty funny, considering the obvious interpretation of that particular phrase. 'You could build a new slogan around that,' I remember telling him, and we had a good laugh together playing with a dog owners' ad campaign and the

'Watch where you're stepping in a Lyons' angle. Of course, we never actually trotted it out."

Mr. Choppy had no doubt whatsoever now that they had accomplished their objective with Petey, who continued to open up to all of them in a congenial manner. But from all reports, Amanda was still not completely onboard, despite everyone's gamest efforts. Then, almost as if she had been reading Mr. Choppy's mind from afar, Amanda appeared in the door frame, gazing rather intently toward the sofa where he and Gaylie Girl were still sampling their drinks and goodies.

"Mother, I need to talk to you for a moment," she said, her tone decidedly edgy. "In private."

Gaylie Girl frowned and put her drink on the nearby coffee table. "Right this minute?"

"Yes. Let's go . . . uh, powder our noses."

Off they went—mother and daughter—and Mr. Choppy took a deep breath, expecting to resume the pleasant conversation he had been enjoying with Petey.

But he had another thought coming when Petey said: "Will you all excuse me for a moment? I need to track down my Evening Shadows hostess, Myrtis Troy. Have any of you seen her?"

"I believe she was hanging out in the kitchen with Novie, last I saw," Renza replied. "Is there something I can help you with?"

"No, I just need to touch base with her about something. It won't take long." And with that, Petey left the room, but not before making peculiar eye contact with Meta—decidedly a signal of some sort.

Mr. Choppy continued to observe in silence as those around him moved and spoke as if they were all characters in one of those dinner theater murder mysteries he'd attended up in Memphis now and then. The next line of dialogue and bit of business fell to Meta.

"Don't feel left out, Mother," she told Renza. "I have something I need to talk to you about in private, too. Shall we?"

And yet another mother-and-daughter pair departed Mr. Choppy's corner of the parlor. Despite it all, he found himself smiling while he finished off his chocolate-dipped strawberries and one last cheesecake bite. Damned if he was going to let a mass exodus of party poopers spoil the most elegant desserts he'd enjoyed in years!

When Gaylie Girl finally returned—with Amanda conspicuously absent—her agitation seemed to have escalated.

"Bad news?" Mr. Choppy asked, the worry lines in his face duplicating hers.

"Not sure yet. Amanda wants to talk to me later out at Evening Shadows," she answered. "Last time we huddled out there, things got pretty heated up."

Then Renza returned alone, her customary hauteur very much in evidence, and she was anything but forthcoming about what had transpired between herself and her own daughter. Instead, she put her hostess hat back on and forged ahead as if nothing had happened. "Anyone for more fondue or coffee?" There were no takers, but Renza did offer up one last enigmatic aside. "This seems to be a night for indulgence."

MR. CHOPPY HAD BEEN eagerly anticipating Gaylie Girl's return from Evening Shadows for some time now. The two of them had driven home from Renza's in his Dodge, and then she had taken her own car out to Evening Shadows for the mother-daughter interaction Amanda had requested during the dessert course. He was way past ready for feedback now. Not to mention a plausible explanation for the rest of those "excuse me, please" mini-dramas he had witnessed and puzzled over there near the end. If all went well, he was certain everything would come into sharp focus when Gaylie Girl sat down with him at the kitchen table on Pond Street.

He had begun his vigil shortly after ten o'clock on an already eventful Saturday evening. Ten-thirty came and went. Then eleven. Gaylie Girl had still not darkened their doorstep. Though the hour was late, Mr. Choppy rang up Evening Shadows to check on things. Myrtis had answered, confirmed that Gaylie Girl and Amanda were still upstairs talking, and suggested that he put on a pot of coffee for what could turn out to be a long night.

"They haven't been fighting all this time, have they, Myrtis? Can't you tell me anything more?" he managed.

She told him she had nothing further for him, and he had signed off reluctantly. "Have Gaylie Girl call me before she heads back," he said. And then he had resumed the waiting game.

By quarter to midnight he found himself reduced to singing bits and pieces of a children's ditty that he just couldn't get out of his head. It had been one of his childhood birthday-party favorites, even though he hadn't really thought of it since puberty appeared. Whatever the case, it seemed to sum up the hectic evening of food, drink, and confounding fun and games perfectly:

Here we go looby lou
Here we go looby light
Here we go looby lou
All on a Saturday night.

When the wall phone finally rang, he nearly jumped out of his skin. Of course, it was Gaylie Girl telling him she was headed home. She showed up just past midnight, looking as weary as he'd ever seen her look—which wasn't often, considering the impeccable care she always took with her appearance. Mr. Choppy poured her a cup of the coffee he'd just brewed, and the two of them eyed each other across the table.

"We can do this in the mornin' if you're too tired," he said, studying her face closely while offering up a solicitous smile.

She took a sip of her coffee and waved him off. "No. I'll soon be your wife, so you have the right to know all about the dirty laundry in my family."

"Somethin' tells me Amanda's still not completely on-board."

Gaylie Girl's smile was wry and exaggerated, and there was an air of incredulity in her tone of voice. "We hardly even discussed the wedding, believe it or not. I thought I knew my daughter, but I was dead wrong. It seems Petey's whirlwind encounter with Meta Belford forced the truth to the surface for Amanda at last. She told me that it's been all about maintaining the illusion instead of the real thing for her lately. She's also betting that Petey's found the right woman at last. Not that I hope she's wrong, but I guess I'll believe it when I see it, considering his track record."

Mr. Choppy was more curious than ever. "Right now, I'm havin' trouble followin' all this. Can you simplify it for me just a tad bit?"

"Just hang on. I'll connect all the loose ends." She took another sip of coffee and seemed to be working things out in her head. "First revelation: Petey and Meta Belford are spending the night at the Second Creek Hotel. This, according to Myrtis, who says Petey told her at Renza's not to expect him for breakfast in the morning. Which is just as well since we're all headed over to Greenwood for Sunday brunch with Wittsie."

"So that's what all the maneuvering was about just before we left. Wow! Another generation—another rendezvous at the Second Creek Hotel! Not the best of precedents, in my book."

Gaylie Girl shuddered slightly. "Agreed. And I hope it doesn't take Petey and Meta a half-century to work things out the way we did. Of course, Renza just had to call while I was out at Evening Shadows to say that she wasn't pleased at all with the way her daughter was acting with *my* son. Like a schoolgirl with a mad crush, she said. She vented for about fifteen minutes about the hotel thing. 'Well, would you rather they spent the night at your house right under your nose?' I said to her. That finally shut her up."

"Petey and Meta are hardly teenagers, though. Not like we were—back in the day."

Mr. Choppy's last remark had a sobering effect on both of them, and there was a period of thoughtful silence before Gaylie Girl spoke again. "Anyway, getting back to the issue of keeping up appearances—that's the second revelation. Amanda has not been telling me the truth. All this time she's touted the perfection of her marriage to Richard, he's been running around on her and spending lots of her money. Apparently, he's not the paragon we all thought he was, but she's been superb at keeping up those perfect nuclear-family appearances. To a fault."

"Keep goin'," Mr. Choppy said, the frown on his face still very much in evidence.

Gaylie Girl put down her cup and began tearing up, unable to speak for a few moments.

"Take your time, sweetheart."

She finally regained her composure and said: "There we were, commiserating in her guest room, and Amanda got it all out in the open, and it nearly knocked me off my feet. Her insecurities about my marriage to you have much more to do with Richard and his philandering ways—not to mention the unsatisfactory money situation. I never saw any of that coming, but it all makes sense now. She's been fibbing a little about some of those trips she's taken, too. Many of them have been without Richard—just the kids—as it turns out. She needed to get away and get a different perspective, hoping that would somehow improve things. What really got me was when she started crying and said, 'Mother, I'm a fraud, and so is my marriage to Richard!' Then she asked me for a big hug, and it felt like years of tension between us were wiped away in an instant. And I understood why she's been so concerned about the company and my will— especially if a divorce from Richard should happen to enter the picture."

"Is she seriously considering it?"

Gaylie Girl wiped away a tear or two but managed a fledgling smile. "She hasn't decided yet, but she says she's glad she made the trip down here now. She sees clearly that I really am happy with you and all the Nitwitts. I truly think we've finally gotten past that part. I'm just sorry she felt she couldn't come to me with the truth long before now. Keeping up silver-spoon appearances can get you in a lot of trouble. I should know—I did quite a bit of it myself up in Lake Forest."

Mr. Choppy almost seemed to be preening. "So you think you'll be able to have that family wedding out at Evening Shadows the way you wanted it? I mean, with the part about Petey givin' you away and Amanda as your matron of honor?"

"As I said, we actually didn't get around to discussing the details of the wedding. This thing with Richard really threw me, but it finally put everything in the proper perspective. I've been racking my brain these past few years for an explanation as to why Amanda had gotten so mean-spirited and concerned with money all the time. I read it as aloofness and immaturity—even snobbery—but I couldn't have been more wrong."

"I've said it before, and I'll say it again. You really don't have a thing to worry about regarding the money angle."

Gaylie Girl drew back and squinted. "You've been speaking to that subject like a Tarot reader all weekend. Are you ever going to tell me what you know that I don't know? Because, to tell the truth, I'm not even sure yet what changes I want to make in my will once we get married. And if I don't know, myself, how can you possibly know anything?"

"I promise you'll know what you need to know by Sunday evening," Mr. Choppy said. He could tell by the way she widened her eyes, arched her brows, and shrugged her shoulders that she had no intention of pursuing his cryptic remarks any further.

"Very well. Let's go get some sleep, then," she said instead.

"We've got another big day ahead of us tomorrow." She brought her hands up in front of her face and wiggled her fingers playfully. "After all, Laurie and I will make our debut as the concert pianists supreme of the entire Mississippi Delta."

"Sure you don't wanna run over to our new house and get in a little last-minute practice? For once, you'll probably be able to hear yourself without the workmen poundin' away."

Gaylie Girl's grin was sly, her eyes half-lidded and full of promise. "Tomorrow, my talent will be unveiled to the world, thanks to Euterpe's unsurpassed instruction. Besides, knowing Renza the way I do now, she'll probably be up at all hours worrying about both our children, see the lights on in the middle of the night, and call the police about a possible burglary down the street. I'll probably be arrested for breaking and entering, or at the very least for disturbing the peace."

"You know I'll bail you out!"

"My irresistible, courageous, and loyal Hale Dunbar Junior," she answered with a broad sweep of her hand. "You already have."

9.

"HEART AND SOUL"

*I*t was no coincidence that Delta Sunset Village just outside Greenwood reminded everyone of Mount Vernon—with a couple of extra floors and a few cypress knees in the front yard thrown into the mix. The Memphis owners of the state-of-the-art retirement home with its assisted-living and memory-care wings were relentless in their pursuit of flag-waving Americana. They had also built two condo developments over on Lake Ferguson with all the units resembling scaled-down versions of either Monti-cello or Jefferson Davis's home, Beauvoir, down in Biloxi; and then a singles apartment complex modeled after the Alamo that was within a great tee shot of Tunica's largest casinos; and finally a theme park near Vicksburg with a concrete mock-up of Mount Rushmore that had been poured into the side of one of the many loess bluffs that characterized the area's topography.

"I know the home looks a little like a Hollywood set on the outside, but it's really quite unique inside," Gaylie Girl was saying to Mr. Choppy as he pulled into a parking space near the white-columned front entrance. He had driven her car over on this sultry Sunday morning from Second Creek, leading a veritable motorcade that included the rest of the Nitwitts, Powell Hampton, Euterpe—without her poodle, for once—and finally Amanda, Petey, and Meta Belford bringing up the rear in Mr. Choppy's Dodge.

"The important thing is the quality of care Wittsie is getting round the clock. The staff is no-nonsense and prepared to deal with any health crisis that arises. That's really the only thing that helps me keep my emotions under control whenever I come over to visit her," Gaylie Girl continued. "I can pull a cord, and someone appears like magic."

Mr. Choppy unhooked his seat belt. "Well, I sure hope they have plenty of food for everyone. Judgin' by last night's progressive dinner, this crowd can really put it away."

Gaylie Girl soon joined him in the parking lot, watching the rest of the Nitwitts emerge from their cars all atwitter and dressed in their Sunday best. "That's been taken care of. We've reserved a private dining room and ordered up some extras, including small glasses of watered-down champagne. Of course, in true Nitwitt fashion some of the girls were lobbying for the full-strength variety, but the staff said no, better not tempt fate with all the people wandering around on medication during mealtime, including our dear Wittsie."

Several minutes later, everyone had gathered in the spacious lobby of the facility, and there was a healthy amount of stargazing for those who had never been under its roof before. The first thing that caught the eye was a mini-atrium that reached all the way up to the third floor, supported by four white columns that echoed the style on the façade outside. In the exact center of the room was the elegant grand piano where Gaylie Girl and Laurie's duet would later be staged. On the wall to the right was a large, high-definition TV monitor displaying the extensive Sunday brunch menu. Against the customary blue background, someone had even gone to the trouble of matching up the day's choices with their approximate colors. Glazed carrots glowed a garish orange; steamed broccoli a bilious green; buttered corn a bright gold; sautéed shrimp a sizzling pink; even cranberry sauce was attractively announced in a maroon italic font.

"Oh, goody gumdrops!" Denver Lee exclaimed while wandering over to scan the list. "Lots and lots of veggies for me to eat today!"

"Yes. Who would have guessed?" Renza said, stepping up from behind and unable to resist yet another opportunity to tease her friend. "Elderly people. Roughage. Regularity. The mind boggles. Anyway, let's all go give the management our name, rank, and serial number."

She pointed to the sprawling front desk at her left where all visitors were required to register for security purposes, and the line quickly formed.

"Now, where is the old girl this morning?" Renza said after everyone had finished signing in. "Whenever I come over for my Tuesday visits, Wittsie's always waiting for me right here in the lobby. I always think of her as a little puppy just wagging her tail. But that's a good sign, since it means she knows who I am and why I've come to see her."

Just then, the director of the complex emerged from her office adjacent to the front desk. She was an attractive, middle-aged woman with a tangle of curly hair and a welcoming air about her. "Good morning, everyone!" she announced, her voice clear and crisp. "Some of you know me quite well by now, but for those who don't, I'm Mrs. Lisa Holstrom, and I pretty much make all the executive decisions here at Delta Sunset Village. Of course, we're delighted to have all of you out here today for this special event. Miz Wittsie, as we've all come to call her, has been looking forward to this so much. It's all she's been able to talk about."

"Well, where is she, then?" said Renza, pursuing her earlier question with customary impatience. "I trust nothing's wrong. Please don't tell us we've come all this way and Wittsie can't even get out of bed."

"Nothing's wrong in the least," Mrs. Holstrom answered with her usual efficiency. "We just didn't want to bring Miz Wittsie out of the memory-care unit until everyone was here and ready to go on into the brunch. Disturbing her daily schedule any more than necessary upsets her. Routine is very important to our memory-care patients. Don't worry, though. One of the staff is bringing her over from the unit right now. I'm sure she'll be raring to go when she gets here."

And raring to go she was. Unlike many of the other residents, who were creeping along toward the dining room with their walkers or making somewhat better time in their wheelchairs and scooters, Wittsie appeared on the arm of one of the orderlies, waving at everyone with a smile of utter delight on her face. She had definitely dressed for the occasion just like the other Nitwitts, looking as if she were going to or coming from church.

"Oh, my!" she declared, surveying the group before her in amazement. "Have all of you come over just to see me today? . . . I've never had this many visitors . . . at least I don't think I have!"

Many hugs, pecks on the cheek, kissless kisses, and near misses followed, as well as introductions to the people Wittsie had never met—Petey, Amanda, Euterpe, and Meta Belford. Predictably, Wittsie had trouble keeping the newcomers straight.

"Now . . . is this young lady . . . Amanda, was it? . . . your daughter, Gaylie Girl? I thought she was my April for a second there. . . . You see, I thought April was comin' today and bringin' my little Meagan with her. . . . Meagan's come for many a visit over the years. . . . Now, where did I get that impression?"

"I don't know, Wittsie," Gaylie Girl replied as gently as possible. "Your daughter and granddaughter are not here today. But my daughter, Amanda, and my son, Petey, are definitely here—down from Lake Forest, Illinois—for a weekend visit with bells on their toes."

Then Wittsie focused on Meta as the group headed en masse toward the dining room. "And whose daughter were you now? . . . I seem to have forgotten already. . . . My, but you have pretty blond hair."

"I'm Renza's daughter, Miz Wittsie. I just bebopped into town on the spur of the moment. My mother has told me so much about you and how you started up the Nitwitts after your husband died a few years back. I just love how you all look after each other."

Wittsie seemed to make the connection at last, brightening further. "Oh, speakin' of bebop, will there be any dancin' today? . . . Can I dance like I did at the Piggly Wiggly last summer?"

"Maybe we can sneak something in," said Powell, who had picked up where the orderly left off, personally escorting Wittsie into the dining room on his arm. "And you're as sharp as a tack there remembering our time together in the aisles of the Piggly Wiggly."

Wittsie was still smiling even as she was shaking her head. "Wish I could say that about myself all the time, Powell . . . but I go hot and cold like a faucet. . . . I mean, you know your Laurie and the rest of my Nitwitt friends come over to visit me like clockwork. . . . They've all been so sweet

to me . . . but they never know which Wittsie will show
up . . . and I don't, either."

Powell gave her arm an affectionate little squeeze. "Well,
I'm convinced we've got the A-list Wittsie with us today."

Several smaller tables had been pushed together and
covered with starched white tablecloths to accommodate
the group in the private dining area used for special occa-
sions, and it took a few minutes for everyone to pick their
seats and settle in. Laurie and Powell decided that Wittsie
should preside at the head of the long, makeshift table, and
they chose seats on either side of her. Gaylie Girl and Mr.
Choppy were next closest, and then Euterpe, the rest of the
Nitwitts, and their offspring spread themselves out from
there. A few minutes later, Powell stood up tall and said:
"Well, folks, let's don't let this sumptuous spread go to
waste. I for one can't wait to get at those blueberry waffles!"
At which point everyone began heading over to the buffet
by twos and threes to select from the dazzling array of
choices.

"FOR SOME REASON, I keep thinkin' you're already
married," Wittsie was saying to Gaylie Girl while taking a
first bite of her eggs Benedict a few minutes later. "Now,
why did I think that? . . . Did I dream it? . . . The truth is,
things get so jumbled up for me sometimes . . . but I try
hard, I really do."

Gaylie Girl and Mr. Choppy quickly exchanged glances,

but it was Mr. Choppy who answered Wittsie's questions. "Gaylie Girl and I aren't married yet, Miz Wittsie. But that'll be comin' up around Labor Day in just a few more weeks, God willin'. We've already had a little talk with your doctor, and he's agreed to consider lettin' one of the Nitwitt ladies come and pick you up for the ceremony. Now, it's not a done deal, you understand. But he did say he'd take it under consideration. A change of pace like that might be just the thing you need."

"Yes, and we've decided to draw straws if it's a go, Wittsie," Myrtis said. "Otherwise, we'd be fighting over you for so long, we'd all miss the actual wedding."

Wittsie put down her fork and clasped her hands together in rapturous fashion. "Oh, that would be wonderful . . . you don't know how much that means to me. . . . I know I'd love to attend. . . . It's just that I thought you'd gotten married last year in the Piggly Wiggly, Mr. Choppy."

Laurie intervened, reaching over to pat Wittsie's hand gently. "No, that was me and Powell, Wittsie. I can still hardly believe we exchanged vows in the grocery store, myself. But we had the time of our life, thanks to Mr. Choppy, you, and all the rest of the girls. Your little Meagan was even in it as the maid of honor, remember?"

Wittsie seemed to be trying her best to follow along, but the creases in her face showed that she was going through a bad patch. "My Meagan was in a wedding here last summer? . . . I just don't remember that, I'm afraid."

"Don't you worry about it for a single second," Laurie

said, waving her off. "That's all over and done with, and Powell and I have been happily married for about a year now."

Wittsie took another bite of her eggs and shrugged. "Uh . . . imagine that. Time flies, I suppose." There were concerned but understanding faces all around the table as Wittsie continued in that rambling manner of hers. "I was hopin' my daughter, April, would be here today so she could tell me how long I've been here. . . . This is not my real home, you know. . . . I think she is definitely plannin' to take me home soon. . . . At least I think she wrote that in a letter . . . but I don't know for sure." Then Wittsie suddenly started tearing up in her confusion.

It was Laurie who quickly thought on her feet in an obvious attempt to defuse the situation. "Just don't let it upset you, sweetie. April couldn't come. I know she wanted to, but she just couldn't swing it. I'm sure she'll be coming down to visit you soon, though."

"I hope so. I haven't seen her in a while. . . . Do you think she's forgotten that I'm not at home anymore? . . . I wonder if she has my new address here."

"Oh, I'm sure she has it, Wittsie, and I know she hasn't forgotten anything as important as that."

Wittsie sighed and stabbed a couple of carrots with her fork, staring down at them with utter disdain. "Vegetables. That's all we have here—orange vegetables, green vegetables, yellow vegetables."

"The more colorful the vegetable, the more nutrition in

it!" Laurie exclaimed. "And the glaze on these carrots is absolutely delicious. I have half a mind to get their recipe."

The remark brought an immediate smile to Wittsie's face. "Oh, Laurie, you don't need it, I'm sure. You've always had the lowdown on everything from cookin' to dancin'."

"Yes, she has," Powell added. "And I bet you didn't know she has a surprise floor show planned for you after brunch. She and Gaylie Girl as a one-two punch, that is."

"My two best pupils," Euterpe interjected from the other end of the table. "No offense to you other ladies. You're all making splendid progress at this early date—so says the Mistress of the Scales."

Wittsie leaned in to Laurie and whispered, "Who is that lady down there in the blue? . . . Did she say she was a teacher of some kind . . . or somebody's mistress? . . . That's a bit brazen, I think."

Laurie winced ever so slightly. "No, that's our piano teacher—Mrs. Euterpe Simon. I introduced you to her out in the lobby just before we headed over here. You even commented on that lovely peacock blue dress she's wearing. It's her signature color, you know."

"Yes, it certainly is beautiful . . . but I don't seem to remember you introducin' me to her . . . oh, dear!"

"At any rate," Laurie continued without batting an eyelash, "we've all been taking piano lessons from her, and Gaylie Girl and I have worked up a little duet for you. Now, don't expect Liberace or Henry Mancini or anything as accomplished as that. We've barely mastered our scales, but we've been practicing day and night just for you—together and separately. Just a little something to let you know we're always thinking about you."

Then the pendulum of recognition seemed to swing to the other extreme. "Oh, yes, I do remember one of you tellin' me about the piano lessons a couple of weeks ago. . . . I wish I could take them, too. . . . I think I might be good at it . . . but maybe that's just not possible . . ."

"Oh, I find that anything's possible," Euterpe replied, acknowledging the attention. "That's my motto."

Wittsie suddenly seemed more focused, if a bit giddy. "Well, I can hardly wait to hear your little recital, girls. What a wonderful treat!"

MRS. HOLSTROM had instructed the activities director to have extra chairs brought into the lobby so that all the residents who had gotten wind of it through the grapevine could become part of the audience for Laurie and Gaylie Girl's musical moment in time. She had not underestimated the demand one iota, either, as every seat in the impromptu house was taken by the time Euterpe stepped to the piano to introduce her latest handiwork. The Nitwitts and the rest of the brunch contingent had managed to claim everything across the front row—placing Wittsie in the exact center. They were all soon noisily chattering away, of course, forcing Euterpe to shush them politely several times before she could launch into her spiel.

"And now, ladies and gentlemen," she began at last. "It is my distinct pleasure to present two of my current pupils in a lighthearted little number in honor of their great friend Wittsie Chadwick. I'm quite sure that each of you will remember this time-honored ditty from somewhere back in your childhood. Perhaps it was at summer camp that you first encountered it, as I did. My first experience with this sweetest of songs coincided with the first crush I ever had on a boy. His name was John Rogers Healy, and he was a dark-haired little devil with a cowlick that no amount of spit could ever tame. I shall never forget the way he and I memorized the lyrics and sang them to each other over and over again out on the pier whenever we got together during our free periods.

"I firmly believe this particular song was meant to be played for and sung by the sweetest people on earth. And there is absolutely no doubt in my mind from the way your friends care about you, Wittsie Chadwick, that you definitely fit that description. And so without further ado, I give you Laurie Hampton and Gaylie Girl Lyons together at the piano playing that sentimental standby 'Heart and Soul.'"

Both Laurie and Gaylie Girl, who were already seated at the piano, stood up and executed brief little bows to the polite applause of the audience; although Denver Lee indulged a bit of raucous cheerleading in the form of "Tickle those ivories, you tried-and-true Nitwitts! Work those manicured fingers to the bone!"

And then, with Laurie energetically taking on the bass

part that rocked back and forth so playfully, and Gaylie Girl sounding the cheerful melody in the treble clef—simple key of C, of course—they were off to the races. It all went surprisingly well for the most part. Gaylie Girl hit a B natural instead of an A natural once by mistake, but other than that, the performance was very easy on the ears.

"Oh, please play it again, won't you, girls?!" Wittsie exclaimed, obviously enjoying herself to the hilt. "And this time maybe some of us can sing along. . . . I mean, I may forget what day it is sometimes, but I think I can remember most of the lyrics. . . . How about the rest of you?"

The second time around, there was vigorous communal singing led by Euterpe, who announced that she remembered all the lyrics and invited everyone to follow her. Even those like Renza and Mr. Choppy, who couldn't carry a tune as simple as "Happy Birthday," were doing their best to contribute. The entire room was overflowing with camaraderie; and a relaxed and joyful Wittsie stood at the center of it all, swaying her arms in the air to and fro as if she were at a tent revival about to be anointed.

"I don't know when I've had so much fun!" Wittsie called out to both Laurie and Gaylie Girl as they rose from the piano to take their final bows. The entire audience was soon pressing in on the performers with congratulations and smiles.

"An unqualified success!" Euterpe proclaimed after most of the residents had returned to their rooms and things had settled down. Only the rest of the Second Creek contingent remained huddled around Wittsie, Laurie, and Gaylie Girl. "I continue to believe that mastering an instrument like the piano opens up new ways for people to connect with each other, and a moment like the one we just enjoyed is the primary reason I've chosen to travel and teach."

"You truly are the Mistress of the Scales," Laurie replied. "Although I have to confess, it almost feels like you're walking around naked without your little Pan on your shoulder."

"Oh, Sarah's looking after him back at Evening Shadows. I wanted to be able to concentrate fully on Wittsie and your recital today. Even precious poodles have to take a backseat from time to time."

MR. CHOPPY AND GAYLIE GIRL had no idea what Wittsie was up to. After everyone else had said their good-byes and headed toward the parking lot in various combinations, she had asked the orderly to wait in the hallway for a few more minutes. Then she had tugged at Mr. Choppy's sleeve insistently. "I don't want you and Gaylie Girl to leave just yet. . . . I, uh, have somethin' very important to tell you. . . . I mean, it's slipped my mind a few times when Gaylie Girl has come out to visit me on Saturdays . . . but it won't happen this time. . . . I've held on to it like a dog at a postman's trousers . . . and I'm pretty darned proud of myself, too."

The three of them had moved to a serviceable sofa near

the grand piano and were now seated together comfortably. "What's on your mind, Miz Wittsie?" Mr. Choppy asked with an expectant expression on his face.

Predictably, Wittsie took her own sweet time before speaking, ratcheting up the curiosity level a few notches. "Well . . . how to put this? . . . There's this incredible thing I've noticed . . . and you can ask Mrs. Holstrom about it if you don't believe what I'm goin' to tell you, but—"

Gaylie Girl interrupted, gently rubbing Wittsie's arm a few times. "Now, why wouldn't we believe whatever you have to say to us?"

"Yes," Mr. Choppy chimed in. "We're all ears and open minds."

"I'm . . . I'm countin' on that." Then Wittsie began to unveil her revelation in earnest. "Well . . . it's . . . it's the fireflies. . . ."

Mr. Choppy was clearly amused, offering up a reassuring tone. "Oh, that. You mean the fact that they've been missin' all summer, right? We've all noticed that over in Second Creek, too."

Gaylie Girl seconded the observation. "Hale has me on the lookout for them all the time. Unfortunately, there's never anything to report. Hale's maybe spotted one, but I haven't seen any since I came down here."

But Wittsie was shaking her head emphatically. "No, that's not what I was gettin' at. . . . I mean, I did know the fireflies have been missin' over there in Second Creek . . . you've mentioned it to me a couple of times on your visits,

Gaylie Girl . . . you told me that Mr. Choppy seemed to be frettin' over it now and then. . . . Of course, I haven't seen it for myself because April moved me over here to Delta Sunset Village, and I wasn't payin' much attention before that."

"Then what are you getting at?" Gaylie Girl said, her voice now tinged with concern.

"What I mean to say is that the fireflies are all over here now . . . it's like they've migrated . . . there are lots of them outside my window every night just blinkin' away . . . and some of the others in the independent-living wing say the fireflies are in the front yard and backyard as far as the eye can see, whenever they go out for a late walk. . . . They light up the night everywhere around us . . . ask Mrs. Holstrom, she'll tell you. She says she's lived in Greenwood all her life and has never seen so many before. . . . She says it wasn't like this last summer, to her recollection."

"We don't need to ask her," Gaylie Girl responded quickly. "We'll take your word, sweetie."

But Mr. Choppy pressed further while shaking his head. "I didn't think fireflies could be so territorial."

"They sure seem to be now."

"Excuse my language, Miz Wittsie—but I'll be damned!"

"It doesn't make any sense, I know, but . . ." Wittsie paused to offer up an endearing little giggle. "I do have a theory . . . I mean, I have all this time on my hands over here . . . I spend a lot of it thinkin' about the craziest things . . . things that don't make sense to other people make all the sense in the world to me now . . . my brain—well, it works different these days . . . I can't explain it, but I know it's true . . . scary but true."

Gaylie Girl reached over and patted Wittsie's hand. "So what's your theory, sweetie?"

"I . . . I know I don't have all that much time left . . . I don't kid myself about that . . . so I think the fireflies have all gathered to wish me well when the time comes. . . . I think they're here for me, I really do. . . . You see, when I was a little girl gettin' ready for bed during the summertime, I used to send up a little prayer every time I saw one blinkin' at me outside my window. I asked them each and every one if they'd be so kind as to always light my way in life . . . so I think what happened was they couldn't find me at first when April took me away from Second Creek, but now they've found me again . . . and I was thinkin' that maybe all those prayers backed up from my childhood have been answered now . . . when I need them the most."

Gaylie Girl moved closer to give Wittsie a heartfelt hug, but it was Mr. Choppy who felt something almost electric surging throughout his body from head to toe. Images of his mother telling him boyhood stories about bracelets made of fireflies and using them to actually learn how to fly swirled inside his brain. Something in his deepest core was pleased that Wittsie had worked it all out as only a lifelong Second Creeker could. Even so, Mr. Choppy thought the moment needed a bit of levity.

"You best keep all that magical Second Creek stuff to yourself, Miz Wittsie. They may take you away, you know."

The remark had the desired effect, acting like a balm and bringing a smile to everyone's lips. Then Mr. Choppy gently took Wittsie into his arms, closed his eyes, and whispered to her softly: "Thank God for angels like you."

"I THINK THIS has turned out to be a phenomenal weekend so far," Gaylie Girl said on the ride back to Second Creek. "I only wish Amanda and Petey could have been with us when Wittsie unburdened herself back there. That's the sort of thing about Second Creek that I really want them to get, but it's so hard to convey it to people who don't live here. It just doesn't seem to translate well."

Mr. Choppy drove on through the soybean fields in silence for a half mile or so and decided that the moment had finally arrived. "All I have to say to that is—you're right on cue, sweetheart. You picked the perfect time to mention your children. I think we're gonna be puttin' to bed for good all their concerns about us and the wedding in a few more minutes. I'm about to reveal my ace in the hole."

She looked at him askance and folded her arms. "At last. Are you going to take my breath away like Wittsie just did? I don't know when I've been so moved or how on earth I kept from crying when she went on like that about the fireflies. I got gooseflesh. The good kind, of course."

Mr. Choppy had a ready smile for his Gaylie Girl. "She's a woman after my own heart, that Wittsie Chadwick, and that was the perfect send-off she gave us."

"So where are you going to reveal this epiphany?"

"At my office. I wanted the proper settin' for emphasis. I've asked Petey and Amanda to meet us there at two o'clock sharp."

Gaylie Girl checked her watch and saw that it was one-fifteen. "We have plenty of time, then. But where was I when you put all this together? I thought the game plan was to keep me in the loop about everything important. I'll soon be your First Lady, remember?"

"Oh, you were in the usual places doin' the usual things. The truth is, I had Cherish set everything up long-distance before Petey and Amanda came down from Lake Forest. I figured no matter how things actually went over the weekend, I wanted to get in the last word. And based on Friday, Saturday, and everything that's happened today, I'm thinkin' that this might not be near as hard as I thought it was gonna be a few weeks ago."

Then she unfolded her arms and let out a playful little sigh. "I had no idea I'd be marrying such a cryptic and devious man. You've been having a ball with this all weekend, haven't you? It's been one big tease after another."

"I just wanted to play it conservatively. I certainly didn't want to take anything for granted, and I was only goin' by what you'd been tellin' me about Petey and Amanda these past few months. You gotta admit they weren't exactly turnin' cartwheels when they stepped off the plane the other day, and I wanted to do everything I could to help 'em see the light."

"Our efforts have paid off, too. I do think we've made substantial progress with both of them, particularly Petey. Meanwhile, Amanda's made me take a long, hard look at some financial matters I've needed to address anyway regarding Lyons Insole and my will."

Mr. Choppy heaved a triumphant sigh. "Perfect. That's exactly what I wanted to hear from you. As I've been sayin' all along—I think we'll soon be home free."

IT WAS JUST a few minutes past two o'clock, but Mr. Choppy felt as if he had been waiting for hours for his session with Petey, Amanda, and Gaylie Girl to begin. Truth to tell, he had been waiting for months—ever since he had made a crucial decision regarding his proper place in Gaylie Girl's former Lake Forest–Lyons Insole universe. He had chosen to keep that decision to himself, however, no matter how much his Gaylie Girl had pressed him about his mysterious mutterings. The whirlwind weekend with her children had to play itself out first—there was no other way around it.

"I don't wanna take up too much time with this today," Mr. Choppy began from behind his office desk. Gaylie Girl and her children were seated directly across from him, their expressions reflecting a curious impatience. In fact, Petey took it one step further, glancing down at his watch every now and then—very likely in anticipation of the evening flight from Memphis to Chicago that he and Amanda would be catching in a little less than five hours.

"I know you have some packin' to do out at Evening Shadows," he continued, "so I'll try to get y'all outta here as quickly as possible." Then he drew himself up in his chair and exhaled slowly, centering himself as he had managed so superbly during his election campaign. "First, I wanted to say that I've truly enjoyed meetin' and gettin' to know both of you, Petey and Amanda. At this time in my life, I never expected that I'd be dealin' with stepchildren, but that's exactly where I find myself. I even went to the library a week or so before y'all came down and got the Book Sheriff— that's our Loveta Grubbs, you know—to find me somethin' to read on the subject." Mr. Choppy paused briefly as Loveta's nickname brought a smile to everyone's face.

"What she came up with made me do a double take. The title of it was *A Blended Family Recipe*. Naturally, I thought it was a cookbook when she first handed it over to me. But I managed to get through it, and I think I collected a few pointers on all the difficulties involved in second marriages—especially when they come with children attached.

"In the end, though, I decided to fall back on a big dose of the common sense I inherited from my parents—Hale and Gladys Dunbar. They were simple, hardworkin' people who ran a small-town grocery store, and it paid off for them in two ways. They earned a respectable livin', and they earned an even more respectable reputation as owners of the local Piggly Wiggly. And I'm very much their son, through and through. I'm proud of who and what I am, and I've never pretended to be anything more. That might even be the reason I got elected mayor over Floyce Hammontree. I've never played games with anybody."

Once again, Mr. Choppy came to a halt, this time glancing affectionately at his Gaylie Girl. Apparently sensing that he might benefit from a show of support, she blew him a kiss, and he resumed his little speech with a renewed sense of purpose. "So, you see, I've never been about money throughout my entire life. Oh, once when I was very young and green around the gills, I thought how neat it would be to become a famous actor with lots and lots of money, but that was a big ole slice a' pie in the sky that was never meant to be." He could see Gaylie Girl dealing with the beginnings of discomfort as she stirred in her seat. But he quickly decided to blow back that kiss she'd just sent his way, and she caught it in splendid form with a generous smile.

"To cut to the chase here," he continued, "I want all three of you to know that I have no intention of acceptin' any part of the Lyons Insole estate that you control, Gaylie Girl. Not now. Not ever. Furthermore, I want you to make no provision at all for me in your will. And I insist that you allow me to sign a prenuptial agreement to that effect. That way there's no doubt about where we'll all stand legally."

The looks of complete surprise from Petey and Amanda

were matched only by the intensity of the frown on Gaylie Girl's face. "Hale . . . I really don't think that's necessary," she said, her tone more animated than he had expected.

Amanda was quick to speak up, however—the relief in her voice quite evident. "I think it's very generous of Hale, Mother. I'm very impressed, and you should be as well. He certainly didn't have to propose something like that."

"But I don't want you to feel pressured about this, Hale," Gaylie Girl replied, completely ignoring her daughter's comment.

"I don't, Gaylie Girl. I see it clearly as the right thing to do. I understand how Petey and Amanda feel about my comin' into their world long-distance and competin' with the memories of their father. I don't think they're bein' unreasonable at all in wantin' to know where they stand on the money issues, either. Me, I'm financially secure for the rest of my life right this instant with my mayoral salary, my savings, and my Social Security. You got yours, and I got mine, and I think we ought to keep it that way. Except we should definitely go ahead with joint ownership of the new house, since that's not a yours or a mine. That's an ours. Kinda like we're pregnant with it."

Petey laughed and waded in. "You're an upstanding guy, Hale. I realized it when we took that little trip out to Pond-Raised Catfish. I had no qualms about your marriage to my mother, after we talked yesterday."

Gaylie Girl still appeared to be conflicted. "I'm glad you think that way, Petey, and I'm very happy you feel so comfortable around Hale now. But I've always thought a prenuptial agreement implied a lack of trust on somebody's part. Are you absolutely sure that's the way you want to go, Hale? Because you must believe me when I tell you that I trust you—implicitly."

"I know you do, but I've been sure about this for months now. I want you to respect my wishes here. As far as I'm concerned, it's the last hurdle we have to clear to say our *I do*'s when Labor Day rolls around."

Gaylie Girl was silent for a while, exchanging cursory glances with both her children before speaking her mind. "So this was your ace in the hole, Hale? I have to admit I had no idea what you were going to say this afternoon. But now that I've had a chance to think about it a bit, I have to say it makes me love you even more. I know exactly what I'm getting in you, Hale Dunbar Junior, and I trust Petey and Amanda know that now, too."

"I guess I should apologize for my misconceptions about you and Second Creek, Mississippi, Hale," Amanda said. "All the hospitality has been an amazing revelation to me. I've been so impressed by the food and the architecture and most of all by the companionship. I think I'll be a very lucky woman if I'm surrounded by the kind of friends Mother has made down here, when I'm her age. I was very touched by what went on this morning over in Greenwood. You folks don't do things by the book, but that's what makes it all so fascinating. In some ways it's been the ultimate travel experience for me."

"And it's been a no-brainer for me," Petey added. "You've got a good thing going, Mother, and Hale is the main reason. Maybe—just maybe—I can get something going just like it with Meta."

Gaylie Girl looked momentarily startled. "I appreciate your enthusiasm, son, but you and Meta have only just met. I know the sparks have been flying, but I hope you'll take your time with this relationship."

"I intend to, Mother. We're both going to be patient and practical about it. Meta's practicing even as we speak, as a matter of fact—nursing a latte at the Town Square Café. I'm sure she's going to like hearing about what happened in this office today—on top of what we decided last night. She'll be flying up to visit me in Lake Forest soon, and then I'll be seeing her again for your wedding after that." He rose from his chair deliberately and moved to hers, taking her hand and kissing it softly. "Where I will be giving you away just as you've requested."

Gaylie Girl stood up and embraced her son warmly. "Oh, Petey, that's just wonderful!"

"And, yes, Mother, I'll be your matron of honor," Amanda put in, getting to her feet as well. "I'm sorry I've been so difficult about everything. Just don't make me wear some hideous, froufrou outfit that will make my grandchildren cringe when they thumb through the scrapbooks someday."

"You'll wear whatever strikes your fancy—the parlor drapes in deference to Scarlett O'Hara, if you like." Amanda hugged her mother even longer than Petey had, and then

Gaylie Girl finally drew back. "This is all I wanted from both of you. To be a real family again in the midst of all this change. It means so much to me to have you understand and accept it."

"Same here," Mr. Choppy said, watching the display of family affection and believing for the first time ever that he might be able to blend in, as Loveta's library book had trumpeted so often throughout its pages. Maybe not blend in right away, but somewhere down the line when everyone truly got to know one another.

Somehow, he found just the right words to sum it all up. "I think there's no question we got to the heart and soul of the matter today."

10.

Broken Hands and Magic Fingers

Sunday gave way to Monday at last. There was an undeniable feeling of accomplishment among the Nitwitts. Another of their legendary projects had been executed to perfection over the busy weekend. Following her return from the Memphis Airport to see her children off, Gaylie Girl had stayed on the phone the better part of Sunday evening, spreading the word to everyone about Petey and Amanda being fully onboard the wedding at last. Now the countdown to the long-awaited festivities could begin in earnest.

"Tomorrow, let's hoist a few Bloody Marys to our success," Renza had suggested on the spur of the moment during Gaylie Girl's call. "How about an impromptu meeting and a bite to eat at my place around noon? We can make doubly sure we're all on the same page regarding the next two weeks leading up to the wedding."

Of course, there was no such thing as having to twist any Nitwitt's arm to gather for "laughter, liquor, and lolly-gaggin'." It was a phrase one of them had coined during the club's earliest days, though nobody could quite remember who it was. So twelve noon Monday arrived, and Belford Place was yet again the hitching post for the social horses of Second Creek. Could there possibly be anything more important looming on their horizon?

"No one can resist the Nitwitt cavalry riding in," Renza reminded them all as they were sampling her corn-and-shrimp bisque with jalapeño corn bread at the dining room table. "I've always said General Douglas MacArthur would never have announced his return had we all been there blocking his way."

"We've won our share of battles, that's for sure," Laurie added, her expression slightly conspiratorial. "Or ripped our panty hose trying. And I'm so glad you called us all together, Renza. As you all know, Powell and I will be leaving for Paris to visit his good friend the Great Buddha Magruder on Wednesday, so we'll be out of the loop for at least a week—maybe longer. This meeting will enable me to jet away from my obligations without the slightest hint of guilt."

Novie put down her spoon and shuddered with delight. "Ah! Paree! What a divine destination! I must return before I'm too feeble to walk the streets of Montmartre or the Latin Quarter again. And could there be anything more romantic than riding one of those lovely *bateaux-mouches* down the Seine? It's the only way to see the city unfold in a leisurely manner, believe me. Everything begins and ends along the Seine. Now, I did give you my list of 'must-sees,' didn't I, Laurie?"

"That you did. It's one of the first things I'm going to pack, and I definitely plan to follow through with those walks around the . . ." Laurie hesitated as she worked the muscles of her face and the pronunciations in her head. "The Île Saint-Louis and Rue d'Auteuil . . . Those didn't sound too 'ugly American,' did they? I've been practicing with one of those *French for Travelers* books that Loveta Grubbs recommended to me."

"Not a syllable out of place—pronounced or silent."

"Anyway, our Buddha has a lovely little house on the Avenue Junot, and since we'll be staying there with him, we won't miss all those painters' studios in the neighborhood, either."

Novie gently wagged a finger at her friend. "I absolutely insist that you take pictures, of course. We'll get together and compare."

"I already know mine will pale up against yours," Laurie returned, tactfully deferring to Novie's ego in the matter.

"We'll miss you, of course," Renza added. "But we know you and Powell will be back in time for the wedding. That's all that counts." Renza swallowed a spoonful of her bisque and then wiped the corners of her mouth with her napkin. "Meanwhile, girls, I have an idea I just had to run past you all. There's something that's been gnawing at me for a good while, and I think the time has come for me to do something about it. So—here goes."

Everyone straightened up a bit in their chairs, giving her their undivided attention. "It's that gold-plated hand that the storm blew off the First Presbyterian Church so long ago. When Mr. Choppy told us how he'd been led to it last year by some mysterious force, I just couldn't let go of that image. How he walked through somebody's pecan orchard to a cattle pond to discover the index finger sticking out of the water big as you please. How he considered the whole thing a sign that he should run for mayor. But every time I've asked him about an expedition to retrace his steps and locate it again, he just shrugs his shoulders and gets quiet on me."

Laurie was the first to break the thoughtful silence that followed. "Maybe he doesn't want to find it, Renza. Maybe he thinks it's found its proper resting place. To remove it now would be like exhuming it. Have you thought of that?"

Renza sighed. "The thought has occurred to me in some form, yes. But I also had another thought coming. Wouldn't it be too fantastic if we were able to go out and find that hand again, clean it up, and bring it back as the ultimate center-piece of Mr. Choppy's wedding?"

"You mean like the ice carving of the hand and the index finger that Vester Morrow did for Myrtis's election night to-do?" Laurie said.

"Well, not exactly. I don't think we would actually want something that heavy on the table."

"Damned right, you wouldn't!" Myrtis interrupted, flashing on her rival. "That table's been in my family for three generations. It was hidden in the hayloft from the Yankees during the Civil War and has survived everything from lovemaking to childbirth on top of it. I'm not about to allow it to be done in now!"

"Oh, calm down! I was thinking maybe we could feature it in the center of your boxwood maze outside, Myrtis. Why, we could lead Mr. Choppy right to it. Imagine his surprise! It would be the ultimate party favor!"

"Are you planning to blindfold him and spin him around a few times? This isn't pin-the-tail-on-the-donkey, Renza. Besides, I don't think it would be the right kind of surprise. I don't think you should pursue this. Somethin' about it just feels wrong to me. I mean, First Presbyterian replaced the original hand a long time ago, so perhaps you should just let missing hands and their pointing index fingers lie."

"If that was supposed to be funny, I fail to see the humor."

Myrtis drew herself up, clearly taking offense. "It wasn't meant to be funny. It was meant to make us all stop and think. Besides, there are practical considerations. How are you going to go about this? Mr. Choppy told us he didn't think he could find that pond again in a million years, so how do you plan to locate it? A divining rod?"

"I was thinking about putting an ad in *The Citizen*."

Myrtis's laugh had an unmistakable element of derision in it. "An ad? You mean like, 'Pond Wanted. Must Have Broken Gold-Plated Hand with Index Finger Pointing to Heaven Resting on Bottom'?"

As she had done so often in the past, Laurie stepped in to keep the exchange from escalating further between the two rivals. "Now, ladies. Let's remember we're here to make sure the wedding goes off without a hitch." Then she turned to Gaylie Girl. "Has Mr. Choppy said anything to you about the location of the hand or expressed any interest in it at all?"

"Not a word. He hasn't brought it up once since I came down. I've had him so focused on my children and the wedding, he hasn't had time to think about much of anything else, I'm afraid."

But Renza had clearly gotten her back up and plowed ahead. "There can't be that many pecan orchards in the county, can there? I thought the ad could be worded so the owner of any land remotely fitting that description might step forward."

"What about the legal issues involved?" Myrtis put in. "Think about it. If you actually found the thing, who would it belong to? The owner whose pond it splashed into like Dorothy's house tumbling down from Kansas, or the First Presbyterian Church it was blown off of many decades ago?"

Renza's eyes narrowed as she homed in on her rival. "Believe it or not, I've already thought of that. I paid a visit to the Reverend Hiram Greenlea at First Presbyterian about a week or so ago, and I broached the subject with him. First of all, he said he doubted the church would really be interested in the broken hand at this late date, since what would they do with it now? He said they'd forgotten all about it long ago. Plus, three-quarters of the congregation from way back then is either dead or can't remember who they are. So he leaned toward negotiating with the pond owner—that is, if I could actually manage to track it down."

Myrtis bristled. "You mean pay somebody for the right to raise a big ole tarnished ornament out of the muck? At whose expense? I realize you're the president of the Nitwitts right now, Renza, but you just don't have Laurie's knack for ideas. That is, unless you want to go on an expedition in chest-waders all by yourself like some latter-day Hernando De Soto. I can just see you now, traipsing all over the county, going from door to door. I think you'd have better luck as a Jehovah's Witness. For the record, however, I would certainly not be in favor of using any of our club's slush fund money for this."

"Could we at least take a vote?" Renza said, surveying the table with an almost pleading expression and tone of voice.

There was a general shaking of heads, causing Renza to throw her hands up in the air with an exasperated sigh. "Well, it seems when I try to come up with something different or off-the-wall like Laurie did when she was president, everyone digs in their heels. I really don't think my idea is that off-base."

"You really shouldn't feel like you're in competition with me," Laurie replied. "All those ideas of mine were just moments in time that struck everyone the right way. Given different circumstances, I could easily have struck out. Maybe we should move on to the wedding details again. What about Larry Lorrison and His Big Bad Swing Band? Are they definitely still onboard? Myrtis, you said you were going to put down the deposit since that was your brainstorm."

Myrtis nodded crisply. "Done. They're definitely booked, as I promised. We'll be setting up the stage and a little dance floor beneath the tent on the other side of the maze."

"I'm just overwhelmed, ladies!" Gaylie Girl exclaimed. "All of these wonderful touches you're adding for me and Hale. Now, please—don't you dare go out of your way with elaborate wedding presents for us."

"I had been thinking of the gold-plated hand as a souvenir of sorts," Renza said, determined to get one last airing for her suggestion. "But it seems I've been advised that my intentions were misplaced. So horse apples to that!" She paused briefly, and the looks around the table indicated no one knew what was coming next. "There's another proposal I'd like for us to consider, however."

The others winced, but Renza immediately chastised them. "You all needn't have those 'time for a tetanus shot' expressions on your faces. You'll be happy to know that this is Myrtis's idea. So I'll quietly defer to her."

Myrtis finished up with a bite of her corn bread and daintily cleared her throat. "Thank you, Renza. As you all know, Euterpe is still livin' with me out at Evening Shadows. I thought she'd have found a place of her own by now, but she doesn't even seem to be looking. It's almost as if she's found her niche as a permanent resident. Money seems to be no object for her. The other guests who come and go just love her. Every night before dinner, she sits at the piano and plays requests for them. I've just been astounded by her repertoire—everything from Rodgers and Hammerstein to 'Moonlight Sonata.' She knows them all.

"As you are also aware, each of us has made incredible progress with our piano lessons in just a short time. We'll soon be beyond the 'Heart and Soul' and 'follow the metronome' stage and on to greater musical glory. Euterpe has the touch, or rather—the magic fingers, I should say. I think she's a very unique addition to Second Creek, and I'd like for us to invite her to join the Nitwitts in recognition of the new dimension she brings to our little universe here."

Where Renza's dissertation on going to questionable lengths to track down the broken hand had elicited everything from scorn to disinterest, Myrtis's nomination keenly stirred the gathering. There was a virtual explosion of positive feedback.

"I don't know why we haven't thought of it before now," Denver Lee offered first. "Euterpe is certainly patient with me and all the bangin' I do every time I sit down at her bench. And there's something about her that seems to soothe me when I walk in all depressed after goin' a rough round or two with my blood sugar. I just despise it when I get bad readings. I'll tell her what I've been dealin' with, and she'll listen to all my ramblings with a smile on her face—and every bit as attentively as a psychiatrist, I might add. In the short time I've taken lessons, I've come to think of my sessions with her as—well, therapy almost."

"I know exactly what you mean," Novie chimed in. "She was so thoughtful giving Marc and Michael that huge houseplant order for her studio to help How's Plants? get off to such a fast start. She still drops in on their shop whenever she gets a little free time in between lessons or on her lunch hour. Catching a glimpse of Michael's freckles and red hair just makes her day, she says. I find the interest she takes in my family so reassuring. As you know, I tried to sweep Marc under the rug for so long, and now I'm just so proud that he can be who he is right here in Second Creek. I just wish Geoffrey could have lived to see it."

Then Laurie, Gaylie Girl, and finally Renza took turns with their own enthusiastic testimonials. No one sounded a discordant note.

"I'm guessing we do want to vote on this one," Renza said as evenly as possible. "Everyone's here except Wittsie, and I'll take it upon myself to phone her up and let her know the results. I'm quite sure after what took place at Delta Sunset Village yesterday, she'd approve wholeheartedly. And I don't mean this unkindly, but that's assuming she remembers."

To no one's surprise, the group unanimously voted to invite Euterpe to join; Novie recorded the proceedings in her notebook, and Myrtis volunteered to inform Euterpe over dinner that evening.

"Do you think she'll accept?" Renza asked, still the tiniest bit miffed about Myrtis's nomination coup.

"I don't see why not," Myrtis replied. "Imagine being the only person in town who is Mistress of the Scales and a Nitwitt to boot."

MR. CHOPPY COULD TELL Cherish had something on her mind. She'd been a bit distracted all morning—forgetting who was holding on the other end of the line at one point and making some uncharacteristic mistakes in the letters she had typed up for him. She had even made the same typo on one of the letters the second time around. Finally, he found a moment to invite her into his office and sound her out.

"I know you too well by now," he told her as she took her seat across from him. "You just haven't been here with me in spirit most of the day. Would you like to talk about what's goin' on?"

"Oh, Mr. Dunbar!" she began, blushing a bright pink. "I'm so sorry about that. I'm pretty bad at concealin' things. I should just always come right out and say what I have to say."

"You're just so efficient ordinarily. Are you still worried about Henry's job out at Pond-Raised Catfish?"

Cherish fidgeted with the sleeve of her bright orange sundress, looking as if she were picking off tiny pieces of lint. "Oh, well . . . that, too, I guess. Have you gotten any more inside information out there?"

"I should have brought you up to speed about the weekend when you first walked in," Mr. Choppy began, giving her his most paternal smile. "But you'll be pleased to hear that Miz Lyons's son, Petey, is seriously lookin' over the proposal that Curtis Ray Keyes gave him on behalf of the owner. No agreement yet to buy the plant, of course, but he seems definitely interested."

"That's . . . good to hear. I'll pass that along to Henry. But—there was somethin' else I needed to tell you. I've been goin' around and around about it in my head all morning."

Mr. Choppy studied her face closely before speaking. "I'm always so surprised when you don't smile, Cherish. I can always count on two things every day, no matter what problems I have to handle as mayor of Second Creek—the sun'll come up and you'll come to work smilin'.'"

She managed to conjure up a smile for him, but he could

clearly sense the effort involved. "I feel guilty about what I'm gonna tell you, though, Mr. Dunbar."

"Guilty? That's the last word I ever expected to hear from you."

"I understand how strange that must sound, but it has to do with somethin' my obstetrician just suggested to me. Because of my history of miscarriages, he wants me to look into takin' maternity leave in the third trimester. He wants me to pamper myself a little and not take any more chances than absolutely necessary. So . . ." Cherish tailed off, unable to look Mr. Choppy in the eye. "Does Second Creek even have a maternity leave policy? I realize I haven't worked here that long."

"I can't answer that right now. This is the first time such a request has come up. But I promise I'll look into it for you, Cherish. And if there isn't one already in place, maybe I can negotiate with the councilmen," he responded quickly. "At any rate, why should you feel guilty about requestin' it? There's no harm in askin', I assure you."

She finally resumed eye contact but still looked decidedly uncomfortable. "I really like workin' for you, Mr. Dunbar. You're a wonderful boss—truly almost like a father to me—and I don't want to let you down. It would seem like I'm runnin' out on you. And with the baby bein' unplanned and all, I would just feel . . . well, guilty about not workin' as long as I can."

Mr. Choppy was polite but firm. "Nonsense. You shouldn't feel that way at all. Particularly with doctor's orders on your side. You think I'm gonna go against that? But let me get the time frame straight, if you don't mind. Would you be wantin' to leave, say, around Thanksgiving?"

"Right around then, yes. Maybe a little after, if necessary."

He didn't hesitate, giving her a reassuring wink. "I'm sure we can work somethin' out. Matter of fact, I just this second got a brainstorm like Miz Laurie Hampton always does about who I can get to replace you. How does my very own Gaylie Girl strike you?"

Cherish drew back, her bright eyes widening in surprise. "Oh my, Mr. Dunbar! It'll be interesting to see what Miz Lyons says when you run that past her. There are aspects of this job she might not like. Some of the people I have to deal with over the phone are just downright rude."

"No one in my administration, I trust. You need to tell me if anyone ever crosses the line with you."

"Oh, no. Everyone in the building treats me like a queen. I'm always tellin' Henry about my routine around here, and he thinks they even treat me like a prom queen. Ha! I do get that special feelin' from some of the men, if you know what I mean. It's just that some of the people that want to bend your ear all the time over the phone need a refresher course in manners. For instance, whenever Lady Roth calls up for you, demandin' to know why you can't stop what you're doin' and come out to Cypress Knees and meet with her at that very minute, I know I'm in for some serious di-plomacy. Call-screening in general is not as easy as it looks and sounds."

Mr. Choppy had a big smirk on his face. "No doubt. But you do it beautifully. I can't help but overhear how you handle people like Lady Roth all the time. And I trust my Gaylie Girl can be just as diplomatic when push comes to shove. I have a hunch she'll want to lend a helpin' hand when the time comes. She's all about wantin' to fit in down here."

He thought for a moment, propping up his right elbow on the desk and cupping his chin in his hand. "Inciden-tally, I've been meanin' to invite you and Henry to our wed-ding out at Evening Shadows on Labor Day. We're keepin' the numbers small, and we're not mailin' out invitations. We don't even care if Erlene Gossaler and her sarcastic social column stay away. In fact, we're hopin' they will. Just word of mouth is what we're gonna use. I hope you don't have any plans weekend after next."

Cherish regained her usual cheerful demeanor and be-gan gushing. "Oh, I don't think we do! That's so kind of you, Mr. Dunbar. And Henry will have the day off from the plant—that is, if he still has his job. I know we'd both love to come!"

"Great! And I have a feelin' things will work out at the catfish plant. No guarantees, you understand. But from my reading of what went on this weekend, it's possible you'll have new management and new ideas out there soon. Maybe it'll mean job security for Henry, too."

LATER THAT EVENING, Mr. Choppy and Gaylie Girl were sitting out on one of the side screen porches at 34 Pond Street, enjoying the whirring of the ceiling fan above them. It had seen better days but still managed to keep the air circulating and the August humidity at bay. They weren't doing much more than watching traffic go by while they finished up a bottle of Delta muscadine wine. But as usual they made time to maintain their vigil for fireflies as the shank of the evening arrived. For the umpteenth time, however, there was nothing to see—either at eye level or higher up in the tree branches—and it triggered some unfinished business for Gaylie Girl.

"We never actually got around to discussing this, Hale, but do you think Wittsie was on the up-and-up about the fireflies setting up shop over in Greenwood? I was so taken aback by what she said that I just let it go yesterday. I felt it was so much more important at the time to be supportive of her, no matter what. But we never said a word about it on the ride home."

Mr. Choppy ran a finger around the rim of his wineglass several times while he carefully formulated his response. "The reason I didn't mention it any further was because of my upbringin' in Second Creek. We're so used to bizarre and mysterious things goin' on around here. Wittsie's little revelation only seemed to be business as usual to me. It really never crossed my mind that it might be her Alzheimer's talkin'. The truth of the matter is, if you pressed me to the wall, I'd have to say I honestly don't think it was. By the same token—and me not bein' a doctor—I can't prove anything one way or the other."

He paused for a self-satisfied chuckle. "Maybe this'll make more sense to you. Daddy once told me never to question Second Creek when it spoke to you, however crazy it sounded. The way he put it was, 'This town has a true heart and soul to it. Now and then it stumbles, but it's never down for the count long. So when you're puzzled about somethin', trust the signs that are sure to come your way.' And I never forgot that. I've more or less lived my life by those words, and the last time Second Creek took the trouble to speak to me, I listened closely, decided to run for mayor, and won."

Gaylie Girl took another sip of her wine and considered for quite a while. "I was comparing that to my life in Lake Forest. How I lived on the ritzy surface all the time. I had a glittering, sophisticated run up there all those years, and it truly was about keeping up appearances for Peter. I tried to convince myself it was what I really wanted. But I think I'm ready for a little substance, and Second Creek seems like a place I could really sink my teeth into now."

"Well, that was just about the perfect segue," Mr. Choppy said. Then he told her all about Cherish's request for maternity leave and his first choice for her temporary replacement. She couldn't have looked more surprised.

"You really think I could do it when the time comes, Hale? I've never had any real responsibility like that. I don't count all the many charitable endeavors I've contributed to every year or the library board meetings or my museum docent duties. All of those things could and did go on perfectly well without me. But I'm thrilled you really want me to be your girl Friday. An honest-to-goodness working First Lady! None of that Queen Elizabeth, hand-waving figurehead stuff for me!"

"I'm happy you like the idea so much. I wasn't completely sure you would. Cherish pointed out there would be people like Lady Roth to deal with over the phone, for starters."

Gaylie Girl waved him off quickly with a smirk. "Oh, I think I can handle Lady Roth. After that vaudeville routine of hers I witnessed out at Cypress Knees over the weekend, I can vouch for the fact that she's basically harmless. She's just looking for a little attention."

"And she knows how to get it, too."

What happened next made Mr. Choppy wish that Cherish's third trimester would begin tomorrow. Gaylie Girl finished off her wine, got to her feet, stretched out her arms toward the street in a very theatrical gesture, and shouted: "Second Creek, Mississippi, I love you! And I can't wait to become your First Lady!"

"It all seems to be fallin' into place for us, doesn't it? Your children onboard after one helluva sociable weekend on our part, our wedding just around the corner, and, down the road a bit, a chance for you to help me run the mayoral office smoothly every day. Are we livin' right, or what?" He rose and put his arm around Gaylie Girl's waist, managing a peck on the cheek as an exclamation point.

"I'd have to agree with you there," she added, gazing at him affectionately. Then she gave a little gasp. "Oh, I meant to tell you. Renza went off on a tangent today about trying to get everyone interested in locating the infamous gold-plated hand. The rest of us pretty much scotched the idea. I told them that you never brought up the subject."

"I do think about it now and then, though," Mr. Choppy said. "One of those Second Creek signs that Daddy told me to be on the lookout for. But I think it needs to stay right where it fell to earth—stuck in the mud but still pointing the way to heaven."

Gaylie Girl's smile was assured and serene. "I think I finally understand what a Second Creek solution is all about."

MYRTIS AND EUTERPE were seated across from each other in the drawing room of Evening Shadows, swirling their snifters of brandy following a sumptuous dinner of peppered pork tenderloin, consommé-flavored brown rice, and sweet potato soufflé. The other guests in the house, a giggly young honeymoon couple from Helena, Arkansas, with the typical Deep South monikers of Newmie and Har-rilyn Trendon, had just retired to the four-poster delights awaiting them upstairs. This, after politely taking a pass on further piano selections from the Mistress of the Scales. Euterpe had thought it just as well, since she hadn't been able to conjure up their requests for Willie Nelson's signature hits before dinner. For once, it seemed, she had been found musically wanting.

Myrtis had a dreamy, distant look about her as she let the brandy work its magic. "Raymond and I were just like those young people when we were first married. Well, maybe we didn't giggle that much. That silly business of theirs was beginning to get on my nerves by the time Sarah brought out the poached pears. I'd say Raymond and I were more touchy-feely and not quite so verbal. What about you and David?"

Euterpe briefly gazed down to check on Pan, who was curled up at her feet, and said: "Let's just say we spent an awful lot of time silently in the dark."

"Are you referring to his miserly ways with the electricity you've told us all about, or did you intend a more romantic interpretation of the phrase this time?"

Euterpe dismissed the question with a roll of her eyes and a brief hissing gesture. "Both, actually. David preferred to make love to me quietly in the dark. I, on the other hand, was always of the opinion that romance should occasionally see the light of day and offer up a few huzzahs for variety's sake. But let's don't talk about our husbands, shall we? Not when I have my new Nitwitt title to celebrate."

"Oh, I'm so pleased you accepted our invitation. You've got our numbers back up with Wittsie mostly unable to participate anymore. Of course, that's not why we invited you. We're all just fascinated with your talent and style. How do you account for the rapid progress we've all made at the piano? I read somewhere that the older you get, the harder it is to learn things like languages—and I suppose music. We've all been joking that you have the magic touch. Or at least a magic metronome. Do you? Is your secret that you really hypnotize us?"

"You flatter me. But I do think I have a gift for teaching. I seem to be able to connect with people in the areas of their greatest concerns. That just seems to move the learning process along light-years. Once you clear your head and rinse out the ole sponge, you'd be surprised how easy it is to soak up something new."

Myrtis looked impressed and downed more of her brandy. "A very Second Creek–ish answer. I hope you stay here with us a long, long time—a practicing Nitwitt forever."

"Oh, I believe I can contribute substantially to the club as time goes by. As for the here and now, I want very much to do something special for Gaylie Girl's wedding. Perhaps play the 'Wedding March' or some other traditional selection."

"I was counting on it. I think having Gaylie Girl jitterbug down the drawing room aisle to Larry Lorrison's Swing music would be a bit over the top. The band will be there strictly for the dancing out in the tent—hubba hubba!"

The two women finished off the rest of their brandy,

alternating more wedding talk with periods of contented silence, and then Myrtis checked her watch. "Oh, I must go and call up all the ladies before it gets too late. Some of them can snap like terrapins if you disturb them after they've packed in their faces and hair for the evening. But I know they'll all be so pleased to hear you've officially accepted our invitation and boosted our Nitwitt power by leaps and bounds."

Euterpe smiled graciously as she reached down and gathered up her Pan, shifting him to his favorite spot on her shoulder. Then she made her manners and headed upstairs to claim her own portion of rest, complete with sweet, healing dreams.

11

THEY COULD HAVE
DANCED ALL NIGHT

No one was anticipating Laurie's return from Paris more eagerly than Gaylie Girl. Throughout the course of the week that Laurie and Powell were spending with the Great Buddha Magruder enjoying the City of Lights, the intimate little wedding that Myrtis had been planning out at Evening Shadows had quickly morphed into a typical Nitwitt competition to see who could fatten the guest list the most. Gaylie Girl had been reluctant to apply the brakes because she felt she was still too new to the group to say no to anyone. The runaway train that the wedding was threatening to become needed the engineering touch of the only member who had ever really managed to rein in Second

Creek's most diverse group of busybodies—Laurie Lepanto Hampton.

Renza was the first to phone Gaylie Girl to ask if she could add some of Meta's friends to the roster. "I don't want to be pushy about this," Renza had begun, completely ignoring the fact that she was being exactly that. "But, as I don't have to tell you, my daughter has gone gaga over your son, and she would just adore having some of her artsy-craftsy friends down in Saint Augustine come up to meet him during the wedding. I hope it won't be an imposition if two other couples enjoy the Labor Day weekend. I have plenty of room here to put them all up. Getting Meta to come visit me at all over the years has been like pulling eye-teeth, so naturally I'm thrilled she wants to bring some of her friends with her, too."

At first, Gaylie Girl saw no threat in the request, approving it good-naturedly without hesitation. But then Novie called her up, not too long after, about Marc and Michael. Somehow, they had been omitted from the original list, probably an oversight due to the fact that they hadn't been in town all that long and were hardly the first to come to mind.

"I know you aren't issuing formal invitations," Novie had said. "But Marc and Michael keep askin' me over and over if they're invited. I don't want to make it sound like they're being overly sensitive prima donnas about this, but I was sure you didn't want to overlook them." And, of course, Gaylie Girl had accommodated Novie immediately.

But it had not stopped there. Denver Lee had lobbied for her daughter Nita, her son-in-law Carter Hewes, and her grandson, Christopher, who just happened to be coming to Second Creek for a visit. "They all had so much fun down at headquarters helpin' Mr. Choppy get elected that they naturally wanted to see him get married, too. I always say the more the merrier."

But Gaylie Girl wasn't so sure that would be the case. Every time she told Mr. Choppy about the newest additions to the guest list, she felt tense and compromised. She had also become quite adept at reading distraction in his face, and eventually he got around to expressing his concerns.

"It's not that I think all these additional people shouldn't be invited," he was saying one evening over a supper of leftover cold chicken and cheese grits that Gaylie Girl had thrown together. "And I certainly don't believe in hurtin' other people's feelings. No sir. Not with the way I was brought up, and certainly not now that I'm smack dab in the middle of politics. But I was just thinkin' today at the office: whatever happened to the private civil ceremony we talked about in the beginning? I know we moved away from that almost immediately as you got more and more involved with the Nitwitt ladies. And I know I went and invited the councilmen and the department heads at my end. But too many more, and Evening Shadows will be choked with people."

Gaylie Girl took a bite of cheese grits before answering him. As a Yankee, she was justifiably proud of her rapid mastery of this Southern staple he'd taught her to prepare. "I know what you're saying, Hale. The words *overkill* and *Nitwitt* do seem to go hand in hand, as I've discovered in my short tenure in the club. Another way of looking at it, though, is that they're all just trying to show their support for us. I don't think we should fault them for that. But don't forget—you just recently invited Cherish and Henry Hempstead. Not that I don't think you should have."

And he had deferred to her as all good soon-to-be husbands should. "Good point. I guess we'll both have to continue to walk that fine line."

But the stream of guest list additions had continued to flow. It was as if a Hoover Dam of propriety had burst somewhere. Proceeding full-throttle now, Renza informed Gaylie Girl that Meta had a few more of her friends she wanted to bring along. "It would be so much more fun for all the young people," seemed to be the rationalization. This, in turn, was creating some unexpected friction between Gaylie Girl and Myrtis, who had to take the amount of food being prepared into consideration as the wedding weekend inched ever closer.

"Couldn't you just call her back and tell her no, Gaylie Girl?" Myrtis suggested during the latest phone update. "Can't you reason with her?" There was an awkward pause. "Now, what the hell am I saying? I should know better than that. Renza will eventually invite everyone she hasn't antagonized over the years. Fortunately for us, that does narrow down the possibilities a bit."

Both women managed a chuckle, easing the tension between them somewhat. "It's just that Sarah and I have got to get started on the ordering for all that curried chicken we're goin' to turn out. Not to mention the boiled shrimp and all the hors d'oeuvres. We need to settle on a quantity per person and stick to it. I have a sneaking suspicion that Renza's doing this on purpose just to annoy me. I think she's still ticked off that I was the one who thought of nominating Euterpe for Nitwitt membership."

"Let's not get paranoid. It's been my observation that Renza applies that self-absorbed attitude of hers on an equal-opportunity basis."

Myrtis went silent for a while, but Gaylie Girl could still hear the dramatic breathing at the other end. "Please remember that I'm on your side here, Gaylie Girl. You've got to be careful not to let this get out of hand. I've tried to pay strict attention to your guidelines about keeping everything small and manageable, but it's going in the opposite direction fast."

Gaylie Girl sighed emphatically. "I just wish Laurie were here. She'd give me an injection of backbone vaccine. Novie also called to say she might have a few more last-minute additions, and all I did was hem and haw and tell her things like not to wait too long to let me know. This is all bringing home in a very dramatic way how different the social norms of Second Creek really are. People think they can get away with just about everything down here."

"And they do. You've simply got to learn to put your foot down and step on a few toes when necessary."

AFTER WHAT SEEMED more like a month than a week, Laurie and Powell were safely back from their Paris sojourn, and Gaylie Girl was the first to call up and welcome them home the very next day, ulterior motives and all.

"Are you still jet-lagged?" Gaylie Girl was saying after the usual warm greetings had been exchanged.

"Me, not so much. But Powell definitely is. He's conked out on the bed right now, and there's a lot of unpacking left to do. We were just too tired to do much when we got in late last night."

Despite the fact that Gaylie Girl had carefully rehearsed what she was going to say to Laurie about the latest wedding developments, the words decided to fly out of her head at the last moment. Instead, she fell back on spontaneity.

"Do you feel up to a cup of coffee and a little bite to eat at the Town Square Café? I could meet you over there in about half an hour. Why don't you take a break?"

Laurie's dramatic sigh told the tale. "I really should, you know. No reason to exhaust myself hanging things up and moving them around until I feel up to it. But there's something I need to tell you. It's on the order of a surprise."

No sooner had that last word escaped Laurie's lips than a booming, basso profundo voice began singing in the background, clearly audible to Gaylie Girl through the receiver.

"Oh . . . sounds like Powell's up," Gaylie Girl observed. "I didn't know he could sing that well."

"He can't. His talent is in his feet."

The vigorous singing continued, and Gaylie Girl recognized the tune after a few more bars. "Isn't that 'Crazy World' from *Victor/Victoria*? I just loved Julie Andrews in that film!"

"You have a good ear there, Gaylie Girl."

"I once sold sheet music and hit records up in Evanston, remember? Anyway, what gives, and who is that singing his head off? I assume you didn't bring Pavarotti back with you."

Laurie laughed brightly. "No, but we did coax the Great Buddha Magruder into returning with us for the wedding. He simply couldn't resist the opportunity to sweep all you Nitwitts off your feet when I gave him a thumbnail of our club. I also told him about how you and Mr. Choppy had managed to get back together after more than half a century. It seems he's a sucker for a good romance novel come to life."

"How delightful!" Gaylie Girl exclaimed. "I'm sure all the ladies will be thrilled to meet him." But a quizzical look soon appeared on her face. "It's just that I truly thought the Great Buddha Magruder's specialty was dancing—not singing."

"Oh, it still is. I can assure you I got quite a workout at some of the nightclubs we attended. And Powell already knew about Buddha's incredibly deep speaking voice, but neither of us knew that he was quite an accomplished singer. The only thing is . . ." Laurie's pause was lengthy and puzzling. But seconds later, the singing stopped, and the conversation resumed with Laurie having lowered her voice. "Good, he went back into the guest room for a while. It's just that he seems to go around singing 'Crazy World' and nothing else all the time. We could hear him singing it in the shower last night before we all crashed from the long trip. Now it's caught in one of those maddening loops in my head."

Gaylie Girl managed an empathetic chuckle but then remembered the purpose of her call. Yet another person had been added to the guest list, although she could not see how the presence of the Great Buddha Magruder could do anything other than enhance the celebration ahead. Whatever the case, she decided to postpone discussion of the expanding guest list until she and Laurie were settled comfortably beneath the big pastel umbrella of one of the Town Square Café's alfresco tables.

"THAT'S NOT A VERY big lunch, Laurie," Gaylie Girl remarked after the clean-cut young waiter at the Town Square Café had walked away with their orders. "Only rabbits can survive on side salads."

Laurie rolled her eyes and gestured toward her waistline. "Yes, well, my self-imposed rabbit diet is justified. I overindulged supremely all week in Paris. Buddha may dance and sing 'Crazy World' to distraction, but he doesn't like to cook. So we constantly ate out, and no matter what I ordered, everything seemed to have a sauce poured over it and was just packed with calories. Not that it wasn't worth it, of course. Buddha took us to his favorite spots— La Coupole, Beauvilliers, and Ladurée, where we stuffed ourselves with the macaroons. And that's just the tip of the iceberg, since the other bistros and restaurants have blended together and blurred nicely in my head. But they all put a few unnecessary pounds on me."

An expression of slight disgust flashed into her face as she continued. "Sometimes I just hate Powell and that male metabolism of his. That's what happens when you're tall as a redwood. He ate everything in sight, and it was all rich and sinful. He had way more of those macaroons at Ladurée than I did, and I'm positive he didn't gain an ounce. He never does."

"Men, huh? My Peter was the same way, but that figure of yours looks as darling as ever to me," Gaylie Girl insisted.

"Thanks, but you aren't the one breathing inside this dress. I've just got to make amends for being a bad girl, I'm afraid."

The iced coffees they had ordered arrived, and they both took a moment to refresh themselves with generous sips amid the August heat. "I did have a question for you, though,"

Gaylie Girl eventually resumed. "Why didn't you bring your houseguest with you? I can't wait to meet him."

"I did suggest it to him," Laurie said. "But he decided that Powell had the right idea about the jet lag and opted for a nap in the guest room instead. At some point I'm sure they'll both be up and about and hungry as wolves, and I'll have to defrost something from the freezer. I don't feel like cooking from scratch yet. But I did have one of my brainstorms as soon as Buddha closed his door. What would you think about a little cocktail to-do at my place tomorrow to introduce him to all the other Nitwitts? And if by chance it resulted in an exhibition of world-class dancing, I'm sure no one would object." She hesitated, looking momentarily conflicted. "Although Buddha might object eventually. The girls wore Powell to a frazzle at the Piggly Wiggly last summer."

Gaylie Girl leaned back in her chair and eyed Laurie skeptically. "Never mind how Buddha would come off. Are you sure you have the energy for something like that so soon after your trip?"

"I'm just talking about opening a couple of bottles of wine and letting Powell bartend the rest."

"In that case, why not?"

It was only after their lunches had arrived and Laurie had exhausted her enthusiastic accounts of all the palaces, museums, churches, boulevards, and bridges across the Seine she had toured that Gaylie Girl decided to broach the subject of the out-of-control wedding list.

"I've been reminding myself lately of that character in *Oklahoma*," she was explaining at one point. "What was her name? The one with the bad reputation, I mean."

"I believe you're referring to Ado Annie, if I remember my Rodgers and Hammerstein correctly."

"Right you are. I just can't say no to any of them, Laurie. I can't imagine you having any trouble doing so, though." At which point Gaylie Girl seemed to shut down completely, looking too embarrassed to continue.

"I'm reading between the lines here and guessing that you want me to say something to all of them?"

"They'll listen to you, Laurie. They always have. There's not a one of them that hasn't told me at one time or another that the Nitwitts wouldn't have lasted too much longer had you not taken over as president when Wittsie stepped down."

Laurie's smile had an air of resignation about it. "I suppose I should own up to that, since it happens to be the truth. At any rate, I'll be happy to read the riot act to the girls—very politely, of course. Why not tomorrow evening at my Great Buddha Magruder to-do?"

They both laughed at the sound of that, but Gaylie Girl soon adopted a more somber demeanor. "Do you think Hale and I are wrong in wanting to keep this under control? We never intended it to become the social event of the season. I've had way more than enough of that sort of thing up in Lake Forest."

"It's your wedding. For Mr. Choppy especially, it's been a long time coming, I might add. The most important thing now is what the two of you want."

TO SAY THAT THE Great Buddha Magruder was a big-boned specimen was truly an understatement. He sported a sturdiness and width about his shoulders typical of an offensive lineman playing the professional game. At the same time, the bulge around his middle suggested he had long ago forsaken any training regimen in the gym for the conspicuous consumption his adopted hometown of Paris offered in the way of food and drink. For all his size, however, he had a certain proud carriage that effortlessly induced people to concentrate on other aspects of his personality.

He never slumped—holding his head and neck as if he were posing for a great, dignified portrait. Despite the fleshiness of his face, it nonetheless remained an arresting one with dramatic dark eyebrows slanting away from his rather prominent nose and complementing a full head of salt-and-pepper hair. Finally, a well-trimmed dark mustache and goatee punctuated a devilish smile that the man was seldom without as he went about the everyday business of teaching and charming women on the ballroom dance floor.

From the moment he made his entrance in Laurie's parlor the following evening for the casual cocktail party she

had decided to host for him, the Great Buddha Magruder—
gold guayabera shirt, matching pants and all—had the Nitwitts swooning and fantasizing. This, despite the fact that
a detractor might have likened him to a gigantic Christmas
tree ornament.

"Such a profound pleasure to meet all of you fabulous
ladies at last," were the first words out of Buddha's mouth
following Laurie's brief introduction. "My interest in you
has been stimulated by your gregarious Laurie, and the
picture she painted of your charmed lives here in your
mysterious Second Creek was just too much for me to resist. So voilà! I've flown all the way across the ocean to
help you celebrate the marriage of one of your very own
Nitwitts. I trust we shall all dance the night away on that
very special evening. And in case you didn't know, my
specialty is the tango."

"Now, that's a well-spoken, healthy-looking man," Renza
whispered to Myrtis while Buddha was making the rounds
with his customary panache. "He could make two of Lewis
Ralston Belford. I can't wait to have him show me a step or
two. Then we'll see what develops after that."

Myrtis drew back, giving her rival an incredulous look.
"Down, girl. You do know he's gay, don't you?"

"Says who?"

"Says Laurie, for one. And I thought somebody had
mentioned it at one of our meetings as well. Anyway, I
called her up today to ask about the trip, and she told me
that she and Powell had spent several evenings in some

quarter of Paris called the Marais, I believe it was. They visited with several of Buddha's close gay friends, including one or two of his former lovers. Laurie said she can't remember when she's laughed so hard and been so thoroughly entertained by such witty banter."

"I don't recall anyone mentioning at one of our meetings on which side the Great Buddha Magruder likes to butter his toast." Renza continued to look Buddha up and down as he moved through the crowd with cocktail in hand. "In any case, I would never have guessed he was gay. He has that marvelously deep voice and such a masculine air about him."

"That's a lot of gold for a regular fellow to be wearing. Anyhow, you'd better not let Novie hear you slingin' around such stereotypes," Myrtis said, aggressively rattling the ice cubes in her Bloody Mary at her rival. "She's gone from being totally embarrassed by Marc to touting him for out-of-the-closet poster boy."

Renza shrugged off the remark while eyeing Buddha shrewdly across the room. "I'm truly not interested in what Novie thinks or does. I'm only interested in a tango or two with that mountain of a man—no matter who he likes to sleep with. Do you think we can talk him into it?"

"Who is 'we'?"

"Oh, horse apples, Myrtis! I meant myself—and Laurie, if necessary. You can fade into the wallpaper for all I care!"

Renza was, in fact, the first to wheedle a tango demonstration out of the man, wresting him away from Gaylie Girl, who was settling for mere conversation at the time. Unbeknownst to Buddha, however, Renza had actually paid attention to the lessons Powell had given to the club a couple of years earlier, enabling her to feign the part of novice and apt pupil to the hilt.

"You certainly do catch on fast, Mrs. Belford," he was saying as the two of them paused and dipped at a strategic point in the *Tango Nuevo* CD Buddha had brought along at Laurie's urging. They were working their way through "Cherry Pink and Apple Blossom White" in the space Laurie had managed to clear out in the middle of the parlor.

"Please. You must call me Renza. I noticed you were on a first-name basis with our Laurie and Gaylie Girl, so why not with me as well?"

"Renza it is, then. Such an unusual name. But then, so is mine."

Renza maintained her intense eye contact and her flirtatious grin. "I was named after my grandmother, who emigrated from Poland aeons ago. I know that may sound a bit unusual for Mississippi, but there's also a little town in our state called Kosciusko, and it was named for a famous Polish soldier of Revolutionary War fame. So there's my bit of Southern trivia for the day—and my rarely discussed Polish connection as well."

Buddha continued to lead with his polished maneuvers even as he fed her a large chunk of his own backstory. "And I was named Buddha because both my father and mother decided to up and leave the Roman Catholic Church to become Buddhists as a show of defiance to their parents. As if the dramatic change of faith weren't enough. But I'm not complaining, you understand. Somewhere along the way, I realized my personality was just as flamboyant as my parents' religious rebellion. They named me more wisely than they knew, and ever since I've enthusiastically embraced my moniker. Even lifted it to greater heights as the Great Buddha Magruder."

"Utterly fascinating!" Renza exclaimed just as the music came to an end. "Oh, could we do this at least one more time?"

But a kibitzing Laurie stepped in with a firm directive. "Why don't we give our Buddha a breather for a few minutes? I can assure you he's not going anywhere. Meanwhile, Renza, I'd like for you to join me along with the rest of the girls in the kitchen."

Renza blinked at first but took note of Laurie's authoritative tone and quickly conjured up a wink to accompany her suggestive exit line. "Be back soon, Buddha—you big dipper, you!"

ALL THE NITWITTS except for Gaylie Girl had gathered around Laurie's kitchen table for the impromptu meeting she had just called. Even Euterpe and her poodle had been summoned to participate in what would be her first official Nitwitt confab. Not surprisingly, however, it was Renza who could not refrain from throwing her weight around in the beginning.

"Why is Gaylie Girl excused from this little gathering, and how long are we going to be holed up in here like this?" she was saying, fidgeting with her little foxes. "We're missin' all the big fun out there with Buddha. And I do mean big."

Laurie maintained her customary patience, knowing all too well how crucial it was to douse Nitwitt brush fires early on. "This won't take long, ladies. To answer your question, Renza, Gaylie Girl did not need to hear what I'm going to say—although it does concern her since I'm speaking on her behalf. It's just this. Some of you have been padding the guest list for the wedding, and you don't seem to know where to stop. Gaylie Girl is way too polite to say anything on her own, but all of you know I can and will."

Laurie paused and acknowledged Myrtis with a brief gesture in her direction. "And then there's also this. We're less than a week away from the event, and Myrtis has the responsibility of getting an accurate head count for the menu and the booze. So I'm asking each of you to take stock and realize that Gaylie Girl, Mr. Choppy, and our Myrtis would prefer to keep the crowd size manageable. I'm sure you can appreciate that. So, please. No more last-minute additions. That is all. End of friendly lecture. Please take it in that spirit."

"I had no idea this was such an issue," Renza said, after an awkward moment of silence.

But Myrtis was having none of it. "Oh, for heaven's sake, Renza. Stop being so disingenuous. You know very well what's been going on with my head counts and such. We've all of us thrown enough successful parties in our lifetimes."

It was Euterpe, not Laurie, who spoke up next, however. "Being a Nitwitt is certainly a lively proposition, isn't it? I think I'm going to enjoy being a part of it all very much."

The remark caught everyone off-guard, defusing the tension, and Laurie said: "You know what, ladies? Euterpe just put her finger on something we sometimes forget. We all came together originally to help each other out and to have good times in the face of our widowhood. Perhaps we ought to get back to that spirit starting right now. Sometimes it takes a newcomer to help us put things in the proper perspective."

"Well, that is a good point," Denver Lee added, hanging her head slightly. "I didn't intend to make more work for you, Myrtis. I don't think any of us did. It's just that we're so fond of Mr. Choppy and our own Gaylie Girl that we want this wedding to be unforgettable for them."

Novie sounded properly chastised as well. "I suppose I got a little carried away, too. You just have to understand that I'm so thrilled about my new relationship with Marc that it spills over into the rest of my life. I'll reel in the additions, though."

That left only Renza to reconcile with the gathering. To Laurie's great relief, however, she did not buck the trend.

"Meta's Saint Augustine contingent will be gravely disappointed, I'm sure. But I suppose I can deal with it. Now, does that conclude our business? I really do want to get back to the Great Buddha Magruder. I can't remember when I've been so taken with a man before. Not even my Lewis."

"Oh, yes, we're all done here," Laurie said. "Go right back in and enjoy yourselves."

But as the others headed toward the parlor, Renza was the one who stayed back, apparently for one last word. "By the way, Laurie, you haven't lost your touch. I still don't know how you do it. My presidency feels like on-the-job training compared to yours."

"Nonsense. Both you and Myrtis have kept the Nitwitts going quite smoothly. But thanks for not making a big stink back there. As you know, Gaylie Girl's been through a lot with her children, and I don't blame her for wanting to stay out of crisis mode now."

"Fair enough," Renza added. "But now, if you'll excuse me, I've got another tango to track down."

OVER THE NEXT FORTY-FIVE minutes or so, the Nitwitts refused to let up on the Great Buddha Magruder and his terpsichorean talents. As good as her word, Renza was successful in talking him into another exhibition on the dance floor. Then he and Denver Lee were the next "two to tango"—with "I Get Ideas" being the music of choice.

The coupling came off decidedly different than Renza's had—what with their combined weight to add to the equation. But it was clear that Denver Lee was casting all self-consciousness aside and following Buddha's lead to the letter.

"I won't tell you what sort of 'ideas I got' while we danced," she told him after they'd finished with a deep dipping flourish that made everyone slightly nervous.

Unfazed by the titters and whispers, Buddha pulled Denver Lee upright while she blushed a bright pink. "Don't worry, dear lady. I have yet to drop one of my dance partners. That would be gauche beyond belief."

Next, Novie took her turn to "Kiss of Fire." Because she was a much smaller and nimbler woman, the couple's energy level rose threefold. She and Buddha were often a blur of sultry technique during various musical strains.

"You are quite accomplished," Buddha was saying to her about halfway through their number. "You're all very capable, in fact. Are you sure none of you have had lessons?"

"Actually, we have in a way. Your friend and mine, Powell, gave us a lecture and demonstration on various Latin dances a while back, and I'd have to say we just lapped it all up. We Nitwitts don't do anything halfway."

"So it seems."

And then, without missing a beat, Buddha found a brief moment to wave at Powell, who was standing in a corner of the parlor next to Mr. Choppy, just taking it all in. "Ah, yes! Powell and I go back a long way, working competitions in

Paris, Madrid, and even one in Buenos Aires. Sometimes he and his first wife, Ann, finished ahead of me and my partner of that particular season, and sometimes it was the other way around. But I can assure you, the four of us were always flirting with the top spots and the gaudy trophies that accompanied them."

"I have no doubt about that," Novie replied as their dance came to an end.

But it was Euterpe who brought all chatter to a jaw-dropping halt with her display of expertise to "Strange Sensation." With a parlor full of friends and her poodle looking on from the sidelines, she was very nearly flawless, anticipating Buddha's every twist and turn without actually leading. The result left everyone breathless and Pan barking out of either jealousy or concern for his mistress's safety as the pair slithered around the floor in an inspired frenzy.

"Oh, thank you, thank you! That was quite an exciting workout!" Euterpe exclaimed to the appreciative applause of her audience. "Hush now, Pan! Mommy's just fine!" Then she caught her breath. "I'm growing rather fond of these Nitwitt perks, I must tell you!"

Gaylie Girl decided to decline her moment in the spotlight, claiming to be exhausted from "just watching everyone else." But there was an informal finale consisting of Laurie and Powell and Buddha and Myrtis as competing couples, just for fun. They again cued up the "Cherry Pink and Apple Blossom White" track from the tango CD and took turns dancing to it as it played all the way through.

"We declare it a tie!" Gaylie Girl shouted as the two couples took their final bows. "Anyone disagree?"

"Two perfect tens!" Mr. Choppy added.

But the insatiable Renza wanted more, sidling up to Buddha with what appeared to be a full-blown case of tango fever. "Do you have enough left for a third go-round with me?"

"Dear lady," he replied, his forehead beaded with sweat and his chest heaving, "I believe I've reached my limit for tonight. But I promise to resume our dazzling partnership at the wedding in just a few more days. And may I make the same promise to the rest of you charming ladies!"

Renza looked disappointed at first but then cocked her head smugly. "We'll all hold you to that. You do realize, of course, that Myrtis has hired Larry Lorrison and His Big Bad Swing Band, don't you? How are you at the jitterbug?"

He offered up that great, booming laugh of his. "I do it all. Jitterbug, the twist—even the minuet, if necessary. I'll be there front and center regardless. You can't miss me!"

MR. CHOPPY AND GAYLIE GIRL were reviewing the evening at Laurie's cottage over another supper of leftovers at 34 Pond Street. For her part, she was still beaming from the report Laurie had given her about the successful wedding list moratorium, and Mr. Choppy had greeted the news with equal enthusiasm.

"Laurie just has the touch with all those women. They're

putty in her hands," Gaylie Girl was saying in between bites of warmed-up pot roast at the kitchen table. "And that's no easy task, believe me. I can only guess at what possessed Renza, for instance. I've never seen her act that way before. Laurie thinks it was a simple case of the 'hots.' She may be right. Maybe you can go only so long murmuring sweet nothings to fox furs as a substitute for romance before you actually explode."

"But how could Miz Renza not have heard that Mr. Magruder limits his tangos with the ladies to the dance floor, so to speak?" Mr. Choppy pointed out. "Powell told me earlier this evening that the man has never even remotely considered the closet as a proper place to hang out."

Gaylie Girl rolled her eyes. "Either Renza wasn't paying attention, or she was playing that delusional game that some women will insist on playing with gay men. My mother's friend Myra Crawford up in Lake Forest was like that, thinking that she had what it took to change this charming confirmed bachelor she'd been dating since—oh, forever. She insisted that all he was missing was the right woman to turn him around. She was mining fool's gold, believe me. It just doesn't work that way."

Mr. Choppy enjoyed a good laugh and took a big swallow of his beer. "Funny you should mention gold, considerin' that outfit Mr. Magruder had on tonight. Powell told me that it was actually one of his more conservative getups."

"Conservative by Parisian gay cabaret standards, I'll wager."

Mr. Choppy dug further into his pot roast and potatoes and mulled things over with a pleasant smile on his face. "So you think we've got things settled down for the final stretch at last?"

"Laurie assured me that the Nitwitts had been properly but tactfully restrained. I think we can proceed with confidence now."

"And you're still set on takin' our honeymoon in Santa Fe, where you and Peter liked to spend the winter?"

Gaylie Girl looked at him askance, playing at being offended. "Winter. Summer. Whenever. The Santa Fe house is ours to enjoy now, Hale. What's mine is yours."

He put down his fork and gently wagged a finger at her. "In spirit only—but not legally. Don't forget the prenuptial agreement we're gonna sign."

"I haven't forgotten. And I'm sure Petey and Amanda won't let me forget, either."

"Does it bother you that they truly quieted down only when the money matters were settled? Because from my point of view, they had every right to know where they stood. I assume you're gonna divide everything between them now."

She gave him a rather stoic sigh. "Mostly. Except for some charitable donations here and there. I do want my grandchildren to have nice things and enjoy life the way I have. Amanda's hints about a divorce from Richard could affect things there. After all, she's the one with the money, and men can be gold diggers, too. But let's don't talk about that anymore."

"Yep, you're right. We got our wedding to look forward to now, and it goes without sayin' there'll be a whole lotta dancin' goin' on."

"Poor Buddha!" Gaylie Girl exclaimed with an emphatic shaking of her head. "I thought the rest of the ladies would run him into the ground tonight, which is why I decided not to add to his workload when he offered me a tango of my own with him. I had this vision of him keeling over in the middle of Laurie's parlor. You know—Great Buddha, great thud! Renza seemed to sum it up best when she came up to me at the end there and took me aside. I've just never seen her so frisky. She was almost like a schoolgirl. 'We could have danced all night,' she said to me. And she really meant it, too!"

12

FIFTY-SOMETHING YEARS
IN THE MAKING

*M*r. Choppy's Labor Day wedding was just three days away now. Only Friday, Saturday, and Sunday remained before that glorious Monday dawned, and the long, lonely decades of his bachelorhood officially came to an end out at Evening Shadows. Still, there were too many secret moments when he felt as nervous and overwhelmed as that sixteen-year-old Piggly Wiggly grocery clerk who had fallen so hard for manipulative nineteen-year-old Gayle Morris—permanently reborn as his Gaylie Girl—in Room 203 of the Second Creek Hotel. So hard, in fact, that he had lost his index finger and every vestige of pride an inexperienced young man of that age could muster.

Mr. Choppy was also prone to dwelling on the enormous positives, however. Incredibly, and otherwise in the category of beyond his wildest dreams, Gaylie Girl was now here living with him, forsaking her cushy Lake Forest existence for the title of First Lady of Second Creek, Mississippi. And as an even more astonishing footnote, she had agreed to replace the pregnant Cherish Hempstead in her third trimester as his very own secretary—doing his bidding and busywork around the office during Cherish's maternity leave.

More than anything else, however, Mr. Choppy wanted time itself to speed up so he could get the actual ceremony behind him and put the stamp of approval on the life-changing events that had made it possible in the first place. He found himself holding his breath hoping that nothing— please, God, but nothing—would go wrong at the last minute.

Then came the mid-morning Friday commotion at work that started the snafu ball rolling. Myrtis Troy appeared in his outer office in what could only be described as a full-fledged Nitwitt dither. "I must see Mr. Choppy at once!" he could hear her saying to Cherish from his vantage point behind his desk. "I've just had the most distressing call on my cell phone!"

Myrtis was immediately shown in, and Mr. Choppy waited for her to take her seat even as he steeled himself for whatever crisis had sent her into such a spiral. "I'm so beside myself that I must look an absolute mess," she began, when she clearly looked nothing of the sort. As usual, she was smartly dressed, perhaps even overly so for a late summer morning in Second Creek when nothing of any import was supposed to be going on.

Mr. Choppy knew better than to let such a calculating remark from a female pass without comment and said: "Nonsense, Miz Troy. It's all in your imagination. You always look like the fashion leader you are."

Myrtis was momentarily pleased by the attention but soon lapsed once again into crisis mode. "Well, it's a wonder I do, considering this awful phone call I've just taken from Larry Lorrison. I had no sooner entered Carla's Candle Shop just off The Square when my 'Big Girls Don't Cry' ringtone started up. It seems several of his musicians were in a wreck early this morning. No fatalities, thank God. But an assortment of broken ribs and such that won't heal anytime soon. The bottom line is that he's going to have to cancel his engagement for our wedding—or rather, your wedding, I should say. So we're going to be out all that wonderful Swing music. I'm so disappointed I could just scream!"

Mr. Choppy leaned forward, offering up his most solicitous demeanor. "Now, don't do that, Miz Troy. It's not the end of the world. I know Gaylie Girl and I were just thrilled as all get-out when you engaged Larry Lorrison for us, but the ceremony can still take place without him and his band, you know."

"Yes, I know. But it just won't be the same. Besides, I've already had that little stage and dance floor constructed out under the maze tent. And with that marvelous Buddha Magruder in town, think of all the possibilities a Swing band like that would have provided for us. Oh, I'm just sick!"

"Have you told Gaylie Girl yet?"

She closed her eyes and shook her head emphatically. "Not yet. I was just so close to your office, I decided to pop in right after I bought two dozen white votive candles for the wedding. Oh, Mr. Choppy, what are we going to do?"

"Get your deposit back, for starters."

Myrtis produced a faint smile. "Well, Mr. Lorrison did say that would be no problem. He's putting it in the mail later today after he visits all his troops in the hospital again. Isn't this just too awful for words?"

That it was, to Mr. Choppy's way of thinking. But he regretfully noted there was also no great sense of surprise on his part. Perhaps he had prayed too hard that nothing would go wrong. He had read somewhere—or was it in one of Reverend Greenlea's sermons at First Presbyterian Church?— that God didn't like whiners. Also that people often attracted their greatest fears by dwelling on them too long. Had he managed both? "Why don't you call up Gaylie Girl and the rest of the Nitwitt ladies and see if any of you can come up with some ideas?" he suggested. "I know it couldn't possibly hurt to get a pro like Miz Laurie Hampton on the case. You can't do better than that."

"Well said."

And so, the dreaded last-minute glitches had begun in

earnest. Mr. Choppy went about his municipal business as best he could, however, feeling somewhat reassured by the fact that the Nitwitts were already out there plotting among themselves. Could a quick fix be far behind?

Just after lunch, Cherish put a phone call through from his Gaylie Girl. "You'll never guess what we've come up with, Hale," she began, her excitement quite evident.

"I assume you're talkin' about the situation with the band?"

"That, and a lot else. We've been talking back and forth all morning, and here's what we've worked out so far. First of all, Euterpe has agreed to play a program of wedding music for the ceremony in the parlor, and Myrtis is going to move all the furniture out except for the piano. Then she'll bring in rows of folding chairs and create a little aisle. There'll be plenty of room. I asked Myrtis if she really wanted to go to all that trouble and wouldn't rather stage the ceremony out under the tent, but she's set on doing it this way. Oh, these Nitwitt ladies! Aren't they just wonderful!"

Mr. Choppy was smiling big now. "Don't forget that you're one of them, sweetheart. I hope you won't think I was bein' too smug about this, but I kinda figured you ladies would find a way to save the day."

"There's more, though," she continued. "Our dependable Laurie told the Great Buddha Magruder what had happened, and he's insisted on doing what he can to make everything as festive as possible. He says there's no reason he couldn't organize the dancing out under the tent, starting with a demonstration onstage using his CD collection. He's got everything covered from tango to Swing and whatever falls in between. Maybe it will turn out to be even more fun than the actual band would have been. In any case, my money's on Magruder."

"My, but all of you Nitwitts have been busy, haven't you?" Mr. Choppy observed. "I should know better by now, though. It seems a Second Creek solution is always around the corner no matter what happens."

NOVIE HAD JUST WALKED into the lobby of Delta Sunset Village and registered for her weekly lunch outing with Wittsie. She was running a little late due to all the phoning back and forth with the other Nitwitts about the Larry Lorrison cancellation, but she knew Wittsie had nowhere else to go and likely wouldn't notice anyway. Nonetheless, it was a bit puzzling that Wittsie was nowhere in sight. She was always there early, faithfully waiting for each of her friends to accompany her to the dining room for what had become the highlight of her daily routine. Not this time.

A few seconds later Mrs. Holstrom emerged from her office and offered her customary efficient greeting. "I needed to have an additional word with you, though," she continued. "It's about Miz Wittsie."

A look of sheer panic gripped Novie's face. "Has something happened to her?"

Mrs. Holstrom reached out and patted Novie's shoulder gently. "Oh, I didn't mean to frighten you. It's nothing like that. One of the nurses has just given Miz Wittsie a little additional medication to calm her down a bit. She's just a little upset today, but it's nothing serious. She's being brought over from the memory-care unit right now. Why don't we make ourselves more comfortable while we're waiting, and I'll bring you up to date on everything that's happened."

The two of them moved to one of the lobby sofas, and Mrs. Holstrom continued in a soothing, confidential tone. "After careful consideration, Dr. Milburne has decided that allowing Miz Wittsie to attend the wedding over in Second Creek would be too disorienting for her. He doesn't feel she should be subjected to all the hoopla and confusion, even if she's under the watchful eye of you and your friends the entire time. The reason Miz Wittsie wasn't here to greet you as usual was because she raised quite a ruckus when the doctor put his foot down about it a little earlier." She paused to gesture emphatically toward the floor.

"But we must follow his orders here. We wouldn't want to be responsible for having her get over there and fall apart. It would ruin the festivities for everybody and make her the center of attention in a very negative way, and we never want that for our Alzheimer's patients. As the doctor always says, the cardinal rule is to anticipate and keep them out of trouble."

Novie's disappointment and discomfort were very obvious

as she shifted her weight from side to side. "Well, I can understand why Wittsie took it so hard. She was so excited when Mr. Choppy and Gaylie Girl told her a while back that she might be able to attend."

"But there was a caveat even then. We told them to make it clear to Miz Wittsie that she needed doctor's approval for the trip over to Second Creek. Perhaps it would have been better not to have said anything and get her hopes up like that."

"Then there's no chance at all Wittsie can come?"

Mrs. Holstrom brought her hands together prayerfully and briefly closed her eyes. "I'm sure we both wish it could be otherwise, but I'm afraid it's just not possible. We have to maintain that delicate balance with patients like Miz Wittsie. If it were just a matter of taking her to some local event, it might be different. But the doctor says not for out-of-town travel like that. So I would suggest you soft-pedal the issue with her as best you can from here on out. Try to take her mind off of it."

Just then, the orderly appeared in the hallway with Wittsie in tow. The instant she made eye contact with Novie, she brightened as she always did at the sight of her friends. "Oh, Novie! Is that you? I'm so glad to see you today!"

The orderly released her, and the two friends embraced warmly. "Oh, yes, it's me, Wittsie—reporting for Friday luncheon duty as usual. I was a bad girl and skipped breakfast, so I'm starving."

"I feel like I could eat a little somethin' myself."

"Enjoy the menu, ladies," Mrs. Holstrom said as she headed back to her office.

"BUT . . . I WAS SURE Mr. Choppy told me I'd be able to go to the weddin'," Wittsie was saying after the first course of onion soup had been cleared from the table. "I've been countin' the days." She and Novie had found a two-seater tucked away in the corner of the busy dining room and were now looking forward to their second course of garden salads with ranch dressing. "It's funny what I remember and what slips my mind . . . but I could swear I remembered right this time."

With Mrs. Holstrom's advice still fresh in her mind, Novie tried to be as oblique as possible. "Perhaps you just misinterpreted what Mr. Choppy said, Wittsie. That's so easy to do."

"Easy for me, you mean . . . I can't get anything right. . . . The nurse just gave me a little somethin' extra, and it's made me a bit groggy . . . but honestly, Novie, all I said to Dr. Milburne was that I was sure I could handle goin' over there to Second Creek, and then he told me not to be so testy . . . He had the most peculiar expression on his face . . . like I was a naughty child or somethin' . . . I didn't feel he liked me much. . . . Now, when is the weddin'—this Sunday, right?"

"No, it's Monday."

Wittsie was brought up short—the frown lines deepening across her face. "Oh, dear, I thought it was Sunday."

Novie considered at length, sensing that she needed to do something to lift Wittsie's fragile spirits. "I'll tell you what. I'm planning to bring my video camera with me to Evening Shadows, and I'll tape everything from soup to nuts—the nuts being all of us Nitwitts, of course."

Novie's attempt at humor was met only with silence.

"Anyway, on my next visit over, we can trot out all the footage and watch it together. How does that sound?"

"Not as good as bein' there, Novie, and you know it."

The salads arrived, and they began eating immediately. After a few bites, Wittsie seemed to perk up a bit. "But . . . maybe all is not lost . . ." She tailed off, leaving Novie in the lurch once again.

"Yes?" Novie said. "Were you going to say something else?"

"I just had a lovely idea for a weddin' present, that's all." There was more silence.

"Are you going to share?"

Wittsie speared a couple of croutons with a sly expression. "I have to work it all out in my head . . . this crazy head of mine that's got you all worried to death about me. . . . I know I'm a terrible burden."

Novie was indignant. "That's just not true, Wittsie. There have been times over the years when I've thought of you as the sharpest tack among us Nitwitts. You've always been able to zero in on what's really important in life, and I think you've still got that marvelous quality. All I ask is that you follow doctor's orders and don't do anything foolish."

"Oh, what I'm thinkin' about isn't foolish at all. It would just be my contribution to Mr. Choppy and Gaylie Girl on their special day."

"You've got me on the edge of my seat."

Wittsie leaned in and lowered her voice. "You just tell them that I'll be there in spirit . . . no matter what."

Novie assured her that she would relay the message, but something about the way Wittsie's voice had trembled there at the very end made her strangely uneasy. It had made the words sound remarkably like a farewell.

FRIDAY HAD MOVED along like a glacier—glitches and all—but it finally gave way to Saturday. Fairly early in the morning, Mr. Choppy and Gaylie Girl had driven up to Memphis to pick up Petey and Amanda at the airport and were once again headed south to Second Creek with their wedding passengers and a trunk full of luggage. On this trip, however, the atmosphere in the car was completely different from that first awkward visit earlier in the summer. In the backseat, mother and daughter were discussing their wedding outfits like girlfriends full of the latest gossip, while in the front, Mr. Choppy and Petey were in the midst of reviewing Pond-Raised Catfish as a pressing business proposition.

"So you're gonna make Elston Graves a counterproposal that he can't refuse, huh?" Mr. Choppy said as they crossed the state line into Mississippi. "Curtis Ray made it clear to me that Elston really wants to sell so he can take the money and run—after the ladies, that is."

Petey made a dismissive gesture and chuckled. "Nice work if you can get it. But, hey, what can I say? I really like the give-and-take of business negotiations. Haggling is practically a sport with me. When my first wife and I went to Nassau on our honeymoon, we spent a huge chunk of time at the Straw Market, where we nickel-and-dimed all the vendors to death. Who knows if we really got a good deal on those cheesy hats and trinkets we bought as souvenirs, but it was boatloads of fun driving all those hard bargains."

Mr. Choppy looked impressed. "What's the timetable on this? Is Elston gonna try to get back to you before the weekend is out? I think it'd be kinda neat if you flew back to Chicago with a new business under your belt."

"Don't know the answer to that yet. Mr. Keyes just asked me to drop off the proposal at his office sometime today. Do you think you could find the time to run me out there?"

"At your service. We'll do it as soon as we get you settled. We've got you in Mama and Daddy's old room and Amanda in the guest room."

Having wrapped up her wedding fashion chatter with Amanda, Gaylie Girl chimed in. "Myrtis was full up out at Evening Shadows this time and Laurie brought a guest back with her from Paris, so she's got a houseful, too. Looks like you're stuck with us. It's cozy, but I think you'll like it. And I also think it would be so beneficial to Second Creek if you could make this investment in the catfish plant, Petey. Cherish and Henry Hempstead will need his job securely in place once she goes on maternity leave."

Amanda managed a muted giggle. "I'm sure the rooms will be fine, but I'm still having trouble picturing you as a secretary, Mother. I didn't even know you typed."

"I'll have you know that I got an A in typing back in high school. And now that I'm taking piano lessons three times a week from Euterpe, it'll soon come back to me."

"What do piano lessons have to do with it?" Amanda asked with a frown.

"Well, as Euterpe explained it to me, typing and playing the piano involve the exact same hand-eye coordination. In both cases you're supposed to look straight ahead and not down at your hands. Believe me, she has it all down to a science."

Then Gaylie Girl grew even more excited. "And not only that, I've managed to drag myself screaming into millennium computer skills, thanks to my former assistant, Harriet. She gave me a crash course by default while she was working for me. Oh, she was such a nerd about it all. But just like Euterpe with the piano lessons, she knew what she was doing. Anyway, both Hale and I agree that I'm perfectly capable of taking Cherish's place without turning every day at the office into an *I Love Lucy* episode."

"I like that image, though," Petey said, not bothering to suppress his laughter. "Copy machines out of control, vicious shredders on the rampage, digits missing from critical phone numbers, and Post-it notes stuck to the bottom of your high heels like toilet paper trailing from the bathroom."

Gaylie Girl shifted forward and gave her son a playful slap to the back of his head. "See if I deliver your messages to Hale when the time comes. And speaking of messages, I have one for you from Meta. She phoned just before we left for the airport and said she wants you to meet her at Renza's after you get settled. She wants to introduce you to all her friends, and then you'll all go out for a bite at the Victorian Tea Room. Oh, and Amanda is included."

"That's nice to hear, Mother," Amanda quickly replied. "But I have some things I need to discuss with you about Richard. We had it out last night, and I gave him an ultimatum."

Gaylie Girl looked suddenly apprehensive. "Oh, dear. Are we talking divorce yet?"

"Too soon to tell. But Richard could see that I've had enough, and he tried to make nice by offering to come down with me for the wedding. 'We can bring the kids, too, if you want,' he said. It was pretty obvious to me that I put the fear of God in him but good."

Petey was wagging his brows, his voice full of mischief. "I've always thought you should get tough on Richard, Sis.

He'll get religion pronto if he thinks he's about to lose his cash cow."

"You are such a romantic," Amanda snapped. "I don't think Meta is remotely ready for you."

"Truce, you two!" Gaylie Girl exclaimed. Then she turned to Amanda, sounding vaguely disappointed. "You know, I wouldn't have minded if you had brought my grandchildren with you. I haven't seen the little dears in so long, and I don't want them to forget what I look like."

Amanda threw up her hands and set her jaw firmly. "You haven't missed anything, Mother. They're all going through such hideous phases. Mary Ann, for instance, wants to try out for cheerleader this fall, but I won't let her because her grades were barely passing last year. We'd be at each other's throats all weekend. Anyhow, let's save some of this for later. Besides, I haven't really gotten them to understand why Granny Gayle wanted to move away from them. They all think they've done something wrong."

Gaylie Girl sighed and sank back in her seat. "You're right. We'll just have to take care of all that another time. This weekend is for me and Hale."

SATURDAY WAS BEGINNING to be one big hectic blur for Mr. Choppy. No sooner had he returned from driving Petey out to the catfish plant than Gaylie Girl met him at the front door, dangling her car keys at him. "Oh, good, you're here," she began, sounding relieved to see him. "I'm headed over to Greenwood to keep my lunch date with Wittsie after all, and Amanda is going with me so we can rake my philandering son-in-law over the coals on the way."

"I thought you phoned over there yesterday and told Wittsie that you just had too many things to do for the wedding. I thought lunch was off for this week."

"That was the original plan, yes. But Novie came over while you were gone. You just missed her, in fact. She said Wittsie seemed very depressed yesterday because Dr. Milburne won't allow her to attend the wedding."

Mr. Choppy looked down at the floor and shook his head. "Oh, now, that's a shame."

"Yes, it is. And then Novie delivered a message. She said Wittsie wanted us to know that she'd be with us in spirit on Monday, no matter what."

"Well, that's right sweet—and so typical of Wittsie."

Gaylie Girl briefly shrugged her shoulders. "But Novie said it sounded peculiar, even a bit ominous. She suspects Wittsie might be up to something. Apparently, she raised quite a fuss about the doctor ruling out the wedding and had to be medicated. I just think I ought to go and see her, Hale. She's come to count on me for company every Saturday. Besides, Myrtis seems to have everything under control out at Evening Shadows. So I guess I'll see you whenever."

Mr. Choppy barely managed a good-bye, and then Gaylie

Girl and Amanda were out the door and headed down the sidewalk to her car.

"Is it always like that around here with Mother?" Petey said, more amused than anything else.

"I'm not complainin'. It's been a rush for me from the first moment I laid eyes on her, back in the day."

Petey glanced at his watch and gave a little gasp. "I see it's past twelve, Hale. I'm supposed to get together with Meta about now. Could you run me over there, or should I just call her up? She's got a rental. Maybe I should have gotten one, too. I seem to be putting you to a lot of trouble."

Mr. Choppy didn't have to think about it twice, handing over his keys almost as a reflex action. Petey was already feeling like family to him—the stepson he never dreamed he would have. "Nonsense. You take the car. I could use some time alone anyway before the ladies get back. I'll call over to Miz Renza's if somethin' comes up and I need it."

Petey put his hand on Mr. Choppy's shoulder and smiled. "Thanks, Hale. I really appreciate you. And now, if you'll excuse me, I'm off to make eyes at an extremely pretty girl."

THE HECTIC SATURDAY blur began coming quietly into focus once Mr. Choppy had 34 Pond Street all to himself. It was odd how the silence set him off on an unexpected tangent. He hadn't thought of his mother's letter in years, but now, with his wedding just a day or two away, it had popped into his head with an undeniable timeliness he just couldn't ignore. Perhaps this was the moment Gladys Dunbar had foreseen when she had written it to her son on his twenty-first birthday a half-century ago.

Mr. Choppy moved deliberately to his bedroom closet, scanning the top shelves for the whereabouts of what he referred to as his "boyhood box." It was the one that had "personal" scrawled in marker pen across the lid. He was the only one who had ever rummaged through it, and only he knew how it was organized and what it contained. Finally, he spotted it in a far corner, reached up as far as his height would allow, and pulled it down carefully. It took a while to locate the letter amid all the papers and paraphernalia he'd saved since his eleventh birthday—everything from Valentine's Day cards sent by girlfriends long forgotten to scores of movie ticket stubs from the now-demolished Grande Theater.

But eventually he was able to put his hands on the prize—the pages now significantly yellowed with age. He sat on the edge of the bed, took a deep breath, unfolded the letter, and read the words that had both puzzled and moved him so very long ago:

Dear Son,

I want you to know how proud I am of you on this very special day. You're twenty-one now and have grown into the fine young man I knew you'd become. It won't be that much longer until your daddy turns over the store to you permanently, and I know you'll do our Dunbar family Piggly Wiggly tradition proud—even long after we're gone.

I wish only the best in life for you, son, including a wonderful wife who will love and look after you as long as you're both together. When the right girl comes along, you'll know it, too. So I won't ask you to tell me what really went on that night six years ago when you lost your finger. Your daddy and I knew it wasn't because you were crazy in love with Ava Gardner the way you said. We were sure you had more sense than that. But we figured there probably was a woman involved. A mother would always know when her son's heart was broken. If you feel like it's something better off unexplained and kept private, well, then, you know I'll respect your wishes. Just remember that if you ever want to come to me and unburden yourself, I'll be here for you. I know that whatever happened is the only thing that's really gone wrong in your life so far, and maybe God will bless you and you won't have anything more to deal with. I hope so.

Maybe someday you'll also understand what I mean when I say that things happen and people come into your life for a reason. And sometimes it might take most of a lifetime to discover how it's supposed to work out. And you may never find out why until you're on the other side, so to speak. But there will come a day when you'll pull out this letter and read it and everything in it will make sense the way it never could before. Things will have fallen into place to make it possible for you to understand. Just call it a woman's intuition and a mother's love that's telling you all this. I am so very proud to have

*brought you into this world. You will make your mark, I just
know.*

> *Love always,*
>
> *Mama*

Mr. Choppy rested the letter in his lap and dabbed at the
tears in his eyes. All the good fortune that had come his
way in the last year or so seemed somehow to have been
forecast in his mother's remarkable words. The reconcil-
iation with Gaylie Girl. The acceptance of his marriage
proposal so late in life. Even the fact that he had been
transformed from a grocery store owner into the mayor of
his hometown. Suddenly, all those things took on a new
shine, a certain charmed inevitability that the twenty-one-
year-old Hale Dunbar Junior could never have envisioned.
They were now an integral part of a success story that was
fifty-something years in the making. As much as anyone
could have all the answers in life, the seventy-ish Mr.
Choppy now believed he had them.

He picked up the last page and lightly kissed his mother's
signature. "Thanks, Mama," he said. "Message received—
loud and clear." Then he folded the letter and put it safely
back in the box.

GAYLIE GIRL COULDN'T FIGURE out what had come
over her Hale when she sauntered into the kitchen following her return from Greenwood. Although she was chock-full

of details about that encounter and the conversation with Amanda as well, he didn't seem to want to let her get a word in edgewise. Every time she started up about either one, he kept interrupting her with light, scattered kisses on her arms and neck, catching her completely off-guard.

"Can't this wait?" he finally said, taking her by the arm and pulling her gently in the direction of the bedroom. "We've got the house to ourselves now that Amanda's taken your car and run off to join the others."

Gaylie Girl easily read between the lines. "But what if she or Petey should come back unexpectedly?"

He did not answer the question, murmuring a few endearments instead, and she offered no further resistance. This was earlier in the day than they'd ever done it before, but Gaylie Girl found herself excited by the prospect. She let herself be led the rest of the way to the bed, with a wicked little smile on her face.

There, they threw caution to the wind and made late afternoon love, and she stopped worrying about the whereabouts of her children or their problems or Wittsie's ongoing strange banter and behavior or any of the rest of it. Her Hale was suddenly insatiable and would not be put off, reminding her of their first frenzied encounter half a century ago at the Second Creek Hotel.

In the afterglow, she managed to catch her breath and put her pleasure into words. "To what do I owe this amazing déjà vu, Hale?"

He rolled over and sank back onto his pillow. "My

performance, you mean? If you really want to know the truth, it was a fan letter." But he made no further attempt at clarifying his cryptic remark.

She responded playfully. "So you have groupies now? Should I be jealous?"

Mr. Choppy took it the right way, aiming his hearty laughter at the ceiling. "That's a good one. Let's just say that I got a very special reminder about how you and I were always meant to be. Even if it didn't look that way at first."

"Stop. I'm about to work up a good cry."

But she didn't cry. Instead, she snuggled up to the man she had spent fifty-something years finding her way back to after an improbable and traumatic beginning full of guilt and denial.

Above all, she knew that Monday's ceremony would be a mere formality. She felt more strongly than ever in her heart that they were already very much married.

13.

ONE WITH THE GIRLS

Sunday was supposed to be a day of rest for everyone in the wedding party; a time to take it easy and store up energy for Monday's ceremony and celebration. But an hour or so after a late breakfast with Mr. Choppy, Gaylie Girl began to get suspicious when Amanda kept pointedly asking her to get out of her housecoat and "put something fun on" so the two of them could go see more of the Second Creek sights together.

"I'll even drive, Mother," Amanda insisted. "I'll need to know my way around on my many visits down here anyway."

"What on earth do you mean by 'something fun'?" Gaylie

Girl wanted to know. "I know what I mean, but what did you have in mind?"

"Something you won't be embarrassed to be found in if we're in a wreck. And I really want to snap some more pictures for my scrapbook. Maybe a few street scenes—a cupola here, a veranda there, a lacework balcony or two, things like that."

Although she still felt something was up, Gaylie Girl agreed to go along with Amanda's request, rifled through one of the hang-up bags she'd assigned to Hale's closet and selected one of her more festive outfits.

"Will this do?" she said, modeling it for her daughter in front of the full-length bathroom mirror. It was, indeed, a colorful frock with wavy vertical stripes of orange and yellow running from scalloped neckline to knee.

Amanda stepped back to admire it, overplaying her hand somewhat. "Oh, it's just perfect. I never knew you owned anything this playful."

"What are you up to?"

"Just getting with the program here in Second Creek," Amanda replied. "Isn't that what you've wanted all along?"

Gaylie Girl gave a pleasant little shrug, put her face on, and then mother and daughter headed out together while Mr. Choppy and Petey stood at the front door waving good-bye.

"Have fun!" Mr. Choppy shouted.

Although Gaylie Girl had the sneaking suspicion that Mr. Choppy and Petey might even be in on whatever was happening, she decided to play along. Dutifully, she slid into the front seat of her car while Amanda took the wheel. She was still in a relaxed Sunday mind-set and had no intention of letting go of it, no matter what was afoot.

At first their little junket was uneventful, even boring, as Amanda drove around the downtown area, stopping now and then to get out and snap more photographs. But eventually they veered away from The Square, ending up in front of Belford Place on North Bayou Avenue, where there was not a parking space to be had. Clearly, there was some sort of party going on at Renza's.

"Well, if nothing else, you've made sure I was dressed for the occasion," Gaylie Girl said. "Do you mind telling me what the girls are up to? I recognize all their cars, you know."

"Go on in and find out. I'll find a parking space and catch up with you later." When her mother hesitated slightly, Amanda added, "Go on, Mother. Everyone went to a lot of trouble to set this up."

Gaylie Girl emerged from the car and headed toward the front porch, putting two and two together along the way. The setup had all the earmarks of a so-called surprise shower, even though she had specifically asked every one of her Nitwitt friends not to do anything like that. Their participation in the wedding would be more than enough, she had insisted. In the back of her mind, however, she had suspected that her requests would fall on deaf and devious ears.

Sure enough, the entire club—including Euterpe but without Wittsie, of course—was there in the foyer waiting for her with pointy party hats, noisemakers, and Bloody Marys in hand. "Surprise!" they all shouted, more or less in unison.

"Is it New Year's Eve already?" Gaylie Girl exclaimed, resigning herself to all the extra attention and hoopla with a gracious smile.

"I know you told us not to do something like this," Renza explained, leading the way into the parlor, where several gifts with cards were displayed on one of the antique sofas. "But we just couldn't resist."

"Oh, ladies, not presents on top of everything else. I really didn't want you to, you know!"

Renza gestured toward the sofa and shook her head emphatically. "It's not what you think, Gaylie Girl. You'll see. Meanwhile, someone fetch the woman a Bloody Mary so she can catch up with us. She's way behind."

Novie immediately departed for the kitchen, while the others settled around the room in anticipation of the opening of the presents. But Gaylie Girl still felt slightly uncomfortable about all the organized fuss, turning her attention first toward Myrtis and her generosity.

"Isn't it more than enough that you're staging my wedding for me out at Evening Shadows?"

Myrtis waved her off after taking a healthy sip of her drink. "Don't speak too hastily, dear. Renza's right on target this time, you know. This isn't what it appears to be."

"So if it's not a shower, what is it, then—a magic show?"

Just then, Novie emerged with Gaylie Girl's Bloody Mary and handed it over. "These are pretty potent, so you may want to go easy. Personally, I think Renza's tryin' to slug us."

"Horse apples, Novie! I just want us all to have a good time. So drink up, Gaylie Girl. Have one with the girls. Have two. Hell, have as many as you want in the best Nitwitt tradition!"

Gaylie Girl took a sip of her drink, running her tongue across her lips and offering up an amusing little shudder. "Po-tent, indeed! May I hazard a guess—there's tequila in there somewhere, right?"

"Technically, my Tequila Maria," Renza said, puffing herself up. "Now, don't keep us waiting forever. Get to it. Open those presents."

So Gaylie Girl took a seat on the sofa and got to work, tackling them one by one. First up was Renza's offering, and it definitely lived up to the surprise element of the shower. There, beneath all the tissue paper cushioning it so carefully, was a round, roughly textured bronzed object that Gaylie Girl simply could not recognize.

"It's beautiful and I love it, Renza, but what exactly is it?"

Renza offered up an exaggerated wink and nod of her head. "My artistic daughter, Meta, did it for me. I had the brainstorm when she was here last time and commissioned it then. She'd be here now to take her bows, but she and her friends went out to explore. Anyway, Gaylie Girl, it's a horse apple—isn't that just too clever?"

Renza laughed as a wave of recognition spread across the room. "Just a little something to remind you of me when you finally get settled in your new house and we become neighbors. In fact, the rest of you girls might as well know here and now. I had Meta make up one for each of you for Christmas. Imagine. The essence of your Renza all wrapped up in a dried, bronzed ornament for your tree or mantel or wherever you choose to display it. On the other hand, maybe I shouldn't fool myself. It's the sort of thing that some of you might trot out only when I come over."

Renza's laughter was contagious, and Amanda walked in on it at its peak. "That must have been a great one-liner someone just told," she said. "And good morning, ladies."

The usual greetings were exchanged, and then Gaylie Girl explained the object in her hand to her daughter. "I have to admit this is very original," she concluded.

"That's the point of all this," Renza added. "We actually did respect your wishes here. These little gifts of ours aren't showy or expensive. They're just quirky little reminders of who we are and where we fit into your life. Now, quit dawdling and open some more."

Gaylie Girl fell to, reading the card from Denver Lee. "To the fresh Nitwitt breeze from Chicago. With love, Denver Lee," it read. Although the others knew what it was from the rather large shape and were having trouble restraining themselves, Gaylie Girl tore away at the wrapping paper with abandon. Finally, she pulled out one of Denver Lee's infamous alphabetized oil paintings—this particular one featuring carrots, cauliflower, and corn. If nothing else, it had the vivid colors going for it.

"I know for sure this is something you won't trot out unless I'm coming over. Maybe not even then," Denver Lee said, actually enjoying the buzzing and titters at her expense. "I'm sure you've heard all the girls talk about my god-awful oil painting phase, which has now been put out to pasture, thankfully. As a matter of fact, I probably would have had more success if I'd tackled pastures instead of vegetables. Anyhow, you don't even have to keep it if you don't want to. I just thought it would be a fun reminder of me and all my failed projects. Enjoy!"

Gaylie Girl held up the painting, examined it carefully, and then feigned a gasp. "It is most magnificent, Denver Lee. It reminds me of the frozen vegetable packets at the supermarket. I shall hide it from view proudly."

Denver Lee dramatically clasped her hands together. "That's the spirit! Now, quickly, before you get too hungry from all that realism, on to other things!"

Next up was a plainly wrapped box from Novie. It turned out to be a small potted African violet for the windowsill or bedside table, courtesy of Marc and Michael's How's Plants?; and since it was in bloom, it drew appreciative oohs and ahhs as it once again saw the light of day.

"Oh, I absolutely love it, Novie. How did you know I was crazy about African violets?"

Novie pointed to Amanda and said: "You have your daughter to thank for that. As late as yesterday, I still hadn't thought of just the right simple present for you. So when I came over Saturday to tell you about Wittsie, I found a moment to pick Amanda's brain, and that's what she came up with. I also thought it would remind you of How's Plants? anytime you need something green to take care of and lift your spirits."

"Perfect!" Then Gaylie Girl got to her feet and motioned to Novie and Amanda. "Come. Both of you. Give me a big hug."

Euterpe's present was the next Gaylie Girl chose. It consisted only of a manila envelope with the words "To one of my very best pupils! Love, The Mistress of the Scales!" written across it with exquisite penmanship.

"I trust you'll find this appropriate. I do think it fits the spirit of the occasion," Euterpe said. For some reason, Pan lifted his little head and observed closely while Gaylie Girl opened the envelope.

"Oh, I'm sure I will." Then Gaylie Girl pulled out one of those big blue first-prize ribbons—the kind awarded to jams, jellies, and best pig in show at state fairs—and everyone responded with light applause.

"Each of you has been an outstanding pupil so far," Euterpe continued. "So I have no intention of slighting anyone here. But in honor of the occasion, I've decided to award first prize for progress made at the piano to none other than our Gaylie Girl." Euterpe moved to the sofa, pinned the ribbon to Gaylie Girl's bodice, and then stepped back. "There, now. You hardly needed me to tell you, but you're a winner at whatever you do."

Gaylie Girl warmly embraced her teacher. "We newcomers must stick together, huh?"

"Open mine next," Myrtis called out from across the room. "I just can't wait any longer."

Gaylie Girl retrieved the small flat package that simply had "From Myrtis with love" on the card. What Myrtis had settled on was a CD of Frankie Valli's greatest hits, and Gaylie Girl's eyes lit up immediately. "Now, this is absolutely inspired, Myrtis!"

"Isn't it, though? Do you think I can come over after you've moved into the new house, and we can sing falsetto together?"

"If you can stand it, I can."

Laurie's present was the last to be opened, and Gaylie Girl couldn't resist trotting out the cliché. "Have I saved the best for last?"

"Either that, or you're scraping the bottom of the barrel," Laurie replied, continuing the repartee.

But Laurie had hit paydirt with a framed photo of the Piggly Wiggly in its second incarnation as Hale Dunbar Junior Campaign Headquarters. "I thought you'd like to remember the Piggly Wiggly this way. Not that it isn't lovely now as Euterpe's studio. But you'll officially be First Lady of Second Creek very soon, and this will remind you of how hard we all worked to make that possible. My goodness, but we burned up those phone lines, didn't we, girls?"

There was a general buzzing and nodding of heads, and Renza said: "Yes, we did. Even if there were people I refused to call."

"You and your grudges. You're like an elephant, Renza. You never forget," Myrtis added, unable to resist the opening.

Renza gave her rival a sideways glance with the barest hint of a smile. "I can see you're in great need of one of my bronzed horse apples!"

"Is that going to be your new signature phrase, dear?" Myrtis returned.

This time, it was Gaylie Girl, not Laurie, who stepped in to lighten the mood. "I think it would work. Why not 'Bronzed Horse apples'?" Then she took a deep breath and surveyed the room of well-lubricated friends. "Ladies, I can't tell you how much this little get-together means to me. And you're absolutely right—you went to just the right amount of trouble. You made me feel so special from the moment I first visited Second Creek, and you haven't let up. I can see you've all done a bit of sneaking around to pull this off, and my Hale has even been involved. But that's what makes it feel so special to me. You really are a family to me now, and I'm looking forward to more good times together in the years ahead."

"Well, that was quite a speech," Laurie said. "If Mr. Choppy ever wants to step down, you could run for office yourself."

"Thanks, but no thanks. What I'm doing now just suits me fine. Just think, ladies, you can come to me with your civic projects from here on out, and I'll try to get behind them as First Lady."

Laurie's eyes widened as she enthusiastically nodded. "It'll be a far cry from the bad old days of Floyce Hammontree."

WHEN GAYLIE GIRL and Amanda returned from the shower, they found Petey and Mr. Choppy in the midst of what looked like some sort of celebration. They were drinking beers at the kitchen table in time-honored male-bonding fashion.

"What's going on with you two?" Gaylie Girl asked as she walked into the room with Amanda right behind.

Mr. Choppy rose and gave her a hug and a kiss. "Just a coup for Second Creek, that's all. Shall I tell it, or do you want to, Petey?"

Petey remained seated with the widest of grins plastered on his face. "I defer to you, Mr. Mayor."

"Okay, then. But first you ladies need to sit down for the news." In no time at all, they were both settled around the table with a good idea of what was coming next.

"It's Pond-Raised Catfish, isn't it?" Gaylie Girl said, realizing she might be stealing some thunder.

"You got it. We got the call from Curtis Ray Keyes not too long after you left for your shower—"

"Which you knew all about, you sneaky thing, you!" Gaylie Girl interrupted.

"Guilty. Did you have fun?"

"Maybe the most fun ever. Until tomorrow, that is. And maybe Santa Fe after that."

He leaned over, gave her a peck on the cheek, and then resumed. "Anyway, Curtis Ray called to say that Elston Graves has accepted Petey's counterproposal and wants the lawyers to start talkin' and drawin' up papers and such as soon as possible. I feel really good about the future of the plant with Petey at the helm now. It means a lot to Second Creek."

"Congratulations, son. I'm just thrilled for you!" Gaylie Girl exclaimed.

"Yeah, nice going, Petey," Amanda chimed in. "Are you going to move down here, though?"

Petey swallowed more of his beer as he mulled things over. "I think that's up for grabs right now. I'm a big believer in delegating, so I don't need to be living down here to make sure things are run right. But to be honest with all of you, it depends on how things develop with Meta. She's her own law, and I have to take what she wants into consideration."

"Wow!" Amanda exclaimed. "Talk about your whirlwind romances! Where is she this morning anyway? I thought she might show up at the shower and take her bows for her bronzed horse apples."

"She and her friends are doing some touristy things."
Then Petey blinked. "Her bronzed what?"

"Never mind. Anyway, I hope it all works out between
you two. I'm sure Mother and I would like to see you
settled."

Then Mr. Choppy stepped in with the exclamation point.
"Second Creek has a way of bringing people together.
Eventually."

14.

FLIGHTS OF FANCY

*A*nd then it was Monday. All the waiting, all the planning, even all the last-minute glitches had finally come to an end. The wedding of Hale Dunbar Junior and Gayle Morris Lyons was going to take place at seven o'clock in the evening at the home of Mrs. Raymond Troy of Second Creek, Mississippi. Family members and selected friends would be showing up fashionably attired in a few more hours to witness the joyous and much-anticipated occasion. Despite the best efforts of everyone involved to keep things manageable, however, the celebration had taken on a life of its own and nearly doubled in size.

For their part, Mr. Choppy and Gaylie Girl had decided to abandon that old chestnut about the groom not catching a glimpse of the bride before she walked down the aisle. It would have been impossible to enforce anyway, since he would have had to leave his own house and perhaps check into a room at the nearby Second Creek Hotel; and he was not about to revisit the scene of his traumatic teenage memories on the wedding day he thought he would never see. Not after he'd worked so hard to put them in perspective and rob them of their power to put him off his game.

"It's not like I haven't seen that sizzlin' silver number before," Mr. Choppy said as he sat down to breakfast with his Gaylie Girl around nine-thirty in the morning.

They were joined for omelets and cheese grits by Amanda and Petey, and Gaylie Girl made a big fuss about the fact that she had whipped up the entire menu all by herself. "It's time you put your fear of grits behind you, Amanda. Especially since I made this dish myself with my perfectly manicured little hands. See, I didn't even break a nail."

"Dig in, Sis. They're delicious!" Petey added, having just sampled them and given his mother a thumbs-up with an exaggerated, boyish "Yum, yum!"

Amanda fell to with a modest forkful and ended up agreeing with her brother's enthusiastic verdict. "They taste almost like a cheese soufflé or maybe even a quiche. Kudos to you, Mother!"

"Oh, I really shouldn't take full credit. Hale taught me everything I know about grits."

Mr. Choppy looked skeptical but managed a smile anyway. "Nothin' to it, really, plus your mother was a quick study in the kitchen. Cheese soufflé might be takin' it a bit too far, I think, but we're still mighty glad you like 'em, Amanda."

"They're definitely a treat, but I won't lie to you, Hale. The South has been an acquired taste for someone like myself brought up on the shores of Lake Michigan. But it's been well worth the effort if cheese grits and Nitwitts are any indication."

Gaylie Girl's laughter at her daughter's remark was laced with genuine surprise. "Cheese grits and Nitwitts! Very catchy! Sounds like the title of the club's next cookbook. I'll have to run it past the girls after the honeymoon and see who's willing to give up their deep dark secret recipes."

"Now, that's intriguing," Amanda added. "Food as a metaphor for romantic entanglements. I'd buy it and try it, I do believe."

"The food, the people, the architecture—they're all unique here in Second Creek," said Mr. Choppy, realizing even as he spoke that he sounded like a press release from a tourist bureau.

But Amanda picked up where he had left off, elaborating further on her perceptions of the town she had disdained so in the beginning. "Since I have so many points of comparison in my travels, I can say without hesitation that you have an embarrassment of riches here. I'm a big fan of adaptive restoration, and you obviously have citizens who have taken the time and money to preserve lots of your historical buildings. There's nothing sadder than seeing the wrecking ball get at something irreplaceable. I've always thought it might be a pretty satisfying feeling to personally stop that from happening."

Mr. Choppy was both pleased and surprised at her testimonial. Lately, he had been trying to live up to his campaign promise of strict enforcement of Second Creek's zoning laws, especially as they affected historical preservation. Both issues had been consistently ignored by the previous, Hammontree administration. "You should get together and have a nice long talk with Miz Novie before you leave. She's in charge of the Springtime Tour right now, as you probably know. She could bring you up to date on some of the projects the Tour Committee is lookin' into. New blood and new ideas would be welcome, I'm sure."

"Even though I don't live here? I wouldn't want to seem like some sort of carpetbagger."

"All you really need is the interest and the sense of history, Amanda. I'm impressed with yours already. But good ideas are always welcome. Of course, so is money. Miz Novie says it takes a right nice hunk of change to bring these buildings up to snuff and into the twenty-first century."

"I could keep you in the loop, too," Gaylie Girl added. "I'll know everything that's happening eventually, won't I, Hale?"

"Good First Ladies—and secretaries—always do." Mr. Choppy wiped his mouth with his napkin and glanced at the wall clock. "Well, I guess I'd better get my day started in earnest. I got me a few odds and ends to take care of, includin' a surprise or two for a certain sophisticated someone."

Gaylie Girl reacted with a little shiver of excitement. "Oooh, I just love surprises!"

Petey finished up his omelet and caught his sister's gaze. "And we've got that thing over at Mrs. Belford's coming up." Then he gave Mr. Choppy a quick glance. "Meta talked her mother into throwing a little brunch for her and her friends around one o'clock. It goes without saying that we won't go hungry today with all that wedding food still to come."

"That's the one bad thing about traveling, I find," Amanda noted. "You get out of your exercise routine, indulge yourself in the local cuisine, and pretty soon, your clothes don't fit."

"Well, while you're eating up a storm at Renza's," Gaylie Girl said, "I'll be off to the beauty parlor. Amanda, I think my salon could squeeze you in if you need something touched up. I already swear by my Peggy Anne."

"Thanks, Mother, but I've got it covered. I like to fuss with it myself."

"Men have no idea what it takes for us ladies to look good for them," Gaylie Girl continued, playing at being miffed. "It's a bit more than running a nail file through our curly locks. We don't just fall out of bed with everything in place like in all those Hollywood movies. You men really do have it so easy."

Mr. Choppy rose from his chair and gestured broadly toward his middle. "I'll have you know that I've lost four pounds so I can wow you in my tux. Just wait until you see me in it."

Gaylie Girl was indulging a playful grin. "I'm sure you'll look positively spiffy, but it really does take a woman a long time to get her act together on her wedding day."

"How else would you become my glorious bride?"

And on that note, everyone adjourned from the breakfast table and set out on their separate but busy paths.

OVER AT LAURIE'S COTTAGE, the Great Buddha Magruder was preparing to compliment his hostess on her eggs Benedict. "As delicious as anything I could get in Paris," he insisted, leaning back in his chair at the breakfast nook and patting his substantial belly.

"You flatter me. But I do pride myself on my cooking," Laurie said as she began clearing the table.

Powell was nodding agreeably. "This beautiful lady really will spoil you. It's getting so I hate to eat out—even at the Victorian Tea Room. It just doesn't seem to measure up to what I can get at home."

"What a lucky man you are!" Then he called out to Laurie, who was hovering over the sink. "Leave those dishes for a few minutes, won't you? I have something important to run past the both of you!"

Laurie wiped her hands on a paper towel and headed

over. Soon she and Powell were Buddha's captive audience as he rose from his chair and paced around the room like a professor in the midst of a lecture. "I've had some second thoughts about leading with the tango for my dance demonstration under the tent this evening. I've decided to go with something else a little more offbeat."

Powell quickly sounded the alarm. "What? No tango? The Nitwitt ladies will be heartbroken, Buddha. I'm sure they've all had their calendars circled since you burst upon the scene. I can't imagine that they're going to let you get away with a tango-free wedding reception."

Buddha continued his pacing, his tone becoming even more serious. "No doubt you're right about that, Powell. And I fully intend to include the tango at some point. But the other evening when you first introduced me to the group, I noticed that several of the ladies became rather frenzied and overheated, to say the least. Overcome with a genuine case of the 'vapors,' as you're fond of saying here in the Deep South. I'm wondering if that's the proper note I want to strike right off the bat."

"Then what do you suggest instead?" Powell asked. "Do you really think it matters that much? With a few inappropriate exceptions, I've found that dancing is just dancing for most people. Unless it's in a grocery store, of course."

"I would agree with that. But I was thinking of something more lighthearted—more G-rated and benign, if you will."

"Such as?"

"Such as the Hokey Pokey."

The remark was met with silence while Powell and Laurie exchanged bewildered glances. Finally, Powell said, "As in 'you put your right foot in, you put your right foot out'? That Hokey Pokey?"

"Yes, *that* Hokey Pokey."

"To tell the truth, Buddha, I haven't thought about that little song and dance since childhood. It's been at least that long since I've done it," Powell said as he aimed a thoughtful grin in Laurie's direction. "What about you, sweetheart?"

"Not since before I was wearing a bra," she replied, somewhat amused herself. "Are you sure this is what you want to do, Buddha?"

"Oh, absolutely. It will be a marvelous icebreaker, you'll see. I'll ask for volunteers across the front line—why not the Nitwitts, in fact? They seem to enjoy the spotlight. And it will be a peer pressure thing just like the macarena was a few years back. Everyone will join in and laugh and have a wonderful time. Especially with a drink or two under their belts, and we already know that's going to happen."

"It does seem rather Second Creek–ish," Laurie added. "I think the idea is growing on me."

But Powell was groaning. "I was just flashing back to the heyday of the macarena for a minute there. I sincerely wanted to beat that glorified line dance to death with a baseball bat!"

"*Mais oui!* La macarena was a noisy nuisance over in Europe, *aussi*," Buddha admitted. "But I don't think we're in danger of having the Hokey Pokey sweep the South because we dust it off here in Second Creek for a little wedding reception. Anyway, after everyone's had their fill of it, I'll go on to more adult things, like the tango, and the Nitwitt ladies can get their groove on again."

Powell couldn't help himself and broke out into song. "And that's what it's all about!"

Buddha and Laurie joined him in his laughter, and then Buddha said: "So we're agreed on the Hokey Pokey as our opener under the tent tonight?"

"I assume you have the appropriate CD and all that good stuff?" Powell wanted to know.

"I have CDs for everything, Powell. I am never without appropriate music wherever I go. And that is why I shall forever remain the Great Buddha Magruder of Paris, France, by way of Natick, Massachusetts, and too many other New England towns to name."

"Just one question," Laurie put in. "Do we tell the Nitwitts about this latest development or spring it on them out at Evening Shadows?"

Buddha was emphatic now. "Let's don't give them time to stew and fret. We'll press them into duty when the time comes and make it look like an impulse. I've always found that giving people time to think about being in the spotlight can make them fade into the crowd. If I've done nothing else with my life, I've had quite a bit of success coaxing people out of their shells without them realizing it."

"That's a familiar feeling. And I'd say you did a damned

good job with the Nitwitts and those tangos," Powell added.

GAYLIE GIRL RETURNED from the beauty parlor with every hair of her trademark streaked coiffure in place. Her marvelous Peggy Anne had outdone herself today, adding a few tight ringlets and subtle highlights around the temples to frame her face smartly. But she had begun to worry about the whereabouts of Mr. Choppy. He'd told her he was off to take care of one of those surprises he'd mentioned briefly over breakfast, but he'd been gone for a good three hours now. He wasn't answering his cell phone, either. What was a bride to do?

His prolonged absence gave her time to sit down and reflect upon what was perhaps the most unexpected decision of her life—saying yes to her Hale and his crazy little kingdom of Second Creek. Now that her children were finally onboard, it seemed far less problematic to her. And she knew without a doubt that she loved this very sincere and straightforward man and wanted to help him succeed as mayor in any way possible. She was confident that she could do that. What she wanted out of life at any particular time, she had always pursued and won. But could she keep it all fresh, could she stay involved without getting bored? The far more sophisticated and well-heeled Lake Forest had not held her interest for long, despite all her money.

She looked at the clock on the wall and saw that it was nearly three. The children would soon be back from their brunch at Belford Place and then start to get dressed for the wedding. Amanda had promised to be there for her and help her apply the finishing touches to her makeup and ensemble. Of course, she was perfectly capable of doing it by herself, but the newly found camaraderie between mother and daughter was something she wanted to experience whenever she could. Soon enough, Amanda would be returning to Lake Forest to deal with her marital problems, and who knew how often they would see each other after that?

Then she reminded herself that as First Lady of Second Creek she would be in a position to influence things and make them happen, largely ensuring that she would never be bored if she truly took full advantage of her new role. She was about to make a list of interesting projects to suggest and undertake, in fact, when the phone rang. Much to her relief, it was Mr. Choppy, sounding a bit winded but definitely excited.

"I want you to meet me over here at the new house," he told her. "I have one of your wedding-day surprises ready to unveil!"

His enthusiasm was contagious, and once again she found herself getting goose bumps. "I can't wait. Just let me leave a note for Amanda, and I'll be right on over!"

When she walked into the nearly completed new residence

of Mayor and Mrs. Hale Dunbar Junior on North Bayou Avenue, Mr. Choppy was nowhere to be found, however. She called out his name several times, but there was no answer. She thought it was an odd time to be playing a joke, if that's what it was.

"Out here!" Mr. Choppy finally shouted, and she again felt a wave of relief. "I'm out here in the backyard!"

She moved gingerly down the long central hallway and its recently polished hardwood floor. She was very much aware of the sin of scuffing after all the care they had put into their renovation. There were only a few walls to be painted in a room or two, and then they would be done. The contractor had told them that the house would be ready for a move-in when they returned from their honeymoon in Santa Fe. So they were just a week away from that daunting task, and although she was not looking forward to the inevitable stress and confusion of moving, she couldn't wait to leave all the clutter of 34 Pond Street behind.

"Here I am!" Mr. Choppy shouted as Gaylie Girl emerged from the hallway into the backyard. He was covered with sweat and standing between two cypress trees near the big board fence that separated their property from their neighbors behind them. And right in front of him, now gleaming and looking practically pristine except for the crack through its palm, was the original gold-plated hand with the index finger pointing to heaven. It appeared that Mr. Choppy had spent the better part of the afternoon anchoring it upright in the ground with a bit of cement and a circular arrangement of white marble chips to give it the look of a small monument.

Gaylie Girl approached in awe. "Is that . . . *the* hand?" she said. "The one Renza went on and on about at one of our meetings?"

"The very same. Doesn't it look . . . well, *inspirational* is the word that comes to mind?"

She circled it, admiring Mr. Choppy's handiwork. She knew from the exhilarated look on his face that this was something that meant a great deal to him, and she quickly adopted his reverential demeanor. "So you found it. I want all the details, please."

He put his arm around her shoulder as he began. "Well, I just couldn't shake Miz Renza's idea somehow, no matter how hard I tried. I know I didn't bring up the hand around the house much, but that didn't mean I wasn't thinkin' about it every now and then. It just had such a powerful impact on me. At some point, of course, I realized I had some resources now as mayor that I didn't have as a private citizen when I first stumbled upon it last year stickin' outta that pond."

"Such as?"

"Topographical and satellite maps, for instance. We got 'em for every square inch of the county, basically. So I just went down to engineering, took 'em out and studied 'em. Didn't take me long to isolate a coupla suspects. I've been checkin' 'em out on the sly, and sure enough, there it was, still big as life in the second place I looked. I had it hauled over here a few days ago, and I've been cleanin' it up and makin' it look pretty ever since. Of course, I did get a little help from some of the workmen."

Gaylie Girl leaned down to touch its smooth, shiny surface. It felt very warm to the touch, what with the still steamy weather, but she wasn't inclined to withdraw her finger immediately. "It's beautiful, of course, and I don't want to be a stick-in-the-mud, but who does it officially belong to now?"

"Well, I did just what Renza did and ran it all past the Reverend Greenlea at First Presbyterian, and he confirmed that the church still isn't the least bit interested in claimin' it." He paused, and what could only be described as an impish grin crept into his face. "Then I did a little more research at the courthouse. You're not gonna believe this, but that pond was on land that belongs to Pond-Raised Catfish for future expansion. Apparently, it was sold to them when the plant first moved here. So I pretty much figured I could claim it and haul it over here, since Petey'll soon be the new owner."

"How about that? Looks like you and that hand were meant to be together."

"Just like us."

She stared into his eyes with all the intensity she could muster. "Even though you're hot and sweaty, I'm going to give you a little token of my affection."

"You sure you don't wanna wait until I get home and take a shower?"

"Just be quiet now. I like a hardworking man." And with that, she kissed him warmly on the lips.

IT WAS NOW a little past five-thirty. Wrapped in another of her colorful saris, Myrtis had everything in place for the upcoming ceremony and reception. Marc Mims and Michael Peeler had just placed two dozen potted dwarf gardenias throughout the twists and turns of the maze, and the fragrance was nothing short of heavenly. The makeshift stage and dance floor with tables and chairs scattered about just beyond the maze had also been adorned with potted ferns and palms, giving everything a lush, tropical appearance. Most important, the portable air-conditioning system Myrtis had rented had turned the entire area beneath the big white canvas tent into a more than comfortable extension of Evening Shadows, where the ceremony itself would be held.

Laurie and Powell had arrived early with the Great Buddha Magruder, who took the opportunity to practice his various choreographies in solo fashion before unveiling them to his audience during the reception later on. Though Laurie and Powell were conservatively attired in beige evening gown and tux, respectively, Buddha had chosen one of his most exotic outfits for the illustrious occasion. From the waist down it resembled a pair of toreador pants, and he appeared to be wearing tap shoes; from the waist up, however, he sported a silk blouse of many different garish colors that was open at the neck and featured enormous puffed sleeves. Up top, several peacock feathers had somehow been attached to his salt-and-pepper head of hair. The overall effect was not unlike Carmen Miranda on steroids and in bullfighter drag as well.

"I trust the rank and file of Second Creek are ready for this," Laurie told Myrtis, still withholding the Hokey Pokey revelation from her friend as they watched Buddha silently gliding around the dance floor. He was in a world of his own, stopping now and then to point in this direction and that, working things out in his ornately decorated head.

"Larry Lorrison would have been a blast from the past, of course," Myrtis responded. "I know I was in the mood for a little 'In the Mood,' if you catch my drift. But I think the Great Buddha Magruder will make this an unforgettable evening as well, don't you?"

Laurie offered up her best wide-eyed smile and didn't miss a beat. "Why, I'm sure we'll all be happy as little children at a birthday party!" Then she quickly switched gears. "Are Gaylie Girl and Mr. Choppy here yet?"

Myrtis nodded and gestured across the maze toward the house. "They're both upstairs. I believe she's in one guest room with Amanda, and he's in another with Petey. It looks like they're all one big happy family now."

"And I think we had something to do with that," Laurie added. "The Nitwitts strike again."

By six-thirty, the early birds began arriving to claim

their seats amid the rows of folding chairs Myrtis had moved into the parlor for the ceremony. Only the Steinway remained among the regular pieces, and even that had been moved to a far corner to open up more space. Myrtis had commissioned How's Plants? to bring in more ferns and palms as accents here as well, and the result was every bit as effective as a church setting, minus the altar. Slowly but surely, the room began filling up, mostly with Mr. Choppy's friends and political associates, since Gaylie Girl was still very much a newcomer.

By quarter to seven, Renza, her daughter Meta and friends, Denver Lee, and Novie had made their presence known, arriving en masse and then claiming an entire row that had been reserved for them near the front. Shortly after that, Euterpe strolled down the stairs with Pan on her shoulder, exchanged voluminous greetings with her fellow Nit-witts, and made her way over to the piano, where she placed Pan on the floor and took her seat. She began a program of wedding music, beginning with "Sunrise, Sunset," segueing into "Because You Loved Me," and finally the more traditional "Because."

Next, the Reverend Hiram Greenlea and the tuxedoed Mr. Choppy positioned themselves at the end of the aisle Myrtis had fashioned and awaited the entrance of the bride. Everything was proceeding seamlessly, even though the actual rehearsal had been restricted to a brief walk-through just an hour or so earlier. The usual elaborate rehearsal and dinner had seemed inappropriate to all concerned.

Then, upon a signal from Myrtis, Euterpe began playing the traditional "Wedding March," and Amanda appeared at the parlor entrance as the matron of honor. Matching her mother's impeccable taste in clothes, she was radiant in a silver ensemble that was both understated and charming.

Finally, Gaylie Girl stood before an outburst of oohs and ahhs in her full-length silver gown, carrying a bouquet of fresh gardenias that Marc and Michael had insisted on contributing to the proceedings as lagniappe. Petey made a handsome escort in a gray tuxedo with a silver cummerbund, completing the coordinated fashion statement the ceremony had truly become. Even *The Citizen*'s notorious society columnist, Erlene Gossaler, who had been so catty with her comments about Laurie and Powell's wedding at the Piggly Wiggly the summer before, appeared to be impressed by it all, smiling broadly as Gaylie Girl and her son proceeded down the aisle.

The actual exchanging of vows, however, did not follow a traditional pattern for the most part. Gaylie Girl and Mr. Choppy had chosen to add their own original words to the mix and were soon in the midst of repeating them.

"Gaylie Girl, I stand before you never dreamin' I would be here," Mr. Choppy began with the same sort of confidence he had exhibited during his election campaign. There was not another sound to be heard throughout the room. "But somethin' greater than ourselves brought us back together after half a century had passed us by. I look forward to sharin' the time ahead and seein' where it takes us. From my point of view, the sky's the limit. Whatever happens, I promise to be there for you until the end—with my love, devotion, and companionship—as Second Creek is my witness."

He finished up to a smattering of awws amid the oohs and ahhs of the crowd, and then Gaylie Girl started in.

"Hale, when I first met you fifty-something years ago, I thought you were the most adorable boy I'd ever laid eyes upon. All these years later, *adorable* still sums you up. I willingly enter into this marriage with you, knowing that the best is yet to come. Love has taken its own sweet time getting our attention, but we finally got the message and did it up right. So, here we are, charging into the future together, unafraid. I promise to let Second Creek be my infallible guide in this great adventure of ours until the very end."

There was more appreciative buzzing, and eventually the Reverend Greenlea reached the words that put the stamp of approval on all of it. "By the power vested in me, I now pronounce you husband and wife. You may now kiss the bride."

And then it was done. Sealed with a lingering kiss. Mr. Choppy and his Gaylie Girl were officially married at last. They made a traditional exit to the strains of "The Wedding March" from *A Midsummer Night's Dream*. Euterpe continued to play it while everyone began heading toward the dining room and glassed-in back porch for champagne, boiled shrimp, curried chicken, and crème de menthe black bottom pie.

"YOU MUST BE KIDDING!" Renza exclaimed an hour or so later, wrapping her hauteur tightly around her like a full-length mink. "You want me to get up there on the stage and demonstrate the Hokey Pokey with you? Have you reverted to childhood? Or is this your dotage?" She was standing near the edge of the dance floor after she'd had her fill of Myrtis's delicious food and drink, and the Great Buddha Magruder had just taken her aside and tried to press her into service for his big opener.

"Perhaps a bit of both, Renza," Buddha continued. "At any rate, this is an evening for letting yourself go, for going with the flow. You must trust me just as you did when we tangoed together recently. Won't you join your friends in letting your hair down? Myrtis Troy, Novie Mims, Denver Lee McQueen, and your very own daughter have already agreed to follow my example."

Renza looked unimpressed and shrugged him off. "They must have had too much to drink. I know I have."

"And what if they have, dear lady? This is a celebration, not a trip to the altar for their first communion. All the more reason to express themselves freely."

"To make fools of themselves, you mean."

Buddha remained undaunted and bent near with a

wicked gleam in his eye. He firmly believed there was no woman in the world he could not charm on the dance floor. "Look at it this way. We shall bring out your inner child and amuse it no end with the Hokey Pokey, and that should warm it up nicely for the many tangos to follow." He was prepared to continue his incomparable friendly persuasion when Petey and Meta stepped out of the crowd milling about to do his job for him.

"Come on, Mother," Meta said, indulging her fourth glass of champagne. "It'll be loads of fun. I haven't done the Hokey Pokey in ages. Petey and I are going to get up there and strut our stuff. Let's have two generations on display, why don't we?"

Renza doggedly maintained her skepticism. "Can't I just watch? I mean, when all is said and done, it's tangos I'm after. I want to dance like an honest-to-goodness adult."

"And dance like an adult you shall," Buddha added. "But I implore you to limber up first with the Hokey Pokey." He gestured toward Novie, Myrtis, and Denver Lee, who had just sauntered over. "Ah, here they are! The very first to agree to join me in sticking their right and left feet in and out and shaking them all about. Such playful lyrics! How could you possibly resist?"

Finally, Renza gave in, but only after a dramatic sigh and a firm warning. "I insist that there be no picture-taking of me in some compromising position. This means you, Novie. You know how you get when you have that digital camera in your hands."

"I've taken all the shots I intend to of the ceremony, if you must know," Novie explained, getting her back up a bit. "But I really can't understand why you're making such a big deal out of this, Renza. Since when did you have to be dragged screaming into being the center of attention?"

For a moment or two, it appeared that another Nitwitt altercation was in the making, but Laurie showed up just in time to nip it in the bud. "What are we talking about over here?" she asked. "I saw you all from across the way. Were you two getting into it, by any chance?"

"Good heavens, Laurie!" Renza exclaimed. "Were you hiding in those ferns and spying on us? I think Mr. Magruder should be the one to tell you what we were discussing, however."

"Just a harmless little tiff concerning the Hokey Pokey extravaganza," Buddha replied, cutting to the chase. "We're about to start, though. Why don't you go round up Powell and the bride and groom and anyone else you think might be interested? I'm heading up to the stage right now."

From that point on, the word spread like a flash fire across the dance floor and everyone wanted in. Laurie returned a few minutes later with Powell, Mr. Choppy, and Gaylie Girl, as promised. But Euterpe, Amanda, Cherish and Henry Hempstead, Councilman Morgan Player, Lady Roth, Vester Morrow, and yes, even Erlene Gossaler and the Reverend Greenlea, were among the many others who thought it all sounded like a Second Creek good time they weren't about to miss.

It was a raucous, unforgettable sight, once the entire crowd, both onstage and below, followed the CD and Buddha's lead and began doing the Hokey Pokey in unison. Those less coordinated were soon revealed, but no one cared. Lady Roth, for instance, invariably kept putting her left foot out when the song called for her right foot; and she kept turning herself around counterclockwise instead of clockwise.

"It's my arthritis acting up, I'm afraid," she complained to Myrtis, who was acquitting herself admirably to her left.

Because of her girth, Denver Lee kept bumping into people near her and throwing them off their stride; once she even bumped the slight-of-build Reverend Greenlea so hard that he nearly flew off the stage.

"Oh, I'm so terribly sorry, Reverend!" she exclaimed, rushing to extend a hand to stop him from teetering off the edge.

"No harm done, Mrs. McQueen," he answered with a polite smile. But he quickly moved to another position at the end of the front line.

At times, the very athletic Henry Hempstead seemed a bit more solicitous than he needed to be of his pregnant wife, Cherish, who hadn't even begun to show yet. "Should you be shaking your leg like that and turning around so fast?" he managed as everyone worked their way through additional verses of the song.

But Cherish had no intention of being put off her game.

"I'm just fine, Henry. There's not a thing wrong with gettin' the blood circulatin' a little better, and I'm not the least bit dizzy. Calm down. We've got months and months to get through."

In fact, the younger, more agile guests tackled every phrase and dance step with champagne-induced abandon. Petey and Meta remained in perfect sync throughout, performing nearly as flawlessly as Buddha himself. Amanda had befriended one of Meta's artist pals from Saint Augustine—a gangly young portrait painter with piercings over his eyebrows who called himself simply Power—and they, too, had no trouble demonstrating what the Hokey Pokey was all about.

"This is—like—so awesome!" Power exclaimed at one point. "I had no idea Mississippi people could be so outside-the-box retro!"

Among the adults, Euterpe, the bride and groom, and Laurie and Powell seemed to be enjoying themselves the most. There was hardly a misstep among them. The Great Buddha Magruder had been proven correct in his belief that this delightful reversion to childhood fun and games would be well received and even the highlight of the reception.

When the CD concluded, the tent was filled with thunderous applause, cheering, and laughter, and Buddha took several bows once it had all died down. "And now, ladies and gentlemen, for your dancing pleasure, we shall offer a tango or two for those so inclined. If I may be so bold, I'd like to ask Mayor Dunbar's permission in leading off with his beautiful bride and the new First Lady of Second Creek."

"Permission granted," Mr. Choppy said. "But, if you would, Buddha, I'd like for you to play a simple, old-fashioned waltz for me and my special lady. I'd like to uphold that tradition of the first dance, if you don't mind."

Buddha bowed low with a flourish. "I stand before you reprimanded for this grievous oversight, sir. Let me think now. Did I bring any waltzes? Oh, yes, I believe I have one on my *Fabulous Fifties Hits*." He quickly moved to the small table where he had placed his CD player and located the proper music. "I know we're in Second Creek, Mississippi, Mayor Dunbar, but perhaps you'd enjoy dancing to Patti Page and the 'Tennessee Waltz.'" Then he paused for a moment before cueing up the track. "Oh, I see 'Allegheny Moon' is on here, too. Would you rather dance to that?"

"Why not both? Patti Page always did the trick for me," Mr. Choppy said, clearly delighted with the selections. "I grew up listenin' to her over the radio and singin' along. No better way to celebrate waltzin' with my darlin', as far as I'm concerned."

And the crowd looked on with unanimous approval as the new First Couple moved graciously about the stage to the strains of the "Tennessee Waltz" and "Allegheny Moon."

After that, it was tango time for Buddha and the many ladies who lined up for his services, starting with Gaylie Girl. Fortunately, there were a few men in attendance who either knew how to slink around the floor suggestively or were quick studies. Others proved to be game but pale imitators. In any event, practically every possible coupling was attempted sooner or later.

Among the more intriguing: Lady Roth—first with Vester Morrow, then with his partner, Mal Davis—both of them laboring mightily but with enormous tact and sensitivity to deal with her physical limitations;

Amanda with Power, then with Michael Peeler, and finally with her brother—off-the-wall pairings one and all;

An insistent, possessive Renza with Buddha—not once, not twice, but three times, as it turned out, while drawing the ire of the other Nitwitts, who were champing at the bit for a single go-round with him;

Denver Lee cornering the Reverend Greenlea—who looked terrified initially, but she was determined to make up for her earlier clumsiness and managed to calm him with a reassuring smile and a promise to show up at church the following Sunday after what had been a long absence;

Councilman Player and Cherish Hempstead—with Henry stalking them nervously throughout the dance, in case "something happened," he kept saying;

And perhaps the most mind-blowing of all combinations— the towering, plus-size Erlene Gossaler with the diminutive Marc Mims. It came as no surprise to anyone that Erlene actually led the entire way, while Marc just shrugged his shoulders helplessly every time he caught Michael's gaze as he passed by firmly under her control.

Growing wearier by the dance, however, Buddha

eventually decided to retire the tango in favor of less taxing music, and the crowd settled into enjoying more conventional waltzes and fox-trots as the time neared for Mayor and Mrs. Hale Dunbar to depart for their Santa Fe honeymoon.

COUNCILMAN MORGAN PLAYER was the only member of Mr. Choppy's administration whom he trusted to take over his extensive mayoral duties during the week of his upcoming absence. A lean, intense-looking man with high-maintenance and perfectionist tendencies, Morgan was devoted to Second Creek and had seriously considered running for mayor himself at various stages of his political career. As long as Floyce Hammontree had maintained his stranglehold over Second Creek, however, he had disdained it, hoping to outlast the former mayor and his corrupt machine. No one had been more surprised than Morgan, of course, when Mr. Choppy appeared on the horizon with his unlikely campaign; and Morgan was all but shaken to his roots when Mr. Choppy had actually won.

Morgan had managed to put all that behind him quickly, clearly understanding that he needed to try his best to ingratiate himself with the new head honcho. He had achieved that goal in the few short months since the inauguration, and for the moment his reward was spelling Mr. Choppy while he and his Gaylie Girl enjoyed their much-deserved honeymoon.

Morgan had only one vice, however, and that was smoking like a fiend. As part of his daily routine, he frequently had to step outside the courthouse to get his nicotine fixes while strolling around The Square. Thirty minutes or so was about as long as he could go without taking a drag. The celebration at Evening Shadows proved to be no exception for him, and it was around eight-thirty or so that he left the comfort of the air-conditioned tent to enjoy a cigarette in the heat of the Labor Day evening.

He walked a short distance into the elaborately landscaped front yard, leaned against a cypress trunk, and lit up. That first drag was always the best one, and he sent the smoke streaming out of his nostrils with the customary feelings of ecstasy and relief washing over him. He was so intensely involved with his nicotine fix that he didn't notice at first.

Finally, he looked skyward, and that was when he did a double take. It was beyond him how he had missed it the instant he stepped out of the tent, but he frequently missed a lot of things when he was craving his nicotine.

They were everywhere. High and low. In the trees. Hovering just above the grass. Some more green than yellow. Others more yellow than green. There were dozens and dozens dotting the night, blinking on and off like moving, mini–neon signs. At any rate, there were way too many to count.

Fireflies. The entire town had been without them all summer, but now they seemed to be back in droves. Second Creek was no longer without fireflies.

Morgan finished his cigarette and headed back in, puzzled and excited at the same time. He made his way through the crowd until he had tracked down Myrtis Troy.

"You've got to come see this," he said. Then, in the same breath: "How did you manage it, by the way?"

Myrtis looked perplexed. "See what? How did I manage what?"

Then he told her about the fireflies that were massing outside like some Hollywood special effect.

"I don't believe you, Morgan," she answered. "Are you sure you haven't had too much champagne?"

"I expect we all have. But just come see for yourself. It's incredible!"

So Myrtis and Morgan proceeded together this time, saying nothing to anyone along the way. Once outside, Myrtis was quickly overwhelmed by the dazzling sight.

"It's so unbelievably beautiful and delicate. Where do you suppose they came from?"

"Better question—where do you suppose they've been all this time?"

Myrtis shrugged but continued her stargazing with delight. "Well, I couldn't have anything more spectacular to show off if I'd paid through the nose for fireworks. I'm going to tell everyone to come out and enjoy it while it lasts."

IT DID NOT TAKE long for word to spread that something unusual, something Second Creek–ish, was going on outside, and soon the tent had virtually emptied.

When Mr. Choppy and Gaylie Girl finally witnessed the spectacle, they froze in their tracks, looking around in awe. "It's just beautiful, isn't it?" he said. "Almost as if it was tailor-made for us like some kinda finale."

They stood there in silence for the next several minutes while others came and went after getting their fill. But when Novie joined them with a solemn expression on her face, the one word she uttered completely changed their focus: "Wittsie."

It was Gaylie Girl who recognized the implications first. "Oh, my goodness, Novie, I hadn't even thought of her. Hale, you remember all those things Wittsie said, don't you?"

And then it rushed in on him as well. "Like finding a way to be here in spirit? You don't think—"

But Novie interrupted. "I think we should go back in and call Delta Sunset Village right this instant. I have an uneasy feeling about this."

Gaylie Girl was shaking her head emphatically. "Oh, you're probably overthinking this, Novie. Hale and I got a sweet little card from Wittsie yesterday that said, 'Wish I could be there with you on your special day. All my love.'"

Nonetheless, the three of them headed back to the house to find Myrtis. "We need some peace and quiet to make a phone call," Mr. Choppy said, once they had tracked her down in the kitchen helping Sarah put a few things away.

"The upstairs guest room to your left is empty. You can get some privacy up there," Myrtis explained. "Is something wrong?"

Gaylie Girl decided it was time to think positively, so she immediately abandoned her look of concern for a smile. "We thought it would be a nice touch to check in with Wittsie and tell her how much we missed her this evening. Would you like to come with us to say hello?"

Myrtis clasped her hands together emphatically. "Of course I would. Should we go and round up the rest of the girls, too?"

"Oh, they're scattered all over the place," Gaylie Girl replied. "It would take forever. Let's don't dawdle too much longer. I think we should make the call before Wittsie goes to bed. She usually turns in around nine-thirty, she told me on one of my visits."

The four of them made their way upstairs, where Myrtis pointed out the available guest room. Once inside, Gaylie Girl sat on the edge of the four-poster and checked her watch. It was ten minutes to nine. Then she dialed the number on her cell phone, while the others stood nearby waiting patiently.

A sturdy male voice belonging to the night clerk in the closed ward answered, and Gaylie Girl used her new name for the very first time: "This is Mrs. Hale Dunbar Junior calling for Mrs. Wittsie Chadwick. Could you check and see if she's available to come to the phone?"

The clerk put down the receiver and returned after a few minutes. "I believe she went to bed early this evening, Mrs. Dunbar. She complained of being very tired. Could you call back in the morning, please?"

Suddenly, Gaylie Girl was in the grip of the uneasy feeling that Novie had mentioned before. "I wonder if you could just do me one small favor, though . . ." She asked for the clerk's name before proceeding further.

"Marcus Foster," the man said.

"Marcus, it would be a great relief to me if you would just go knock on Mrs. Chadwick's door and see if she's all right. It's really important that you do that for me. And if there's any way she can come to the phone, it would be greatly appreciated."

Evidently responding to the sense of urgency in her voice, Marcus told her to please hold on, and he'd go check on things personally this time.

"What's going on?" Myrtis said, picking up on the tension in Gaylie Girl's voice. "Is something wrong with Wittsie? What are you not telling me?"

Mr. Choppy quickly summarized the conversations that he, Gaylie Girl, and Novie had had with Wittsie about fireflies and migrations and childhood prayers backing up and all the rest of it.

"But you don't really think there's anything wrong, do you?" Myrtis said.

Gaylie Girl just shrugged, and none of them could think of anything to say for a while.

"Are you on hold?" Novie wanted to know, having worked her fingers into a nervous tangle.

Gaylie Girl shook her head. "No, he just put the phone down. I can hear voices in the background. They're discuss-

ing something, and I can hear Wittsie's name being mentioned every now and then."

Another full minute passed. Myrtis asked Mr. Choppy
what he really thought of Wittsie's ramblings.

"I think this is Second Creek, Miz Myrtis. Anything's
possible. I stopped tryin' to explain our flukish weather and
the fallout it's caused a long time ago."

Gaylie Girl fidgeted in place, expressing her frustrations
out loud. "What's taking so long?"

Now it was Novie who was checking her watch. "Aren't
you two catching that red-eye out of Memphis around midnight? You better keep an eye on the time so you don't get
too rushed."

"If something has happened to Wittsie," Gaylie Girl said,
covering the mouthpiece with her hand, "I don't think Hale
and I will feel much like going to Santa Fe."

Mr. Choppy agreed, and again silence gripped the room.

Two more minutes passed, during which the four of them
were plagued by morbid thoughts and worst-case scenarios.
It took all the psychic energy that Gaylie Girl in particular
could muster to fight off such persistent demons. Surely,
those fireflies were no more than a serendipitous display, one
of the many flukes of nature that had so often visited Second
Creek down through the years. And Wittsie's ramblings
were just that—the lovely, innocent imaginings of a woman
who could no longer think things through in the real and
earnest world. None of it portended anything more serious.
Or did it?

"Mrs. Dunbar," Marcus said on the other end at last. "Hold just a second, please. I have someone here who wants to tell you something."

Gaylie Girl was on the verge of losing her temper with the man, since he was putting her through an unwitting form of torture. But then she heard that sweet, trembling voice, and what felt like heaven-sent relief spread throughout her body.

"Gaylie Girl?" Wittsie said. "Is that you? . . . They told me you were on the phone for me."

"Wittsie? It's so good to hear your voice!"

Wittsie offered up a giggle. "What are you doin' callin' me up? . . . Didn't you just get married? . . . I didn't get the date wrong, did I?"

Gaylie Girl again covered the mouthpiece as she motioned for the others to move closer to her. "She's talking to me now. She sounds just fine."

"Thank God!" Novie exclaimed, while Myrtis added an "Amen!" and Mr. Choppy just lit up every bit as brightly as he had when the Reverend Greenlea had instructed him to kiss his bride.

"No, Wittsie, you didn't get the date wrong. Hale and I were married a couple of hours ago, and Myrtis put on quite a show over here. We just thought we'd give you a call and let you know we were thinking of you, and if we'd had anything to say about it, you would have been here with us tonight."

"Oh, that's so sweet of you, Gaylie Girl. . . . I wish it had been possible, too . . . but I had to be a good girl and abide by doctor's orders, you know."

Now that she had Wittsie's undivided attention, Gaylie Girl decided to get everything out in the open. "We heard you weren't feeling well tonight. I hope I didn't wake you up."

"Oh, no, I wasn't asleep yet . . . I was just lyin' in bed thinkin' about things. . . . I guess I was havin' one of my tired days . . . they come and go, you know . . . but it's nothin' to worry about . . . I'm still here."

"I'm so happy to hear that. Anyway, there's something I wanted to tell you. Something that happened after the wedding and the reception. I don't know any other way to put it, so here goes. Your fireflies came home tonight. They're all over here now, lighting up the sky for our honeymoon getaway. Isn't that wonderful?"

Wittsie gasped, and at first it startled Gaylie Girl.

"Wittsie, are you okay?"

"Oh, yes, Gaylie Girl . . . I'm fine. Especially now that you've told me that. . . . I mean, I looked out my window about a half hour ago, and the fireflies weren't there anymore . . . and I thought, well, I guess my prayers were answered again. . . . Ever since Dr. Milburne told me I couldn't come, I've been prayin' that all those fireflies would just show up to bless your weddin' and leave me here with my flights of fancy. . . . They've kept me company long enough. . . . You just think of it all as my weddin' present to you and Mr. Choppy."

"It was the most wonderful present I've ever received, Wittsie. I'll treasure the memory of it always."

"You don't know how happy that makes me. . . . I feel like I've contributed somethin' important."

Gaylie Girl had no trouble finding just the right words. "Wittsie . . . *you* are what's important. To all of us. The Nitwitts would never have come into existence without your generous founding spirit. And Second Creek would never begin to feel like home to me without the Nitwitts asking me to join them. You set such a wonderful thing in motion."

Myrtis and Novie were both lobbying for a turn at the phone, so Gaylie Girl gave Wittsie a closing "God bless you!" and handed over the receiver to Myrtis first. Then she and Mr. Choppy moved away, and Gaylie Girl quickly repeated the gist of what Wittsie had said.

"I can't help but ask you this, Hale, since I'm not a Second Creeker by birth. What do you think really happened with those fireflies?" she wanted to know.

He took his time, his expression alternating between thoughtful and smug. But eventually he settled for conventional wisdom. "I'm sure a meteorologist would tell you that their migration patterns changed this year. Now that I'm mayor, I check out the National Weather Service reports for Second Creek every day as I go about my business. None of our strange phenomena ever show up in 'em. If *The Citizen* mentions this at all, it'll be from a scientific viewpoint, I'm

sure. Such as, there was a microclimate here that discour-
aged the fireflies this summer. Hey, we've all been sayin' it
ourselves. It was just too damned hot!"

"So you don't think Wittsie really had anything to do
with any of it—including tonight?"

He put his arm around her waist, drawing her close to
him. "Sweetheart, I don't think we'll ever know the answer
to that question. But there are three things I'm real sure of
right now. That firefly display was the most beautiful thing
I've ever seen; Wittsie's all right; and we're gettin' ready to
head out to Santa Fe for some big fun. So let's get into our
travelin' clothes pronto!" Then he leaned in and gave her a
kiss that made the one at the end of their vows look like he
was kissing his sister.

"Oh, wow, Hale!" she exclaimed, finally breaking away
for air and paraphrasing the old Burt Bacharach hit with
her playful singing. "Do you know the way to Santa
Fe . . . ?"

MR. CHOPPY THOUGHT Gaylie Girl was never going
to stop hugging, kissing, and thanking people as she made
her good-byes downstairs in the parlor. Each of the Nitwitts seemed to take forever with their gushing sentiments.
Myrtis and Laurie, especially, did not seem to want to let go
of Gaylie Girl's hand. Then Lady Roth rambled on about a
relative of her late husband's who had retired near Santa
Fe, and how, oh, they just must look him up while they were

there. Of course, Petey and Amanda took the longest. There were even tears shed between mother and daughter.

The Nitwitts circled Mr. Choppy, too, but after that, he had an easier time of it. Powell gave him a rousing honeymoon pep talk, and then he spent a few minutes with Morgan Player reviewing their last-minute municipal notes. "I know you'll call me if anything of an emergency nature arises. Don't worry about disturbin' us."

Morgan shook his hand firmly and said: "Will do. And y'all just enjoy yourselves."

Finally, Mr. Choppy and Gaylie Girl were able to put all the emotions to bed, head out to the driveway, and slide into the honeymoon car. Several friends and family members continued to linger in the doorway shouting things and waving furiously, and the fireflies continued hovering high and low over it all.

"I'm real happy no one junked up the car," Mr. Choppy said, just after they had pulled away and begun their journey to the Memphis Airport.

Gaylie Girl laughed and leaned toward him. "At our age I think it would have been ludicrous, to say the least. Although it was beyond ludicrous that Erlene Gossaler caught the bouquet. And to be completely honest with you, I was afraid Petey might try to soap-sign the car. He's got his father's mischievous streak in him, you know."

As they left Second Creek and drove along Highway 61 through the soybean fields, they noticed that fireflies were now everywhere they had been missing before.

"It's almost like they're tryin' to make up for all that lost time," Mr. Choppy observed.

"Or maybe they're just escorting us all the way up to Memphis."

It was an intriguing thought, and it reminded Mr. Choppy of his mother's firefly stories that had fired his imagination so as a small boy. In some peculiar fashion he could not comprehend but clearly sensed, Wittsie's ramblings and Gladys Dunbar's mythical descriptions were connected in that special Second Creek way. His life seemed almost to have come full circle. And then he remembered that he had one last surprise for his Gaylie Girl. To his way of thinking, their wedding would not be complete without it.

She caught the nearly exalted expression on his face. "You look like you just won the lottery."

"Nah. Just a little somethin' I wanted to give you as a reminder of where we started," he told her. "Look behind you on the backseat."

She unbuckled her seat belt and turned around, craning her neck. She spotted something oddly shaped and wrapped in tissue paper on top of one of their overnight bags and retrieved it. "Is this it?"

He nodded, his grin turning impish now. "Go ahead. Open it."

She lost no time noisily tearing away at the paper and then gasped. "Oh, my God, Hale! Zinnias!"

He was preening now, feeding off of her excitement. "What else?"

"No one but you will probably ever understand why, but they'll always be the most beautiful flowers in the world to me."

"I thought about givin' 'em to you when you walked down the aisle, but maybe this is better. More private. Just between the two of us."

She thought for a moment and frowned. "I don't think I'll be able to take them on the plane, though."

"Got that covered, sweetheart. There's practically a whole roomful of 'em waitin' for you at the house in Santa Fe. I don't miss a trick."

The sigh she gave him was perhaps the most romantic he'd ever had the pleasure of hearing, and she leaned over to give him a peck on the cheek. Then the two of them fell into a contented silence, still basking in the glow of all the fireflies and festivities at Evening Shadows.

Their time together as Mayor and First Lady of Second Creek had officially begun.

ACKNOWLEDGMENTS

It would be impossible for me to put this third novel in my *Piggly Wiggly* series to bed without acknowledging once again the exceptional input of my agents—Meg Ruley and Christina Hogrebe. These women at Jane Rotrosen know the business and keep me centered and on track before, during, and after working on a manuscript. They help me deliver the most publishable product possible to my editor at Putnam—Rachel Beard Kahan. Working with Rachel is a dream come true—a learning-curve experience unrivaled and one that has steadily improved my work.

I would also like to acknowledge the anecdotal input of my cousin, Margaret K. Fulton, who has always been one of the biggest supporters of my writing career. And finally the citizens of my hometown of Natchez, Mississippi, who over many generations have largely been the inspiration for my Second Creek universe. I trust that their idiosyncrasies, speech patterns, anecdotes, foibles, and unique triumphs have been captured and preserved forever in my writing.